I AM TOYON SUTAK.

I am rich, the owner of a fleet of freighters. I regulate the flow of grain and gold from planet to planet. When I visit among my worlds, I am welcomed to cavalcades and crescendoes. Now I circle above a planet that holds my dreams—a small planet, one ocean, one continent and a lost city I have yearned to visit since my childhood—Hoep Tashik.

I AM ALIN KENNERIN.

I am Toyon's wife, competitor, lover, companion, enemy; but, most of all, I am myself. Empire-builder, pilot, painter, ethnologist. I plan to study the strange, simian inhabitants of this small planet. Perhaps this journey will bring Toyon and me together again. It has been so long since I have trusted him.

A CITY
IN THE
NORTH

by

Marta Randall

WARNER BOOKS

A Warner Communications Company

WARNER BOOKS EDITION

Copyright © 1976 by Marta Randall
All rights reserved

ISBN: 0-446-94062-3

Cover art by Vincent DiFate

Warner Books, Inc., 75 Rockefeller Plaza, New York, N.Y. 10019

A Warner Communications Company

Printed in the United States of America

Not associated with Warner Press, Inc. of Anderson, Indiana

First Printing: May, 1976

Reissued: March, 1979

10 9 8 7 6 5 4 3 2

for
Harris Zimmerman
a man of great kindness and greater patience
with love

"The devil hath established
his cities in the north."

St. Augustine

Chapter 1

And so we're finally in the shuttle, orbiting down toward a planet so backward that its port isn't big enough to handle the bulk of an interstellar freighter, and has to be serviced by these smaller and lighter vessels. We pursue the curve of Hoep-Hanninah, and the dark blue sheen of the planet-girdling ocean breaks to reveal the banded rectangle of the world's only continent. I lean forward, pull at and curse the restraining web about me, crane to see through the infuriatingly small port. The shuttle angles in, and I look not so much down as out toward the land, at the brown and white of the southern range of mountains, the darkening greens as the forest blends into the midcontinental jungle, darkness broken by the silver lines of rivers, the glimmer of lake and swamp, and the jungle breaking against another brown-white jag of mountains. Beyond this northern chain, at the northwestern corner of the continent, a further block of land, rectangular and gaunt, thrusts itself into the ocean, and I murmur its name as I gaze on the brown, gray, golden hues of it. Hoep-Tashik, Hoep-Tashik, odd words in an alien tongue, meaning a place as familiar to me as my own body, as never-before-seen as the jungles, forest, or stone peaks. Gazing, I forget the maddening restraints, the tiny port, and am seized by the mingled excitement of beginnings and ends.

I was a child when the first expeditions returned

from this place, and the news of its discovery did not touch me. Then, in my tenth year, one of the original explorers came to my home-world on tour, spoke before an assembly of my learning-group, and for the first time the lure of alien planets was born in me. A world of one island, high mountains and thick jungle, desert and forest that I had never seen, air I had never breathed, smells and sights and sounds and sensations completely new; I sat entranced while the short, stocky sorcerer in a blue uniform poured an alien world through my mind. My home-world was barren of native sapients, but she spoke of an indigenous intelligent race, she showed holos of squat, square creatures with long arms and bowed legs, covered with dark hair save for face, palms, soles, belly; their waists wrapped in long, pleated sashes, knife-hilts gleaming from the folds of cloth. Creatures that stared blankly at me from the shimmering edges of the holographs. Apes, they looked; apes, they walked, yet they had a name for themselves and their world, engaged in incomprehensible rituals, were sentient, aware of their own condition as living creatures on the way to death. The Hanninah, of Hoep-Hanninah, standing in sullen review before my wondering eyes. Then the stocky sorcerer in Survey blue capped the wonder and captured me entire, for she showed holos of a desert city, ancient and deserted, half in ruins yet exhibiting designs so advanced that they were hard to comprehend, architecture that even in ruin defied gravity and the laws of time as it rose and swept, arched and spired through the desert air. Murals on walls, carvings on fountain-lips, tall abstract creations that may have been sculpture, may have been shelter, shapes that dazed and confused the mind. Could this city have been the product of the simian Hanninah? Impossible! Unthinkable! Mystery!

And mystery it would stay, for the Hanninah, being sapient, requested that access to their planet be limited and, being sapient, were granted their request. Terrans were confined to a small area on the western coast, with jungle to the north, forest to the east, and mountain to the south. Hoep-Tashik, the desert, the city, were forbidden to man.

I did not accept the restriction, and for the next twenty-five years I did not accept. My home-world is rich and green, its most intelligent native is a small, now-domesticated reptile that cackles and stinks and is good for boot-making; the lizards of my home build no cities, speak no language, leave nothing to mark their days and the passing of their days but turds and stenches. The Hanninah named their world: Place of the Hanninah, Place of the People. The Hanninah built a city in the north, a spired and static wonder straining with the undeciphered, the mysterious, the new. Hoep-Tashik, what does it mean? Place of whom? Land of what? In my dreams I've walked the alleys and halls of the city, felt the texture of fountain-lips beneath my palms, smelled the tang of desert air and antiquity combined. How old is Hoep-Tashik? In the screens of my mind, the arches and curves have lofted high above me, pale stone against an incomprehensibility of blue sky. I want it. A startling ting of water-drops striking hollowness, somewhere out of sight. I want it. The taste of dryness tight behind my teeth, the press of ground stones fashioned by races other than my own, in times so distant I can barely comprehend them. Oh, I want it, all of it, down to the last crack and whispering of stone, the last pale trace of dust, the slightest chip and cut and break. And now, finally, it circles below me, after twenty-five years of clawing my way toward this moment, from the rich sticky fields of my home, from the shrieks and clutter of distant ports, from the dense air of merchants' quarters on a freighter, from work and sweat and plans and politics, from the final, hushed quiet of sealed offices perched on shafts of gleaming metal in a city in the center of my Sector. I am rich. I am Toyon Sutak, owner of a fleet of freighters, I regulate the flow of grain and gold from planet to planet within my Sector, when I visit among my worlds

I am welcomed with cavalcades and crescendos, feasted on fine wines and the best dishes, slept in soft beds with soft bodies, praised in loud voices. And here I circle a backworlds planet, light-years from homes and offices and empire, a planet where my name means no more than a set of sounds, where my worlds are so distant that they lack even the flavor of the exotic. I would not be elsewhere.

The shuttle drops lower, the continent disappears behind us, but it will come again as we circle toward landing. I lie back in the webbing, tense, eager, and Alin beside me looks up from her checklists, smiles, returns her cool brown gaze to the shifting cubes again. I glance at her, obliquely, for the truce between us is too new, too fragile, to bear the burden of a longer gaze. Competitor, lover, wife, companion, enemy; wife again, now, after so long? The data-cubes shimmer between her long brown fingers, occasionally she presses a small red dot into place beside one item or another, working rapidly, working well. Twenty years ago she controlled ships and cargo as well, as quickly, handling with energy and intelligence the empire that her family had left her, and I, the upstart, gazed across at her from the shaky eminence of my own hegemony, lusted after her domain, lusted after her self. Three years later we married, but I am never sure that I gained either woman or empire, for she has always been, pre-eminently, herself; wife, empire-builder, pilot, painter are secondary. Our marriage has always been fragile, and many times has shattered; I thought the last time was truly the end. But she understands my obsessions, more completely than I, perhaps. And she has let Hoep-Hanninah create a bond between us. Tenuous, granted; delicate, weak, but perhaps the planet will hold that bond for us until we are strong enough to hold it for ourselves. Another beginning, another end. The continent leaps to meet us, and Alin puts aside her cubes, smiles at me as the shuttle swoops down toward an alien earth.

ALIN'S JOURNAL

The smell of the planet assaulted us as soon as the shuttle's air-lock door opened. A thick, heavy scent, a mingling of lubricant fumes from the port, sharp salt sea-tang borne on the steady east wind from the nearby breakers and, underlying all the rest, the weighty, miasmic reek of jungle—a smell of decay and corruption that made the other scents seem superfluous, ephemeral. Toyon grimaced at the smell, but the small, morose man who had traveled with us took a deep breath, spat out the open hatch, and muttered "Hoep-Hanninah" in tones of disgust. The door ground open on bottom hinges and locked in place to form a platform; it carried the three of us down the warm sides of the ship to the cracked and steaming pavement. As soon as the platform bumped to a stop, the morose man jumped off and strode toward the distant port building, and we followed. Heat and stench surrounded us, pressing against skin and lungs. We pushed our way through the leaden air, crossed the flat, deserted port.

The port building was a large, empty shed, and although considerably darker than outdoors, was no cooler. The little man strode without slowing toward the back and, after a small hesitation, Toyon shrugged, muttered "When in doubt, mimic," and we followed. Banks of monolithic containers, standing dim in the distance against the walls of the shed, echoed and re-echoed our footsteps as we approached a large slab of table. An indistinct figure rose and moved behind the table; as we came closer he turned up a light globe and the details of his dress showed more clearly. A pale green uniform, tropics standard with baggy pants ending above the knee, sleeveless micromesh shirt and the badge of GalFed Customs slung haphazardly over one shoulder. Worn sandals. Small beard.

Mass of yellowish hair hacked off above his ears. Pants and shirt were both plastered to his body with sweat, outlining the roundness of his belly and the flabbiness of his thighs.

"Anything to declare?" he asked our fellow traveler. The man shrugged. "What you see, Kapl."

"Lost it all again?" The agent grinned. "When are you going to learn better?"

Again the man shrugged. "I'll have better luck next time."

"Not on Xanadu, you won't. Wait a bit and I'll give you a lift into town."

The man nodded and moved aside. We stepped up to the table.

"Let's see," the agent said, glancing down at his databoard. "You're Toyon Sutak and you're Alin Kennerin, right?"

"Yes. I don't think our luggage has come off the shuttle yet," Toyon said.

"You'll have to wait, then," the agent told us. "I have to check it over. From Alta Morena? Okay, let's get the questions over with. Any living plants?"

And down we went, through an interminable list of all the things we weren't supposed to bring to Hoep-Hanninah, and hadn't. Toyon took it all in stride, surprisingly, answering each question patiently and fully. Another facet of his reformation? It's too early to tell, but still it's a good sign.

By the time they had finished with the list, our luggage had arrived. The agent whistled with amazement at the amount. Toyon moved aside and I took over, handing over lading stubs, watching each packaging sack move through the large detectors beneath the table. There were twenty-seven containers in all, and each one packed tightly.

"You folks planning to move in?" the agent asked as we finished.

"No. We're headed up toward Tashik," I said.

"Tashik? You serious?"

14

"Sure," Toyon said. "There's a city up there, some ruins. I want to see them."

"Hell," the agent said. "I don't know about no city. Tashik? You got permission from the apes?"

"The Hanninah? No, but I'll get it."

"Huh. Hey, Weiss, what do you think of this? These two want to get up to Tashik."

"Their business." Weiss mopped his face with a soiled cloth.

"Is there a phone?" Toyon asked. "I want to call a hotel."

"No hotel," Kapl said. "You're staying with the governor."

"The governor?" I said. "Why?"

"Regulations for places with no other accommodations. I'll give you a lift up, but I can't take *all* this stuff."

"Is there a place where I can store it?" Toyon said with heavy politeness. The agent waved toward a bank of lockers beside the table, and I picked out the sacks of our clothes and papers while Toyon stuffed the others into lockers, palmed the doors shut, and stuck his thumb on the seals.

The agent backed a battered black ground-car into the space before the table, and we put our sacks into the hold next to a package which Kapl had carefully removed from the cargo-floater. I glanced curiously at the packaging, noting the use of a newly developed cuddlefield used for transporting fragile medical supplies. Then Toyon tossed in the last of our sacks, and we clambered into the back seat of the car. Weiss sat in front, beside the agent, and the car bumped and ground its way out of the building and toward Tyler's, the one town on the planet. Neither Weiss nor Kapl spoke, and Toyon was busy hanging out the window, staring at the passing landscape. I, too, stared out, at the thick squat plants covered with bright lavender flowers that lined the dirt road, at the far, dim line of blue that was the shore. Clouds of dust billowed up behind us, obscuring the bright shaft of the shuttle

15

as it rose from the port toward the orbiting mother-ship.

The agent wrestled the car through a sharp curve in the road and over a bridge spanning a sluggish flow of river. A few hills with fingerlets of town straggling over them hunkered in the distance, and heavy, flesh-colored trees rose from the banks of the river, cutting off the view to the south. The noise of the car startled a covy of hot-hued birds that rose and winged away toward the west; red, orange, blue, against the darker blue of sky. The squat plants appeared again, their sweet scent riding over the ponderous odor of river and jungle.

"What are those bushes?" I asked, pointing from the glassless window.

"Don't know," the agent replied. "Ask the governor, it's his hobby."

We broke from the tree shadows into heat and light again, and I sat back, blinked, wiped my brow. The road passed through an empty, litter-strewn strip on the edge of the town, over another bridge that seemed to span the same desultory river, and into Tyler's. I leaned forward and peered at the buildings. Each synthacrete and plasteel structure was identical to the one beside it, squat, square, plain, and laid out in the neat, unvarying grid of a company town. Strange plants bloomed in some of the gardens: tall, lilylike stalks topped by deep blue cups with long stamens falling from their lips; ground-covering creepers of an almost purple shade; sprawling orange vines winding over the fronts of houses. Other gardens were baked and bare, or rutted with tire tracks and littered with children's toys. One yard held row upon row of native Terran plants: gardenias, cyclamen, begonias heavy with bright red flowers, caladium, each row carefully arranged and displayed against the alienness of the planet. The streets widened and pedestrian passages appeared before store fronts and company offices. A square park with an awning-covered area in its middle occupied the center of town, and a few children played

16

on the baked dirt. The few loungers in the square stared curiously at the car as it passed, then the street narrowed again, passed through another residential district identical to the first, and Tyler's was behind us. The agent pulled the car over at the last building, a double-level, windowless block with the letters IDC carved over the door, and Weiss clambered from the car. Kapl opened the hold and handed Weiss the package of medical supplies. Weiss tucked the package under his arm and entered the building.

"What's that?" Toyon asked.

"Company offices," Kapl replied, over the grinding of the gears. "Poor bastard's going straight back to work."

The road branched half a kilometer beyond the company building. Kapl urged the car to the left, up a slight rise to a low, sprawling house that covered the top of the hill.

"Governor's mansion, such as it is," he announced, guiding the car under a makeshift wooden roof. He and Toyon began dragging our baggage from the hold, while I stared at the building.

Its center was standard, GalFed issue housing, a block of gray synthacrete with long, narrow windows punctuating the walls, and an energy-saving manual door set squarely in the middle. The original building was not small, for it continued a good ten meters in each direction from the main door, but nonetheless it was almost lost in the confusion of wooden wings and additions that rose around it. A second story reared above the gray block, merging with the sprawling, L-shaped wing clinging to the left of the building. To the right, a stubby, low wing wandered westward, surmounted by a hexagonal cupola of thin wooden beams and latticed windows. A verandah had been tacked to the front of the building, with low steps leading up to it from the drive. A multitude of potted native plants cluttered the steps and rails. The house seemed deserted.

"If you'll follow me," Kapl said, hefting a case, "I'll

17

take you to the guest house. The Governor's probably napping, but he should be up in time for dinner."

"Do you work for him?" Toyon asked as we each grasped a case and followed the man up the creaking verandah steps and into the house.

"Not really. There're only the two of us here, from GalFed I mean. Everyone else is Company. So what the Governor doesn't do, I take care of. Watch the doors here, they're very narrow."

They were. Toyon had to turn sideways to fit both the cases and his wide shoulders through the doors, and I followed, down a long hallway whose once elegant carpets and holos were faded with age and tropic weather and whose light-globes wavered uncertainly. The hall ended abruptly at a second door, and Kapl pushed the door with his hip, leading us into the back garden. It was, for the most part, meticulously kept, with the beds laid in neat patterns along the sides of a small stream, and each plant carefully labeled. One bed, however, contained a tangled mass of dead leaves and branches. Kapl gave me no time to stop and wander, though, for he hurried up the stairs of a small guest house at the back of the garden. The rooms within were light and airy, well shaded, and filled with innocuous furniture. A bowl of bright, fresh flowers glowed from the center of the table. Kapl continued on through the living room and into a bedroom. He dumped his load on the floor and dusted his hands.

"Well, this is it. The Governor'll meet you on the verandah at about eighteen hundred. Vibra's through that door. You want anything, ring and the servant will come. Don't know if that would be any help, though." He turned, passed through the house, and closed the door behind him. The sound of his footsteps crunching through the gravel lasted but a moment, and a sudden, complete silence descended.

Toyon transluced a north-facing window and stared out at the slope of alien trees and shrubs. I sat on

18

the bed, watching him as he leaned forward until his face was almost flattened against the glass.

"Hoep-Tashik," he said with wonder. "Soon, Alin. I'll find us some transport, talk with the Hanninah—it shouldn't take more than four, five days."

I said nothing. He stood, he spoke as he had seventeen years ago, tense and tight, young and yearning, the muscles of his shoulders moving under the light clingsuit, head thrown back, red hair gleaming in the light. I wanted to trust that sudden youth, wanted to touch him, feel the vibrancy, but I kept myself still on the edge of the bed, suspicious of the transformation.

He turned, smiled at me, reached over, and cupped my cheek in his hand.

"Very soon," he promised, and I echoed, silently, "Very soon."

THE GOVERNOR OF HOEP-HANNINAH

Governor Rhodes paused in the dining room on his way to the verandah, checked the placement of the dishes, corrected the angle at which one knife diverged from one spoon, quickly lifted each wineglass in turn and held it to the steady yellow light of the globes, eyes narrowed, looking for stains. His long, pale fingers twirled each glass by its stem in front of his sea-colored eyes before setting it down; pale wrists glimmered under the dark fabric of his robe as he tapped a plate to one side, then tapped it into place again, his thin body arched over the white cloth of the table. He turned to inspect the polarization settings on the windows, fingers dancing over the controls, glance flickering from control panel to windows and back again. The late-afternoon sunlight changed hues as he played with the knobs, so that at one moment his flesh was a pale orange, at the next a deep blue, then a fine, soft shade of gold. The gentle light imbued the room with an unexpected elegance, an air of civility and decorum through which the Governor of Hoep-Hanninah perched and stalked like a long-limbed bird.

A potted moss rested on the ledge below the windows, and the Governor bent to it, frowned, then thrust a finger through the deep green, tightly clustered leaves and into the soil.

"Swamp moss," the Governor muttered. "*Swamp* moss. Needs more water. Humidity. *Rhodontia fulgens.* Wet stuff."

He lifted a pitcher of water from the table, carefully tilted a certain amount of liquid into the plant. The moss tendrils swayed as the liquid seeped into the soil, and the Governor's thin face creased in a smile, lips together, corners barely tilting upwards. He replaced the pitcher, surreptitiously scrubbed his dirty fingers on the inside lining of his robe, smoothed the material over his thighs, and moved toward the verandah.

His guests turned to greet him as he came into the evening air. A tall, broadly built man, red hair clubbed at the nape of his neck, aluminum-gray eyes, pale skin, hard mouth. And a short woman, dark-haired, dark-eyed, dark-skinned, as slim and tiny as her husband was large and heavy. The woman bothered him; her glance was too cool, too much of an inspection, and he automatically slipped on the polite mask of diplomacy as he greeted them, gestured them into their seats again, carefully offered drinks. The governor felt uneasy. He had expected two gushing tourists, come to take pictures of the amusing apes, self-satisfied at having discovered an enchanting little backworlds planet where nobody, my dear, has come at all. This small, dark woman and the tall, farm-handed man with unusual eyes did not fit comfortably in the governor's mind. If not tourists, then what? GalFed inspectors? Was he about to lose yet another post? The governor suffered sudden agonies beneath his politeness, smiled in a polished manner, and turned to call through the door to the servant.

"*Haapati! Hoaki tak bit-bit.*"

"Your servant is a Hannin?" Alin Kennerin asked with interest as the governor leaned back in his woven chair.

"Oh, yes. I'm afraid that GalFed simply doesn't provide the funds to transport a proper Terran servant. It's impossible to hire Company people, especially at the pittance I can afford. One must make do." Kennerin looked sympathetic, Sutak looked bored, neither looked as though they were taking any pains to memorize his comments. GalFed inspectors never looked bored, the governor remembered. Still, best to be careful.

"I can't tell you how pleased I am to see you," the governor said. "I don't often get guests here, and the local company tends to pall after a while."

"We're very grateful for your hospitality," said Kennerin. "We didn't realize that there wouldn't be a hotel."

"No, not a single one on the entire planet," Rhodes replied. "We don't get many offworlders, and the Company maintains hostels only for its own people. But it's my pleasure, really. There's not much for a GalFed governor to do on a Company planet." Sutak's lips curved beneath his thick red beard, gray eyes still opaque. Just sitting there waiting for the interesting part to begin. Should I tell them about my plants? About my garden? About spending more time worrying over the flowering grasses than over the damned Hanninah? Give them a really good excuse this time? Isn't it enough that twenty-seven years ago I made a stupid, youthful mistake, can't they stop prying? Haven't I been sufficiently . . .

Blackmailed. O my God, have they found out about that?

The governor's polite smile did not falter. "Anything I can do for you will be a pleasure."

Sutak leaned forward, suddenly tense. "I want to visit the Hanninah," he said quickly. "I want permis-

21

sion to travel up to Hoep-Tashik, as soon as possible. Can you arrange it?"

What? What? Tashik? Hanninah? Should he call Haecker Or was Haecker in back of it? The governor's hidden rising panic was interrupted by Haapati's entrance, and Rhodes turned with gratitude, motioned the servant to place the tray on the shimmer-top table.

"Ah, here's the tak. It's local, of course, costs are much too high to import liquor. *Baniti, kep-allalal.*"

The Hannin set the tray down. His slender, six-digited hands lifted the decanter and poured yellow liquid into three clear containers, taking care that not a drop should hit the sides of the glasses, nor spill to mar the shifting colors of the tabletop. The dark hair covering head, back, arms, and legs glowed in the light of the setting sun, and when he straightened to present the drinks, the diamond-shaped patch of hair on his stomach gleamed from the pale, yellowish skin. Incongruously, a Terran waist-pouch rested against his brown-furred hip. Kennerin stared at Haapati with deep interest, Sutak with a fascination that bordered almost on repulsion. The governor was ready to concede that Haapati was, by Terran standards, exceedingly ugly, but under any other circumstances he would have taken delight in having shaped the ugliness to this smooth display of courtesy. Now, he simply accepted the break in conversation that Haapati provided, while his mind flickered through lists of possibilities and alternatives. By the time the drinks were poured and distributed, Rhodes had at least calmed himself enough to maintain his diplomatic demeanor. He dismissed the servant with a few brief words, and the Hannin disappeared into the darkness of the house.

"I've seen holos and stills of the Hanninah before," Sutak said. "But there's a distance to that sort of thing. Seeing them up close, in the flesh, is quite another matter." He shook his head. "I'd no idea that the blank expression is, well, their *normal* expression. Like a mask."

22

"*Is* it a mask" Kennerin asked.

"I beg your pardon?"

"A mask, a natural facial immobility. We have mobile faces, for example. We can change our expressions. So can, say, dogs. But, well, you know of the grinning lizards of Nineveh Down? They aren't grinning, that's their natural, immobile expression. They can't *not* grin. A mask. Is the Hanninah face a mask, too?"

"No, I don't believe so. I understand what you mean, but, well, no. They're hard to figure, you know. Not stupid, although that blank face might make them seem so. Just, well, I suspect that 'dense' is the proper term. Deliberately dense. Stolid. Completely incurious."

"I had no idea," Sutak said, and took a sip of the tak. His lips folded at the bitterness of the drink.

"It does take some getting used to," Rhodes said. "The drink, I mean."

Kennerin raised the glass to her lips and drank slowly, and the governor, with equal slow grace, glanced at the watch on his wrist and rose from his chair.

"If you'll kindly excuse me for a few minutes, I'd like to check on our dinner. Native help, you know . . ."

His guests made polite sounds of assent and he glided in the door, then hurried up the stairs to his office, locked the door behind him, lifted the transmitter of his private vidline, and punched a number into the machine.

"Haecker? Rhodes. Are you private? . . . I've some company. . . . Yes, those two. Listen, I think they may be . . . What? . . . No, no, of course not. . . . Well, I can't be sure. You did? What did it say? . . . Well, you never can tell, you know. GalFed doesn't go around announcing these sorts of things, they *would* have a tight cover. . . . Well, they're simply not tourist types, not at all. Listen, I know these things. They want to travel to Tashik. . . . How in hell should I know? . . . What? . . . All right. Tomorrow night, then? . . . Fine. . . . Of course I'll be careful, but I'll have to play along some. . . . Naturally. Fine."

Rhodes replaced the transmitter, twitched at the hem of his robe, then stalked downstairs, peered quickly into the kitchen, and returned to the verandah.

Kennerin finished pouring herself another drink as the governor resumed his seat, and she smiled at him.

"I rather like this tak," she said. "Is it a Hanninah drink?"

"Yes. They do occasionally give, along with all the taking."

"And will they give us permission to travel?" Sutak asked.

"Why, I really don't know." The governor allowed a frown to appear, glanced at Sutak, kept his tone light. "May I ask why you want to travel to Hoep-Tashik? You realize that the planet is semirestricted?"

"Do you know the ruins?" Sutak asked.

"Ruins? Oh, oh, the desert city. Yes, in a way. I've heard of it, read something before I was posted here. Of course, no one's actually been in it, no Terrans, I mean. Restricted, you know. Something of a mystery, I take it."

"And likely to remain so," Sutak said. "I suppose that the Company has no interest in it, since they haven't bothered to see the place. At least, not that I've heard of."

"The Company," Rhodes said firmly, "is here on sufferance, even as you and I. As far as I know, no Company officer or employee has ever set foot into restricted territory."

That, thought the governor, would sound good on crystal.

Sutak gestured impatiently, stood, paced down the verandah, thumped a large hand on the wooden rail, strode back. Big man, huge man, but as intense and quick as a laser. The governor found the contrast disturbing, yet the fair man's intensity did not seem to be an act at all. Kennerin watched her husband, face expressionless, brown eyes cool and calm; Rhodes

24

glanced from one to the other, feeling even the certainty of his suspicions waver. No matter what GalFed suspected, they wouldn't waste talent like this, if this was a setup, on a backwash planet and a backwash administrator. And if they weren't GalFed, then what in the name of the Powers did these people want?

"Listen," Toyon Sutak said. "Listen. When I was a kid, ass deep in manure on my family's farm on a mud-ball planet, a Survey speaker came by on tour. And she showed holos, she talked about a desert city on a planet that we couldn't even see in the sky. She opened a universe for me . . ."

The governor listened as the tall man spoke, walked, waved huge hands for emphasis, pounded a fist on the railing. The evening sea breeze, rising as always with the setting of the sun, floated the smells of night-blooming pillow-vines up to the verandah, and the sky moved through red and golden hues. The governor listened, and when Sutak finished speaking and sat again, Rhodes nodded once, slowly. A brief silence descended as Haapati emerged, moved from lamp to lamp, his long fingers urging a brighter glow from each one. The servant left the porch, and Rhodes sighed, relaxed in his chair.

"Yes, I'll help you, as much as I can," he said. "We can go out tomorrow morning, try to speak to the Hanninah, get your permission to travel."

"And then we'll be able to leave?" Sutak asked.

The governor shook his head. "It may not be that easy. The Hanninah are difficult people to deal with, hard to understand."

"What is there to understand?" Sutak demanded. "All I want is permission to cross their territory. I don't see how that could present any problems."

"You don't know these people," the governor said. "Even after seven years on Hoep-Hanninah, I find them almost incomprehensible. It's something you'll have to understand if you want to deal with them at all. They're simply, well, different."

"In what ways?" Kennerin asked. "Surely there

25

must be some parts of their culture that are accessible."

The governor shrugged. "I can lend you a phrase-book, I can tell you some of my own experiences with the Hanninah, but I'm not at all sure how much that would help you."

"Then tell us," Sutak said with impatience. "Don't just yak about it, tell us something helpful."

The governor's brows gathered, and he moved his thin hands helplessly.

"Surely," Kennerin said. "You must have learned something from your servant."

"From Haapati?" The governor's face cleared. "Yes, of course, I can tell you how I happen to have him with me. I can't promise that it will give you any insights, but at least it may help you know what to expect from these people. Do you mind?"

"No, go ahead, please," Kennerin said, and Sutak nodded. The governor refilled his glass, thought in silence for a moment, then began.

WHAT THE GOVERNOR SAID

"One of my responsibilities is to keep an eye on the natives, make sure that they're not being exploited, haven't any complaints against the company, that sort of thing. About once every three months I pull the hopper from storage and waste fuel flitting about the bush, digging up Hanninah and trying to get across to them. It's not easy. I've picked up a bit of the language, but I don't pretend to have any really firm grasp of it, and they certainly don't help. Not a one of them speaks GalStandard that I know of. Perhaps they can't.

"This one trip, the one that brought Haapati to me, was a trial. I'd been out for three days and not spotted a single Hanninah encampment, not even a single Hannin. They're nomads, of course, but it's fairly unusual not to find at least one small group within ten kilometers or so from the base. Or, at least, it was. These past six, nine months, it's been quite a trial finding the Hanninah. At any rate, it was hot, as always. Sticky. I collect native flora, but there was nothing new in the savannah for me, and after the third day I was ready to give it up and fly home. But the morning of the fourth day I spotted an encampment at the edge of the forest. It didn't look new, but I could have sworn that I'd been over that clearing the day before and not seen a single thing. Still, mysterious Hanninah are better than no Hanninah at all, and I dropped the hopper and walked in for a visit.

"I don't believe the Hanninah spend more than one or two weeks in any particular location, then they're off again. Not terribly cohesive, the Hanninah, always moving about, splitting up, that sort of thing. But it's hard to tell, they all look fairly alike, at least to Terrans. They use porodin for pack animals, have you seen them? No? Well, you certainly shall. Yes, indeed. The Hanninah don't carry much with them: some poles and woven reeds that they use for constructing huts, cooking equipment but not much of that, bedding. No clothing, of course, just some ceremonial stuff, but it's not even protection from the rains. And don't ask me what their ceremonies are, for no Terran to my knowledge has ever seen one.

"They make a camp by tethering the porodin in a rough circle, the goods they don't immediately need go just inside that, then the huts, and in the middle there's always a fire pit and a lot of Hanninah sitting around staring at it silently. I have never, I swear, heard one of them sing.

"I landed the hopper about seven meters from the ring of porodin and walked into the camp between the large, smelly beasts, trying not to step on porodin turds. The animals raised their heads slowly on those thin, snaky necks as I passed, stared at me, then bent to the pasture again. No one guarded the goods, although I spotted quite a few good pelts and a pile of knife-hilts lying about. Oh, have I told you about the

27

knives? Every Hannin wears one, except perhaps the infants, and I'm not entirely sure about them. Stick them through those sashes they have. Folded like pockets, the sashes are, I mean. They carry just about everything in them, you'd be amazed. But the knives, they're long, skinny, sharp things, evil-looking. I'd never *seen* a Hannin raise one against another Hannin, or against a Terran. They use them for killing game, cutting meat and grass, that sort of thing, but they're frightening-looking implements, make you think twice before saying anything that might offend. If you *can* offend these creatures; I'm not convinced that they're capable of finding anything offensive.

"So I passed the goods, and through the ring of huts to the center of camp. This was a fairly small group, no more than maybe thirty Hanninah, all ages, all sexes, and the place smelled like fury. Of course, it might have been only the porodin. Haapati smells acceptable enough, but you get more than two Hanninah together in one place and you can tell by the scent for a kilometer away. All thirty or so were sitting around the fire pit, absolutely silent, staring straight ahead of them. I stood by one of the huts, waiting to be noticed, and trying to peek into the circle. Couldn't see anything, though. Finally one of the older women stared at me and moved herself over a bit, making room for me in the circle. I hesitated, but there seemed to be no help for it, so I went forward and squatted down beside her, tucked up the ends of my tunic so they wouldn't trail in the dirt, then looked into the center of the circle. And stared just like the rest of them.

"The Hanninah, as far as I can tell, are monogamous. That is, they pair up, male and female, and there doesn't seem to be any amount of promiscuity among them at all. Each pair raises its young, and stays together even past the age where the young attain maturity and find another tribe. Doesn't seem to be any affection in the pairings, it's just something that they do, as coldly as anything else. In the middle of

28

the circle of Hanninah, then, there were two males and one female, grouped by the edge of the fire pit. One male, the larger one, stood erect, holding his knife, and staring off into space, at nothing. At his feet lay a female, with a great, gaping hole in her belly, and quite obviously dead. Blood had stopped flowing, but it was still wet along the belly and through the hair; she couldn't have been dead for very long. The second male was holding her body, rocking her back and forth slowly, and in absolute silence. His eyes were closed, and he held her so tightly that the muscles of his arms stood high and hard beneath the black hair. And all the Hanninah were staring, not at the male with the knife, not at the dead female, but at him, the sitting one, watching him with an intensity of blankness that sent shivers down my spine.

"The old female beside me started talking in Hanninee, and the sound of her voice almost made me jump. It took me a moment to realize that she was addressing me, asking what I wanted at the camp. I gave my usual quick spiel, were they happy, had they any complaints against the company, anything that they wanted to let me and GalFed know about, and all the time the sun beat down and the Hanninah stared silently at the dead female and the two males. The old one heard me out, then said that her people had nothing to say to me. She looked at me, then behind me through a gap in the huts, past the porodin, and to my hopper, and asked if I had come alone. The question startled me, I believe it was the first question I had ever heard a Hannin ask about anything so— so personal, and I rather nervously answered that I had. And immediately regretted it. After all, I had no idea what the Hanninah were up to, what had happened, what was likely to happen, and it seemed entirely possible to me that a Terran would be fit meat for whatever ritual or ceremony or, well, *thing* they were up to in that hot clearing by the edges of the forest. I felt for my stunner as inconspicuously as possible, and was vastly relieved to find it nestled in its usual place on my hip, hidden by a fold in the tunic. But the old one turned back to the circle, hunkered and staring with those flat black eyes, then said that Haapati would go back to the base with me. Instantly there was movement in the circle; the standing male dropped his knife with a clatter and strode through the rings of natives, huts, goods and porodin, and disappeared into the woods, still striding along at a distance-eating pace. The second male still sat, eyes closed, holding the dead female, but two Hanninah rose from the circle, came to him and stood at each end of the female's body. The male looked up at them, then slowly loosened his grip on the body and let it down gently. He stood, turned, walked to a young male sitting in the circle. He reached out a hand to the young one, then led him to an older female and sat the child beside her. Then he turned again, walked to me and stood waiting, silent, motionless, endlessly patient in the hot, fierce sunlight. The old female turned her back to me in dismissal, and when I tried to ask her what was going on, who Haapati was, why she expected me to take him, she did not reply, merely walked to her hut, squatted before it, and calmly began to sort through a pile of pelts.

"The rest of them also ignored me, so I finally turned to leave the circle, with Haapati following along behind me. Let me tell you, it was no stroll, that walk through the rings with a black, silent Hannin behind me who, it seemed to me, had been banished from the encampment for reasons I couldn't begin to try to understand. And armed, in addition. As we passed the last of the porodin, Haapati took the knife from his sash, lifted it high above his head and buried it with one swift, powerful thrust in the earth. Then he removed the sash and laid it beside the knife, and followed me, naked, to the hopper. I gestured him to the second seat inside and he entered and sat as though rides in hoppers were part of everyday life for him, and I lifted and headed back for the base. On the way, I tried to get some information from him, but he didn't say a word about what had happened back at the encampment, and never has."

The governor sat back, looked at his two stunned guests with satisfaction, smiled. Kennerin had opened her mouth to comment when the soft sound of a bell floated to them from the darkness of the house.

"Ah, dinner," said the governor. "I trust you'll enjoy it." He stood and lead the way to the dining room, and his guests followed in silence.

TOYON'S JOURNAL

After a final drink with Rhodes, we walked silently through the garden, Alin and I, following the flickering lamp that the Hannin servant held above his head. It was uncanny, watching him as he paced bowlegged through the rows of plants; a small, black body, squat, thick, neckless, and an arching simian arm holding the lantern a good meter above the stolid head. This was what built my city in the north? This creature of graceless body and frozen face? No, I could not believe it. And yet, and yet . . . The light flickered and shook, the sudden shadows of plants writhed and reached for us, and the sense of awe was close upon me. I turned to share it with Alin, but her expression stoppered the sounds in my throat. She stared at the Hannin, her gaze traveling the length of his body, and in her eyes was an almost unholy gleam of curiosity, a swift, voracious light that chilled me, and I turned from her, shaken.

Once inside the guest house, the servant extinguished his lamp, poked at the pale light-globes along the walls, twitched the windows to opacity, and stood as though awaiting a command. What was the formula of dismissal? What was I to say to this alien who didn't speak my language, what could I say that would not sound foolish? But Alin said, calmly, in Standard,

31

"Thank you. You may go now." The Hannin lifted his head to look at her and she gave him a smile of warmth, of friendship, of curiosity, of ease. His pale saffron face remained impassive, and he turned, trudged into the garden.

Alin gazed after him, then walked to the bedroom. After a moment I followed her. She had removed a small rectangle from her hip pouch and lay sprawled on the bed, while deep blue lines reeled across the surface of the rectangle and reflected pale colors on her face. I stood by the bed and she looked up at me, shoulders hunched to her ears, elbows deep in the softness of the blankets, her bushy brown hair framing the oval face.

"Yes? What is it, Toyon?"

What could I say to her? Why did you smile that way at that ape? Where am I in your eyes? It's been ages since you smiled at me, for me, with me, with warmth; why won't you smile for me?

What could I say to her? Oval face uptilted toward my own, slight lifting of the eyebrows, and all she gave me was the shiftings of her copper-colored skin, nothing further, nothing deeper, nothing mine. Why do you chill me from your life? *Why don't you love me anymore?*

What could I say to her? I gestured at the book, tried to smile, said, "What's that?"

"Rhodes's Hanninee phrasebook," she replied, but her eyes gazed through my distress, surgical, aloof. She passed a finger over the smooth rectangle, glanced down. "He mentioned it during dinner, said that he'd lend it to me. It should be useful." Calm. Clear. My wife is a bell in a distant tower.

"Useful? In talking with the apes?"

She put the book down and looked at me again. "They're not apes, Toyon. They're people, like you, like me."

"Maybe," I said, trying to make a joke of it. "But they look like apes to me." She stiffened, and I turned to my desk, moved a small date-cube back and forth.

32

"Apes," I said again, waited without looking for her reaction. Anger? Disgust? Hatred? Anything, anything other than that infuriating, that enraging self-containment.

"Don't be an ass," she said evenly. "You know you don't believe that." And the truth of it pushed fury into my voice.

"Don't try to read my mind," I said, my voice sounding like sandpaper. "Don't you tell me what I think and what I don't think, damn it! I said 'apes' and 'apes' is exactly what I meant."

She turned, disdainful; rolled over onto her side and sat. Not caring, I knew, either for my fraudulent opinions or my expressions of them. I unclenched my fingers, letting the date-cube fall back to the table, and tried again. Gently. Gently.

"Why don't they smile, or laugh, or talk much?"

"We've only met one so far," she said. "And not in context."

"Nonsense. Rhodes said that they're always this dead-faced."

"You have to remember that it's hard to learn alien expressions. They might smile with their hands, or fingertips, or wiggle their ears. We can't make assumptions on the basis of how we do things."

"I suppose that you wiggled your ears at Haapati, then," I said harshly, and tried to cover the pain with a smile. "I've worked with aliens before. And you can usually tell if they have emotions, even if you can't tell what the emotions are. But these people, this Haapati, his face looks dead, even his eyes don't express anything."

"You're making unwarranted assumptions," she said. Calmly.

"So what assumptions are you making? What do you think?"

"I think nothing, I make no assumptions. I simply haven't enough information."

And she sat cool, she spoke cool, completely in possession of herself, her armor intact, finished, and clenched tight against me. I wanted to take her small body in my hands and wrench it, break it, give it pain, make her react to me! To me! Hatred, or fear, or disgust, just so long as *I* created the emotion, so long as she *saw* me.

"*You* haven't the information," I said. "*You* make no assumptions. My God! So gather your information, create your assumptions, as long as I can get to the city, I don't care what your apes are like, I don't care if they make great poetry or eat babies or anything. All I want from them is a yes, and if getting that yes is the only contact I have with them, so much the better."

She shook her head. "That won't do, Toyon. You walk into a Hanninah encampment with Rhodes, feeling like this, and you'll be lucky if they even pay attention to you."

"Just where the hell did you learn so much about alien psychology?" I shouted. "From sharing one heart-deep glance with a monkey?"

And she bit her lip, rolled from the bed, went into the next room. Yes, yes, of course that hurt her, naturally. As I knew it would. Because she did know, she'd trained in ethnology, spent two years in the field before her parents died and she'd come home to manage the empire they had left her. And manage it so well that I too easily forgot her other interests, other passions, the things that called to her soul more strongly than invoices, ladings, runs, and routes. It was not the taunting that broke through her deep calm, not the jibes that hurt, but the forgetting.

Except, of course, that this time I hadn't forgotten. At all.

She kept to herself the remainder of the evening, while I flung objects from sacks to drawers, slapped my traveldesk together, shoved data-cubes around. Silence from the other room. *I* had hurt her, she hurt because of *me!* I howled a song to cover the quiet, spread my maps along the desk top and activated them, one after the other, tracing probable routes in pulsing orange across their surfaces. Silence. Couldn't she even cry? I slammed into the vibra and let the flickering, tickling waves sift the grime from my body, cleaned mouth, crapped, and when I returned to the bedroom Alin was between the covers, her dark back turned to my side of the bed. Silence. And she hurt.

My mother told me, when I was a child, not to fling stones through other people's chapel windows. I climbed into bed, looked at the narrow tilt of my wife's shoulders, listened in shame for the sound of falling glass.

"Tomorrow," she said quietly, "I'll go with Rhodes to talk to the Hanninah. You go into Tyler's to find some transport."

"Yes," I said. "Yes."

Chapter 2

I rose early this morning, before Toyon had awakened. Cool morning sunlight slipped through the edges of the windows, sending long shafts of pale yellow across the desks, floor, wall, bed. Toyon grumbled sleepily, yanked the covers closer about his chin, turned his back against the light. And one arm snaked across the bed, groped through the space I had lately occupied, relaxed against the pillow. I stood, half into my heavy cling-suit, looking down on him. My husband. The phrase, description, had never ceased to feel odd to me, connoting some not entirely believable bond between this man, this volatile child seven years my junior, and myself. Disturbing even from the first, during that space of months when he was constantly at my doorway, clutching exotics in ham-fisted hands, his yearning and determination spread over the planes of his face. So different from the bleakness of my childhood plateau, so different from the mannered sophistication of my parents' home, from the complex academic structures of Dyaan. I wanted him, despite or because of the brashness, the newness, the antithesis of everything I had known before, and eventually I had him. Married. How very odd. When that first burst of passion faded, I found that I could not name the links between us. Habit, perhaps. Love, maybe. Respect? In part, in part. Much bitterness, some violence, a mutual distrust. Shaky foundations, but foundations nonetheless. He turned again, pulled my pillow closer to his face, mumbled against the light. Oh, distrust, and dis-ease, and yet when we laugh together, when we work together, we do it so very well. And so I try yet again. For the sake of the laughter. And, perhaps, for love.

I finished dressing and went out into the garden, to find Rhodes kneeling in the dirt path, clucking over several beds of dead plants. He pulled withered leaves and stalks and placed them carefully in a disposal sack, then signaled to Haapati, who stood behind him, and the Hannin carefully tipped a heat-carrier, pouring boiling water over the flats. Rhodes must have seen my amazement, for he explained that he was sterilizing the soil, on the chance that some disease in the dirt kept killing the plants. He gave me a brief botanical lecture over breakfast on the verandah, called them "prayer plants." *Rhodontia supplex* in his own labeling. The common name, he said, was a direct translation from the Hanninee, but what connection the plants had with prayer, he did not know. They did have a connection with the swamp moss that waved at us through the open dining-room window, though. Rhodes had not been able to raise even a few of the prayer plants himself, could not propagate them, despite his success with the rest of his garden. His perplexity was obvious, as he sat at the table nervously shredding fruit with his long fingers and looking like nothing so much as a distressed stork. It may have been some overnight transition in him, or, perhaps, only his worry about his plants, but I sensed a change in the governor, a loosening of what had seemed to me, last night, to be distrust. His smile this morning was slim, but freely given.

I drank the sweet native tea, nibbled fruit, and waited for Rhodes to remember his promise to take me to a Hanninah encampment. He was so involved in the trials and tribulations of *R. supplex*, however, that eventually I had to remind him. He seemed surprised that Toyon would not be going with us, but was much too well bred to comment on it. An hour after breakfast we were aloft, rising and falling through the sky in the governor's reluctant hopper.

Once in the air, I could see the compact hydroponic gardens that nourished the Terran population. The few slight hills bent and folded away from the town, and then we were over the savannah proper. Large brown and golden fields, with neither dips nor rises, and unbroken save where stands of dusky, spindly trees broke through the ground cover and stood, naked and abandoned, against the sky. To the north, on my left, a faint line of darker green showed the beginnings of the forest and jungle; to the east ahead, and to the south, the savannah rolled unbroken, until it curved over the horizon and away. We fluttered along at a steady altitude of 1.6 km, and the air was clear.

"They should be around here somewhere," the governor shouted over the noise of the machine. "Supply car came in from Eastbase, filed trip-log. Sighted encampment in area. Lucky. Otherwise spend a week finding tribe. There, see it?"

I peered through the transparent shield and saw, in the distance, a series of circles, a bull's-eye amid the rolling brown of the plain. Rhodes maneuvered the hopper toward landing, and the machine bounced, groaned, shook, and eventually was persuaded to settle twenty meters from the ring of porodin. I slid from the high seat and stood in the grasslike plants, rubbing the stiffness of the hard seat from my buttocks, and checked my equipment.

"All in one piece?" the governor asked after closing the connections in the cockpit and joining me.

"Yes. Give me a moment to activate this." I touched the material over my stomach, felt the small pings and shivers as power pulsed through the invisible leads to the visual receptors in my eyelashes, the audio pickup snuggled in each ear, the scent receptors in my nostrils. Everything seemed to be in good order, and the governor and I approached the ring of porodin.

Huge beasts, and as odoriferous as Rhodes had said.

Great, rounded legs seemed planted in the earth, supporting oval torsos and incredibly long and ropy necks. Large, flat heads turned to watch our approach, thick stubby tails swung, swatting at the small insects that buzzed about. The insects swarmed over us as we moved cautiously toward the huts, but our alien scent drove them off and they soon returned to feeding on the colonies of symbiotes and parasites that lived between the brown scales of the porodin.

The trampled mud stuck to our feet as we progressed through the circle of beasts and into the circle of goods, and I paused to scrape the viscous earth from my boots and gaze back at the hopper visible through the ring of animals. It would take only one porod to crush the hopper to sheet metal. I caught up with the governor, and we walked through the piles of goods.

Here were bundles and heaps, strange and exotic, and most of them so unfamiliar as to be incomprehensible to me. For what were those braided lengths of fur? Those tightly seamed pouches, what caused them to bulge so? In the distance lay what appeared to be a cage woven of reeds, with no obvious openings; closer by lay a pile of pelts so fashioned that harsh, prickly fur festooned both sides of the pieces. Surely too uncomfortable for beds or clothing. Most of the goods were of dull earth colors, but my eye was caught by a pile of bright objects in the middle distance. I pointed them out to Rhodes.

"Knife-hilts," he whispered. "No end of trouble from them. Company people always trying to buy them from the natives. Complaints, sometimes. Notice you don't see any blades, and you won't except on the Hanninah."

The goods gave way to the double ring of muddy brown and gray huts; we moved through them and into the central clearing, and stood by a hut waiting to be noticed. Here were Hanninah going about their daily business, some of it easily comprehensible, some of it not. A Hannin sat before the uncovered circular door of a hut, calmly plucking pealike things from podlike things and pitching the results to different piles. Across the circle, three Hanninah young walked impassively back and forth, back and forth, over a length of reeds. The ends of their pale, undyed sashes flapped against hairy buttocks. A half-hearted breeze blew through the circle, swirling small puffs of dust along the ground. Near the circular, mud-walled fire pit, a Hannin sat sharpening a knife. And, as Rhodes had mentioned the night before, a sizable portion of the tribe squatted about the inner circle, staring blankly at the pit. The sun beat down, and the only sound in the camp was the steady scrape-scrape of the knife sharpener. Even the young were silent.

Eventually a maroon-sashed Hannin appeared from one of the huts and spoke with Rhodes. I realized, listening to the conversation, that I had not yet heard Haapati speak, and the governor's version of Hanninee was rough, uneven. The language spoken by the Hannin before us was pure melody, a cascade of liquid sound that took me by surprise. I had expected Hanninee to sound as rough and unkempt as those who spoke it, but the voice lilted from the impassive yellow face, and Rhodes's replies seemed barbaric and harsh in contrast. Music. Melody. Loveliness. Enchantment.

After a number of exchanges, Rhodes turned to me.

"They want to know why you want to visit Hoep-Tashik," he said. "And I must say, it doesn't seem to be going very well."

"Tell them that we have heard reports of their beautiful city to the north," I said slowly, repeating the speech I had prepared the night before. "Tell them that we feel the city will merit, no, will inspire our awe and admiration."

The governor conveyed this to the Hannin, who turned on me an impassive stare. I returned it evenly, staring at brown eyes without whites, whose pupils were vertical slits. Blank, closed, tight, emotionless, yet I felt a sudden kinship with the squat alien who stood no taller than I, a kinship that I could not even begin to explain. Eventually the Hannin grunted and disappeared into the hut. Rhodes turned to me, eyebrows tilted with surprise. "He said he had to confer. We're to wait here."

"Confer?"

"That's as close as I can translate it." Rhodes twitched at the formal collar of his uniform and stepped back into the shade of the hut. "I'll admit that I'm puzzled," he continued, his voice low. "They've never held a conference before, to my knowledge. Don't seem to have any structure for it. Odd."

Odd. A number of adults drifted into the hut, and the conference took quite a while. I began to sweat and tire in the morning heat, and eventually squatted in the slim shade of the hut, undid the topseam of my suit. But Rhodes remained standing, his uniform correct and fully closed, sweltering his authority in the sunlight.

Without warning, the Hanninah emerged from the hut, squatted in a rough circle around us, and one of them produced a flask. Rhodes hesitated, then lowered himself to the ground, tucked the tails of his tunic around his thighs and balanced on heels and hams. The Hannin drank from the flask and passed it around the circle. When it reached the governor, he frowned and, with a look of stern courage, took a very small sip and passed the flask to me. Tak, warm and sharp. I in turn drank and passed, and when the flask had gone round the circle once, the Hannin began speaking. The governor's eyebrows rose, his jaw slackened slightly, shoulders moved back. When the oration was over, he turned to translate.

"They've given you permission," he said, "to visit any part of the continent necessary in your journey to or from the city. Including, but not limited to, the savannah, the river, the jungle, the northern mountains, and the coast. You may take as long as you wish. The single restriction is that you make only one journey in and one journey out again. I'm simply stunned."

As was I, but I kept a careful control of my face,

41

of my movements. "Tell them that we are very grateful for their kind permission," I said. "We consider ourselves in their debt."

The governor told them, and the flask passed around again, counterclockwise this time. As I reached to take it from the flat-breasted Hannin beside me, I glanced at her knife, thrust through her green waist-sash, then, involuntarily, glanced again. The blade was smooth, bright, and looked machine ground rather than hacked or pounded from some native metal. But I did not think it politic to show too much curiosity, and the recording I was making would give me plenty of time to study the blade. I took the flask, drank, and passed it on.

Soon afterward the Hanninah drifted away. Rhodes and I retraced our path through the rings of the camp and into the hopper. I disconnected my recording equipment before entering, and we lifted off.

"A pleasing outcome," Rhodes shouted as the savannah passed below us.

"Yes. And puzzling."

"Indeed. Still, you've your permission. Did you notice that there were no prayer plants anywhere about? Usually an area near a spring is carpeted with them, and I was hoping to pick some up for the garden. Well, perhaps we'll spot some on the way back. . . ."

And the governor shouted happily on about his plants, while I sat impatient to return to Tyler's. For the first time in years, I had something I wanted to share with Toyon.

QUELLAN

Quellan stood spread-legged in the midst of the supply shack, watching the clerk pile box upon box of supplies on the flat counter. Outside, the sun shivered and glared over the pavement of Tyler's main street and the suction pump above the door served only to rearrange the muggy air within the shack. Eleven o'clock, and miserable. Quellan thought grim thoughts about the return to Eastbase, back of the car loaded with supplies, hot sun pounding down from the edge of Tyler's to the eastern forests. It would be cooler at Eastbase, in the shade of the mountains, but coolness was all the base had to offer. Quellan, feeling rebellious, thought mean thoughts about Hoep-Hanninah, about the prissy townsfolk of Tyler's; about the limited entertainments, restricted euphorics, and five daily planet-hours of hard work waiting for her at the base. One break, one lousy, impossible break, and she'd have enough money to get clear, set herself up. Just one small bit of luck.

She arched her shoulders, trying to detach the soaked cloth of her shirt from her back, then barked a few more orders at the scurrying clerk. The clerk paused, passed a hurried fingertip along an order blank, grinned nervously, returned to the storeroom. He obviously remembered Quellan's first visit to the supply shack, when she had decided that the service wasn't fast enough, and had done something about it. Quellan immediately felt better and grinned at the clerk's flutter, baring square white teeth that contrasted sharply with the burnt skin of her face and neck. Hooked a thumb in the pocket of her deliberately dirty work suit. Scraped damp, sun-bleached hair from her neck. Considered the possibilities of beer. Felt better yet.

The bell at the shack's door ponged as someone entered, and Quellan turned from the counter to look at the newcomer. A large red-bearded man stood just within the door, impatiently swatting moisture from his face and staring about the shack. His gray eyes lit on Quellan, and he strode toward her.

"You run this place?" he called as he approached.

"Hell, no," she said, offended. This man obviously didn't know a fielder when he saw one.

"You know where I can get a drink?" he asked. "I'm parched."

43

She gestured toward the icer in the corner, watched as he bent above the spigot, letting cold water rush down his throat. He didn't look like a townie, too big and solid for that, and the beard was no townie ornament. But his face lacked the hard wear of a fielder's skin, and his hands, though large and strong, bore no calluses. Didn't talk like a townie, townies were too polite for their own good. Administration? Government? She speculated, head cocked to one side, hands on hips, as he wiped water from his chin and turned to her again.

"Thanks. Damned hot around here. Who runs this place?"

"I beg your pardon?" the clerk said, returning from the storeroom with still more containers.

"You the clerk here? Good. I need to rent a hopper, something fairly capacious, for three, four months. What can you do for me?"

No, obviously not a company man. An offworlder, newcomer, soft-shoe. Quellan smiled to herself.

"Well, sir, if you'll wait until I finish this order . . ."

"No, you go ahead and take care of this one," Quellan said. "I've got time."

"Well, sir," the clerk said again. He hoisted himself onto the counter and sat with dangling legs, staring at the man. "There is some transport laying about—there always is, of course. Hoppers, ground-cars, light carrying vehicles, even some heavy movers. What exactly are you looking for?"

The clerk, Quellan thought, was being suspiciously helpful. The newcomer smiled and gestured with large hands.

"Oh, nothing terribly big. About two tons capacity, room for two, three people. Fairly long range."

"You want something with self-contained fuel supply?"

"If possible, although I don't mind carrying extra. A C-class hopper with multilanding gear would be perfect."

"Well, I wouldn't know about C-classers. You're from offworld, aren't you?"

"Yes, name's Sutak, Toyon Sutak." The man extended his hand, and the clerk examined it for a moment before taking it, shaking it briefly, and dropping it again.

"Sutak. Yeah. You're the loose-jaw staying up at the Guv's."

"Loose-jaw?"

The clerk mimed someone staring at scenery, hand shading eyes, jaw dropped. Sutak frowned. "I need something to get myself, my wife, and my equipment up to Hoep-Tashik," he said. Quellan frowned suddenly, but kept silent. "A track-free vehicle would be fine, if there aren't any hoppers."

"Three, four months, you say? Um. Your wife's another bug-eye?"

"My wife," Sutak said coldly, "is an ethnologist."

"Well, I'll be. Come to study the apes?"

"Look, can I get it or not?"

"Get what?" the clerk said in surprise.

"A hopper, what else have we been talking about?"

"Did I say there were any hoppers handy?"

Sutak started to flush, then, taking a deep breath, he said very evenly, "What about track-free vehicles? A ground-car?"

"Hell, I wouldn't know about that," the clerk said, a small grin pulling at the corners of his mouth. "I'm just supplies. You'll have to check with company transport."

Quellan watched the big man stiffen, fists balling at his sides, flush deepening under his beard. And watched the hands slowly loosen, the flush subside as the man held tightly to his temper. Bad tactics, Quellan thought.

"Where is company transport?" Sutak said through clenched teeth.

"Pool's east of town," the clerk replied, and waited until Sutak had turned to leave before adding, "But the offices are across the square."

Silent, Sutak stalked toward the door. As he reached it, the clerk called out gleefully, "But they won't be open until thirteen-thirty."

Sutak froze, muscles bunching under the light fabric of his clingsuit. He paused for a full minute, unmoving, and the clerk stopped smiling, slid from the counter and edged toward the storeroom. Sutak pushed open the mesh door, slamming it so hard behind him that it slapped against the frame, and the bell squawked. Sutak gone, the clerk grinned derisively. Quellan stared at the little man, door, clerk again. Perhaps this Sutak wasn't up to it, didn't know the ropes; in his place she would calmly have pasted the clerk at the first untoward comment. After all, if the townies weren't kept in place they'd take all sorts of advantage. But Sutak, being a soft-shoe, probably didn't know about that, probably had big ideas about temper and courtesy and other useless stuff. Still and all, the big man wasn't completely useless, just needed some guidance.

And he was headed for Tashik.

So Quellan glowered at the clerk, said, "You finish my order, I'll be back," and left the shack. On the sidewalk, she squinted against the glare and peered along the street until she saw Sutak's large form moving down the heat-streaked pavement.

"Hey! Hey, Sutak, wait up!" She walked rapidly toward the man. Sweat ran down her face as she approached, and she wiped at it with her sleeve.

"Yeah?"

"Calm down, I'm not going to bite you," she said. "Damn, it's hot. Listen, let me stake you to a beer. There're some things about this setup you've got to learn before you go tackling company."

"So what's in it for you?" He looked at her with suspicion.

"Ease up, will you? I've got a heart of gold. You want that beer?"

He shrugged, his large shoulders lifting in a gesture she was certain he had borrowed from someone else.

"Sure, right," he muttered. "Has this dust-bin even got a bar?"

"Naturally. What else is there to do in Tyler's but drink?" she said, leading him down the street.

BEER AND SYMPATHY

The coolness of the bar was a welcome relief after the muggy scorching outside, and Toyon felt better as he followed the fielder to a far booth. She hollered across to the bar as they sat, and soon two large, frosted mugs of the local brew appeared before them. She lifted the mug to her mouth and poured down about a third of its contents.

"Blessed be the Powers," she sighed. "No matter where you end up, there's always beer."

Sharp, bitter stuff, Toyon thought, but Alin would love it. He lowered his mug, feeling the cold beer slide into his stomach. The woman smiled comfortably and remained silent, letting him relax.

"Who are you?" he asked.

"Name's Quellan. I'm a fielder for the Company, out at Eastbase. Came in to get some supplies, find out what life in the big city's like." She gestured toward the supply shack. "Ticks me to see townies taking off on someone, and just about everyone in Tyler's a townie, one way or another. You're a, what, a tourist?"

"Yeah, a tourist. Slack-jaw. Bug-eye," Toyon muttered. He finished his beer, waved for another.

"Listen, friend, you just don't know how to handle fish." Toyon, thinking of his empire of dockworkers and deckhands, raised an eyebrow, but listened in silence. "They'll try to get your ass every time, unless you paste 'em, and then they lick your boots. No in-between. You've gotta be firm with them."

"Yeah. Listen, who's in transport pool? Can I get anything from them?"

47

"I don't know them, not by name," she said. "And probably not, but let's take things one at a time. Pool's management, at least the people you'll be dealing with. Probably won't be much help. Company's tight with their equipment, even with us. You ought to see the forms I've got to fill out just to take something out on the job, and it's their job, too." She finished her second beer and he ordered more.

"What about top management? Who runs the place, who's in charge?"

She ran a blunt fingertip around the rim of the mug and frowned. "Two guys, basically, topper and next one up. Topper's Leo Haecker, runs things out of Tyler's." She paused.

"Bothers you?"

"Yeah. He's sort of, easy, you know? Not a townie type, polite, that sort of thing. Hard to describe. But not soft, no way. Always get the feeling he thinks double, you know?"

"I think I do. Who's the other one?"

"Jaerek Stover, out at Eastbase. Stover's easy to peg—he's a bastard, pure and simple. Tough, mean, nasty; he's the type of guy when there's an accident, he runs like hell and hopes that the victims are alive and awake when he gets there, so he can watch 'em die. Still, after Haecker, Stover's almost a relief. At least you can always tell where he's at."

"Any chance of getting help from either?"

Quellan shook her head. "Stover, no way. Haecker, I'm not so sure, but you wouldn't know why he helped. You and your wife going to travel alone?"

"That's what we're planning." Toyon watched as she drank, and pinned her: the informative, inquisitive type, slightly bored, good for gossip and information, tends to slack off unless constantly supervised. He employed hundreds of them, had met her, in different guises, under different names and sexes, in any of fifty ports where his liners docked. Not the best worker in the universe, but a gold mine of information. He smiled an encouragement at her, and she settled herself more comfortably into the booth.

"Used to be, transport was pretty easy to get," she said. "You didn't see my buggy, did you? It's pretty battered, a ground-car, takes me two days to get from Eastbase to here, and another two to get back again. Used to take a hopper, long-range thing that made the trip in two, three hours, but about a year ago they pulled in all the hoppers, gave us just ground stuff, and even that's pretty limited. Can't take my buggy anywhere but savannah and road. No bounce treads, no brush-cutters, no floaters, nothing but bare-bones transport with a hole in the back for supplies. And the fuel capacity's worth one trip, one way, that's it. Out at Eastbase, it's got so bad that some stiffs are actually using porodin, you know, the lumber-beasts. You'd probably be able to buy a couple of 'em, but they're at the base and you're here. You planning to be out of Tyler's long?"

"As long as it takes," Toyon said. "What about private transport?"

"Not too likely, either. Oh, there used to be some stuff, mostly town-cars, nothing you could take out-back with you. No new stuff for almost a year, Company put this huge fee on imports, nobody's got that kind of money. IDC runs the shipping here, you know. What they say comes, comes. What they say don't, don't. Not much call for private transport, anyway. Planet's restricted, people stay pretty much in one place, no roving about. Company says it's to make sure no one crosses into restricted territory, but who knows for sure? Company also makes it pretty damned hard to take a leave on-planet. Oh, they don't actually forbid you to stick around, but who's going to spend two months stranded in Tyler's when the Company'll take you to Xanadu for free, and even give you extra spending money while you're there?"

"No one in his right mind," Toyon said, glancing out the window at the baking square. "Well, damn.

49

My wife's getting permission from the Hanninah to visit Hoep-Tashik. . . ."

"You headed up for Tashik? You think Tyler's is bad, you wait until you hit low jungle. I slipped in once, when I still had the hopper. Curious, I guess, but I sure ain't curious anymore. No roads, air's so wet you can damn near take a bath in it. Snake-things and slug-things and swamps and rivers and *all* sorts of crap in there. You sure you want to hit Tashik?"

Toyon thought of telling her of his desert city, then decided against it. "I'll find a way," he said. "Somehow or other."

"Good luck, friend. You'll need it. You haven't talked to the apes yet?"

"No. My wife's out with the governor, trying to do that now."

"Yeah, well that's a whole 'nother problem. Used to be, coming in from Eastbase, I'd pass twenty, thirty different tribes on the savannah, apes all over the lot. Lately, there's maybe one, maybe two tribes, sort of scattered. This last time, I only passed one."

"Shit," Toyon muttered. He tapped the chronometer in his wrist and numerals flashed beneath his skin; thirteen forty-five. He stood and stretched.

"Listen, I appreciate the advice, but I'd better tackle transport before it gets any later."

"Yeah. Sure hope you find something. See you around."

"Are you going to be in Tyler's long?"

"Nope, leaving tonight. But I'll see you at Eastbase, if you make it. Intersects main route to the north, you pretty much have to come through there."

"If we make it," Toyon said wryly. "Thanks for the talk."

She nodded, and he left her to finish her beer, paused at the door of the bar, then hunched his shoulders and strode into the light.

Coming back from the Hanninah encampment, we passed over a field carpeted with white flowers, and Rhodes immediately set the hopper down and climbed out. He removed a number of plasteel flats from the hopper's hold, produced two spades, and offered one to me.

"It's a stunning field," he said with a hint of apology in his voice. "I simply must get some for the garden. *Rhodontia supplex*, you know. Mine don't last, but these do look healthy, don't they?"

He began gathering plants, carefully levering his spade under the greenery and lifting out blocks of dirt. I joined him, and soon we had two flats filled with the small plants. The governor smiled happily and stalked about the flats, his fingers probing into the dirt.

"Yes, they do indeed seem healthy. No rot at the roots, no scale, no fungi, good color, and see here, see the blooms? All perfectly symmetrical. This just may do it."

I helped him load the flats into the hopper, restraining my impatience. After all, half an hour spent digging vegetation for his garden was small enough payment for the flight into the savannah.

Haapati met us as the hopper settled, helped Rhodes remove the flats from the hold and take them into the garden. I followed them on my way to the guest house, watching the laboring Hannin and trying to imagine him amid the group at the camp, being stared at by all those blank and simian faces, while he held a dead Hannin in his arms. I couldn't do it, there seemed to be something about him that set him apart from his race. But I was in too much of a hurry to puzzle it out. I filed the thought away and entered the guest house.

Toyon was not there. The bed was rumpled and its covers strewn on the floor, and his desk was, as usual, in disarray. I took the record-crystals from my equipment and set them to cure in darkness while I stripped and removed the wires and receptors from my gear, replaced each item in its proper niche. I passed through the vibra and dressed in a light tunic, and went to find the governor and some lunch.

Haapati alone occupied the verandah. He put down a bowl of fruit and indicated the second place set at the shimmer-top table. I drew the phrasebook from my pouch before I sat, scanned through it, and made my first attempt to communicate with Haapati in his own language.

I must have murdered the Hanninee phrase for "Where is my mate." Haapati stared at me so long that I began to hunt through the book again, then he said "*Alni*," and disappeared into the house. By the time I had discovered that "*alni*" meant "I don't know," the Hannin was back, bearing a tray of salad. He set the tray on the table, then squatted by the wall, staring at me.

"Have you been here much time?" I asked him in Hanninee. No answer. "Do you go into the town?" "Have you seen the forests?" "Are you leaving soon?" "Is there any water nearby?" "Where are the porodin?" "Is it possible to buy this fine pelt?" I might as well have been speaking to a tree. Finally I thumbed the book off and stared at the Hannin, convinced that I would get no reply from him. Dense. Yes. The stalemate was broken by Rhodes, who stepped lightly onto the verandah, dusted his hands together, and smiled.

"*Haapaeah, kep mahe-maheena*," the governor said. Haapati rose swiftly and went into the house.

"Well, a good morning's work," the governor announced happily. "Your permission, my plants, and Leo Haecker will be able to make it up for dinner."

"I beg your pardon?"

"It's so rare that we get offworlders here," Rhodes explained, carefully checking the arrangements of the

52

dinnerware before reaching for his drink. "I thought it would be pleasant to hold a small dinner party, about fifteen people or so, something to liven up the evening. Perhaps I should have consulted you first?"

"No," I said slowly. "Sounds interesting. But I'd rather like to let Toyon know, he's a bit late sometimes. He doesn't seem to be here."

"He's gone into Tyler's, Haapati told me. Probably trying to find some transport, but I doubt he'll have much luck. Oh, but most of the Company people will be here tonight. Perhaps one of them could help you. People do tend to be more cooperative in a social setting, don't they?"

I nodded, not entirely convinced. "I asked Haapati where Toyon was, and he said he didn't know."

"Oh? What exactly did you say?"

I repeated the phrase, and Rhodes smiled. "Very simple. The Hanninah are quite literal-minded, you know. Haapati knew where your husband went, but he didn't know where he was, do you see the difference?"

I nodded again, and, finally, we ate. Soon after, Rhodes retired to make plans for his dinner party, and I returned to the guest house, spent most of the afternoon going through the recordings of that morning's meeting with the Hanninah and fretting over Toyon's continued absence. Eventually I gave up on the recordings altogether and repaired to the verandah to watch the road, pace, and grow gradually angrier. I knew Toyon's violent temper; a misplaced curse, an avoidable argument, and the Hanninah permission would be useless, we'd find no transport open to us at all, might as well board the next shuttle out and return to Alta Morena. And nagging at the back of my mind was the knowledge that Toyon and I were not special people here, our small territories were tens of light-years away, and should he lose his temper, there were no underlings to smooth things over again, nor any helpful planet managers to cringe and take it. But there might very well be people who would react to his violence with violence of their own. How long had it been since Toyon was actually involved in a fight? Years, certainly. And while he was by no means soft, certain skills grow rusty, certain knowings get lost. So, beset with worries and angers, I paced the verandah while the sun dropped lower and lower, and the evening sea-breeze spilled up the sides of the governor's hill.

Eventually the breeze brought more than the scent of the curiously puffy plants that lined the drive. The hum of a motor, the sound of inflaplast tires on dirt and, riding over this, two voices lifted in song. I stopped pacing, gripped the verandah rail, and squinted into the sunset. The voices drew closer and soon I could make out a ground-car and two people coming erratically up the drive. Their progress was slow, but from a fair distance I could see Toyon in the side-seat of the vehicle, gripping the edge of the car with one hand and, with the other, keeping time to the raucous howling he and his companion emitted. The waving hand looked gloved and pink in the waning light of the sun, then Haapati manipulated the verandah lights to brightness, and I could only see vague shapes as the ground-car halted before the steps and the two drunks reeled forth.

The hand was bandaged, and Toyon held it up for my inspection, the other hand gripping the broad shoulder of the woman beside him.

"Put it through a wall," he said as he mounted the final step into the lamplight.

"I fixed it best I could, not having a med-kit," the woman said apologetically.

"Wall of some bastard at transport pool. Served 'em damned right. Gave me runaround. No one gives Toyon Sutak a runaround. Buy their damned planet. Damned right."

"How much did he have to drink?" I asked the woman.

"Not too much, couple pitchers of beer. Not much else in Tyler's." Together the woman and I levered

Toyon into a chair and I carefully peeled the bandage from his hand. The wound began bleeding again, but did not seem terribly deep. A shadow fell over the hand, and I looked up to see Haapati holding a med-kit out to me. I dropped the bandage to the floor and inserted Toyon's hand into the small clensor.

"Does that hurt?" I asked, not looking at him.

"Not much," he replied, and I remembered my morning's remembrance. Toyon fifteen years ago had said the same thing, in the same tone of voice, under similar circumstances. I was torn between anger and amusement, and, in the end, chose neither. I spread a healer over the wound, applied a shield from the kit, and when I had finished looked up to find Toyon gazing fondly at me, and the woman gone. Haapati removed med-kit and blood-soaked bandage, and I held out a hand for my husband.

"We'd best get cleaned up," I said. "Rhodes has gone and invited half the population of Tyler's to dinner tonight, and you're in no condition for company. And you can tell me what happened."

As we walked through the dark garden, he explained the morning's adventures, introduced Quellan in her absence, told me how he'd gone to the offices of the transport pool after the three beers with her.

"Same damned runaround," he said with anger. "From one idiot clerk to another to another to another, and each one of them taking half an hour to hassle the outworlder before they'd pass me on. None of them actually said No, mind you, they saved that for the honcho, some ass name of Andrea Queens, bitch got me into her office, finally, and gave me the ninety-minute shits and, hell, I got so mad I had to hit something, so I put my fist through her wall and walked out. Her secretary came chasing after me, and I tossed a couple of fifties at him to get the wall fixed. Guess Quellan heard all the commotion, 'cause she was waiting outside the building, hustled me into her ground-car, and we spent the rest of the afternoon in some bar drinking and bitching together. Hell, Alin, you can't blame me, can you?"

I shook my head. "I don't know, Toyon. Rhodes was saying that maybe one of the people tonight could help us out, but after what you did in town, I just don't know."

He pulled clothing from him and dropped it on the bedroom floor. "So to hell with it," he muttered. "Damned fool idea to begin with. We won't get permission from the apes, anyway."

"But I've already got it," I said. "This morning, with Rhodes, I got permission for us to travel from here to Tashik and back again. The only restriction is that we can only make one trip each way."

He stared at me. A huge grin spread over his features, then he lifted me in his arms and waltzed about the room, caroling. Feeling tiny and none too secure in his arms, I nonetheless came close to laughter. "But we've got to get ourselves there and back," I reminded him. "They won't provide any transportation, probably not even porodin. We're not there yet, Toyon."

With which he set me down, stared at me as though trying to pluck some knowledge from my mind, then slapped his bandaged hand against his thigh, yelped with pain, yelped with triumph.

"Hey, listen, Quellan's going back to Eastbase tonight, and she said there's porodin there that some of the Terrans use, we could hitch a ride with her and buy the beasts. Damnation, why didn't I think of that before? Where're my clothes? Alin, I've got to catch up with her before she leaves!" He grabbed clothing, pulled it on and strode to the door, almost colliding with Haapati. The Hannin ducked out of his way, and Toyon ran from the house and through the garden.

I stood, amazed, trying to make sense of Toyon's last speech and rapid exit. Then I turned to the Hannin, wondering how long he'd stood silent in the door of my room.

"Yes?" I said.

And Haapati said to me, in perfect GalStandard, "I intend to go with you."

Chapter 3

THE GOVERNOR'S GOVERNOR

The governor stood amid the shambles of his half-prepared dinner party, a wineglass clutched in his hand, while the sounds of departure echoed from the drive. Eventually the noise quieted to one car running on idle, and he stepped to a window. In the dust outside, Leo Haecker stood bent to the window of Andrea Queen's yellow Land-pacer, and the noise of the engine covered the sounds of their conversation. Rhodes returned to the table and, after a moment of indecision, began stacking the unused plates. The engine sound flared briefly and then diminished, and the governor heard footsteps as the company's planet manager mounted the verandah.

"And what is our governor doing, ah?"

Rhodes straightened, still holding the dishes, and said mildly, "I'm cleaning up. I haven't got a servant anymore, you know."

"Stop it. I'll send someone up tomorrow, this is no time for housekeeping. Do come outside, Governor. And bring me some tea, would you?"

Haecker's small, soft body moved away from the door, and Rhodes set down the dishes, collected a teapot and a cup, then paused, gathered up a bottle of tak and a glass, and followed the planet manager onto the verandah. The sun was well down, but two large, round moons cast a pale light over the landscape. Small flurries of dust from the departing car still floated slowly toward the drive.

"Tell me again," Haecker said once his cup was filled.

The governor patiently recapitulated the events of the past two days. "Then, about an hour ago, this ground-car pulled up, Sutak and Kennerin piled their stuff into it, Kennerin ran up the stairs to tell me they were leaving, they climbed into the ground-car, so did Haapati, and they took off. You saw them leave."

Haecker considered this in silence, stubby fingers steady against the teacup, pudgy body still. Only his tightly-curled hair moved in the fitful twitchings of the night breeze; that, and the occasional flash of his pale gray eyes as he pursued his thoughts. Rhodes glanced at him obliquely, feeling as always that the planet manager's eyes were the only true door to his character. The pudgy body, the mild, sarcastically deferential air, combined to camouflage the deep streak of cruelty that Rhodes had seen once, and that still rested, waiting, in the depths of those cold eyes. The governor rearranged his long, thin legs, sighed inaudibly, and raised his glass of tak to his lips.

"And what did your Mr. Sutak do in town today, ah? Have you heard?"

"I've no idea what anyone did today, other than myself and Kennerin. One moment everything was proceeding smoothly, the next it was complete chaos." The governor twitched at the hem of his tunic. "*I* don't know what's going on."

"I do."

"So I'd suppose."

Haecker glanced swiftly at Rhodes, but the governor's polite expression remained unchanged.

"Well, go on," Rhodes said. "Enlighten me."

"You don't need enlightenment, my dear Governor. You're quite light enough already."

Rhodes twitched his lips. The planet manager settled

himself more comfortably into his chair and cradled the warm cup against his belly.

"You report, simply, that Sutak and Kennerin seemed to have arranged a ride with one of the Company people to Eastbase, you have no idea of their plans, and they're out of your jurisdiction."

"I can't do that," Rhodes said uneasily. "Every single Terran on planet *is* my jurisdiction. You know that as well as I do. I'm supposed to follow through on everything."

"Such a burden. My. Well, then, tell them you'll report further when you know more, tell them you've asked the Company for help in tracing them."

"And the Company will tell me . . . what?"

"The truth, of course," Haecker replied seriously. "The ground-car left Tyler's with unauthorized passengers aboard, the vehicle was known to be unsafe when overweighted, attempts were made to locate the car but without success, and that's all you've got to know. Besides, GalFed will know what happened to them. But they won't be able to prove anything, and they won't dare try."

"You think they're agents?"

"Of course," Haecker said, but his tone of conviction was marred by a slight smile. Rhodes glanced at him nervously.

"No," the governor said. "No, I don't believe they are."

"Really? And what about your call last night? You were certainly convinced enough then."

"I didn't know them very well, I hadn't really had a chance to listen to them. I—I was too quickly suspicious."

"And now you're too quickly unsuspicious, Governor. A dangerous trait." Haecker's voice was cold and sharp.

"I listened to them, I watched them," Rhodes explained. "I'm trained to do that, you know. Watch people. It's—it's a trait we have to have, governors, you understand? They don't have the—the flavor, they lack the bite. I'm not entirely sure what they are, but I know they're not Agents."

"Fascinating. Two complete strangers appear from nowhere, with some lame story about the ruins, go poking about the natives, make a ruckus in town, run off with your servant, illegally make off with one of my ground-cars and one of my employees, and you think they're just tourists. Indeed."

"Not illegally," Rhodes protested. "Against Company regulations, perhaps, but not against GalFed law."

"On this planet, governor, Company regulations *are* the law, and don't you forget it."

Rhodes plucked more quickly at his tunic, refilled his glass, thought of retorting, and finally said fairly meekly, "Besides, no agent would make such a turmoil. It's not the way they operate, they try to attract as little attention as possible."

"Don't be a fool. It's the best possible cover they could have, acting completely out of character. They're Agents, Governor. Prying, long-nosed Agents, trying to turn up all sorts of interesting things." Haecker rose. "You make your report, Rhodes, as I told you, and then forget about it."

"And what about when they reach Eastbase? What report do I make then?"

"What makes you think they'll reach Eastbase, Governor?"

Rhodes rose so abruptly that his chair toppled. "Haecker, what in hell are you planning?"

But the planet manager smiled silently, and allowed his glance to rest on the neat gardens, the comfortable verandah, the dining room visible through the lit window. "You're comfortable here, Rhodes," he said. "Isn't that nice? Come, take a look at my new air-car. It just arrived yesterday, I'm sure a man of your discrimination will appreciate it."

Rhodes shook his head.

"I said, come look at my new car, Governor. Now."

Rhodes forced his knees to strengthen away from

61

fear as he followed Haecker down the steps and to the wooden parking shed. The car was shiny, bright crimson, highly powered, and Haecker gravely made the governor inspect the rows of controls, the banks of meters, while the planet manager talked of its abilities and scope. Rhodes nodded at the appropriate times, made small, forced noises of appreciation, and all the time felt Haecker's sardonic amusement at the puppet show. Finally the planet manager hopped into his car and, with a great, unnecessary roaring of engines, raced into the sky and toward Tyler's. Rhodes stared at the lingering dust-puffs of his passing, then turned and stumbled toward his garden, still clutching the glass of tak.

The door to the empty guest house stood open, a dark rectangle in the white wall. He barely glanced at it, moving instead through the neat plots of the garden. The Terran bed, near the wall, bloomed with gazania, azalea, tulips, a few rosy succulents. Next to it grew the bed of plants from his home world, greenbuds, great straggling pincer-flowers, small delicate thimble-blooms with their sweetly scented, nightblooming flowerets. And the beds of Hannin natives, mosses, bush-monkey trees, pillow-vines, creeping floaters, everything monochromatic in the pale light.

But the prayer plants were dead. He dropped to his knees beside the plot, the glass slipping unnoticed from his grasp, and lifted one of the withered plants from the soil. It lay flaccid in his palm, the roots unnaturally silky, leaves rough along the edges. The pollen sac and nectar basin that grew in the center cup of the plant seemed to have vanished altogether. Rhodes grasped one plant, and another, until he tore wildly through the bed, searching for just one living plant. For a few moments, the moonslight was busy with the passage of flying plants.

Until, finally, the governor crouched motionless in the midst of the ravaged plot, head down, fingers loose, and the wind twitched at the branches and exposed roots of the dead plants.

The savannah spread around us, a flat, dark, immensity whose borders could only be determined by the sudden cessation of stars on the horizon. Occasionally a solitary clump of straggly trees would materialize in the pale moonslight and as quickly recede behind us, and the branches seemed to jounce and shiver from the motion of the car as we went by. I squinted, I looked, and aside from the spectral trees, saw very little. Quellan, beside me, concentrated on driving, creating a small, tuneless humming between her teeth that echoed, in spurts and small silences, the terrain over which we traveled. The instrument board of the ground-car held a small green direction light affixed below the odometer, and its faltering glow barely served to light her face.

Behind me, wedged into the small space in the opened baggage-hold, Alin sat speaking to the Hannin. She held the glowing phrasebook in her hand and repeated, over and over again, a phrase which Haapati completely ignored. Jounce, rattle, phrase, jostle, hum, noise, phrase, and around us the dark savannah with nothing but a small, winking button to tell us where to go. And cold, with sunset some hours behind us and a sharp wind pursuing. I've taken more primitive rides in my life, but none so uncomfortable. I suppose I'm growing old.

I squirmed around in my seat so that I faced, as much as was possible, the back of the car. "What are you trying to do?" I asked my wife, keeping any signs of impatience from my voice.

She glanced at me, pulled her jacket more tightly closed. "Ask Haapati some questions."

"No luck?"

She shook her head and palmed the phrasebook

off. Immediately her face was lost in darkness, and it was out of the darkness that she spoke.

"No, nothing. Maybe Rhodes was right. Dense. Stupid. Dull. He understands Standard, you know."

"What?"

"He understands Standard, he even speaks Standard, when the mood takes him. He told me he was coming along, in Standard. Have you got a switch in your head?" she demanded of Haapati. "Flip it on, flip it off, from smart to idiot and back again?"

"Alin . . ."

But she'd already withdrawn from anger, sat hunched amid the bundles, staring out at the passing night, and I turned to face front. This, the cold lady of the night before? But her fires were banked again, and had flamed for someone other than me. Nothing changed.

Quellan concentrated on the terrain around us, and eventually she said "Hang on," and swung the car to the left. Immediately the green light expired, and the ride became more uneven than before.

"Food stop," she said before I could ask the question. "Shit break. Half an hour."

We banged and clattered under the branches of a strand of trees, and the car shuddered into silence. Gratefully, painfully, we staggered from the car and stood on the baked ground.

Quellan busied herself pulling various packs and boxes from the back of the ground-car, and eventually she had an array of self-heating cans teetering precariously on the front bonnet of the car. We popped the lids and stood shivering together in the darkness, the heating cans that we held providing a bare minimum of warmth. The only one seemingly unaffected by the chill wind was Haapati. He had leaped out of the car when it stopped, walked over to the dispirited trees and leaned against one of the trunks. He dipped a hand into his waist pouch and popped something into his mouth. Then, seeing my glance, he deliberately scratched his thigh.

64

"Can't we stop here for the night and start again tomorrow morning?" Alin asked.

"Too hot," Quellan said. "We'll hole up someplace mid-morning tomorrow and sleep during the worst of it, start again tomorrow evening. Believe me, it's better that way."

Alin looked skeptical. She drank the hot, thick liquid in the can, then picked up another can and took it to Haapati. He accepted and ate, while she stood beside him. I could hear her voice, but the meaning of the words was blown away by the piercing wind.

"What's picking her?" Quellan asked.

"Inconsistency," I said quietly. "She seems to think that Haapati's got more brains than I can see, and she wants him either to be bright or to be stupid, but to be it consistently."

Quellan shrugged, pulled her hat down more firmly, and, removing a small shovel from under the instrument panel, disappeared into the darkness. When she returned, I took the shovel, picked a blackness like to all other blacknesses, and tried to be as fast as I could. When I returned, Alin and Quellan were leaning against the car, as immobile as the still unmoving Hannin. Alin, in turn, stalked into the night.

"What about Haapati?" I asked when she returned.

"Probably did it against the tree," Quellan said, tossing the shovel into the car. "Come on, we've a fair piece to go before sunrise."

This time Alin rode in the front, and I made myself as comfortable as I could in the back. Haapati swung himself into his appointed place, wrapped thick arms around bended knees, and was asleep by the time we reached the light-beaconed track again. Alin's head nodded once or twice, then she wedged herself sideways in the seat, buried her head in her arms, and slept. Quellan made a wide turn and entered what must have been a dried riverbed, for the ride was suddenly smooth, and I fell asleep to the rocking, dark, and silent night.

QUELLAN ON THE PRAIRIE

Quellan leaned back, feeling the purring and thumping of the ground-car vibrating around her, knuckled one eye with her fist, glanced at the other occupants of the car, and shook her head. In the faint, warming light of the dawn, she contemplated the two sleeping offworlders, the crazy pile of sacks and boxes piled and roped to every flat surface of the car, and, worse yet, the dark form of the sleeping Hannin in the back. Again she shook her head, and reminded herself that having the offworlders in her car at all was more than she'd originally expected.

The night before, she had just finished piling the last of the supplies into the ground-car's hold when Sutak came loping and yelling down the street, both arms semaphoring over his head. Quellan had turned, surprised, listened to his rush of words, and agreed to take him and his wife back to Eastbase with her. Within ten minutes they were at the port, dragging Sutak's innumerable sacks from the locker and tossing them into the car. When the hold was full, they piled them on seats, roped them to the back of the vehicle, hung them along the sides, until the car looked like the storage ring of a Hanninah encampment, compressed into one small shape. Then up the hill to the governor's mansion, to hear Rhodes flustering about inconvenient departures, violent guests, and ruined dinner parties. The Hannin helped pile more sacks into the car. Sutak's wife came running from the garden, grabbed the Hannin, and sputtered something incomprehensible in bad Hanninee. The Hannin simply stared blankly at her. She tore up the stairs to the governor, tore back down, vaulted into the car behind her husband, and the ape climbed calmly into the back seat and settled down amid the baggage.

"What the hell?" Quellan demanded, and Kennerin

said, "Haapati is coming with us," in such firm tones that Quellan and Sutak could only gape. Then the governor came spilling down the verandah steps, Leo Haecker's hopper fluttered from the sky, and Quellan slammed the car into gear and took off down the plant-lined drive, unwilling to wait for more confusion. Or for Haecker to have a chance to stop them.

She didn't take her scheduled route, though. A sense of adventure, of challenge, bred by Rhodes's distraught yelling, and the look in Haecker's eyes, prompted her to take a more southerly route, along a seam in the prairie where the track was alternately smooth and bumpy, a few hours longer than the direct path but both unexpected and, amid the dried river-beds and ancient volcanic tucks of earth, affording more cover. If anyone checked the direction/reply posts along the route, they would know which path she had taken, but that would be at least a week later, and she could always make up some excuse, if it came to that. Having decided to take the southern track, Quellan felt that she had the situation well in hand, whichever way it went, and she drove calmly and well.

She had, however, grown impatient with Kennerin's unceasing questioning of the ape, over and over again during the first part of the long night's drive. Kennerin varied the question's structure, its tense, its emphasis, but the ape continued to sit, expressionless, like a large black cliff face against which the questions broke with no discernible effect. "Where have from whom the prayer plants?" "Who doing the prayer plants over?" "Why the prayer plants down becoming?" Quellan had, once or twice, been tempted to correct Kennerin's pronunciation, her phrasing, her grammar, but realized that no matter how clear the accent, no matter how proper the syntax, it would make no difference to the Hannin.

Now the rising sun threw their shadows far before them across the grasslands, and although Sutak grumbled quietly from the back of the ground-car, Quellan's three passengers continued to sleep.

67

An hour later, Quellan nosed the ground-car into a small, oblong dimple in the savannah, overshadowed on all sides by gray-green trees. A spring bubbled in the center of the clearing, and Quellan stopped the car near it. As the engine noise died, Kennerin woke, stretched her arms over her head, yawned, and looked about the clearing.

"Where are we?" she asked.

"About halfway across. We'll take a break here until midafternoon. It's going to get hot soon."

The Hannin rose, left the car, and paced his way to the spring, squatted beside it, splashed water over his face and arms. Sutak, too, was awake, and clambered stiffly from the car.

"I'm in pain," he announced. "I ache. I've been beaten up by experts. I am not happy."

"You can sleep it off now," Quellan said. "Give me a hand unloading some of the bags, okay? I've got to get some sleep before we start out again."

Fortunately, the sleep-sacks were somewhere near the top of the chaotic pile. The offworlders spread theirs out under the coolness of the trees, while Quellan, taking her time, set her own bag at some distance from theirs. When Haapati left the stream, she washed her face, rinsed her mouth, and, finally, taking the shovel, disappeared beyond the rim of the trees.

She climbed the small brow of the dimple and stood leaning against her shovel, staring at the morning-lit savannah around her. Already heat rippled quietly in the distance, and not a cloud marked the increasing blueness of the sky. Closer to hand, a carrion bird hovered on the warm updrafts.

She glanced at her ancient electronic watch, glanced back through the trees to the ground-car, glanced again around the prairie. When she felt that enough time had lapsed, she shouldered the shovel and moved back into the dimple.

Kennerin and Sutak were, finally, in their bags, and seemed quite soundly asleep. Haapati was curled into

68

the grass on the far side of the spring from them. Moving quietly to the car, Quellan lifted a small box from below the instrument panel and took it with her up the lip of the dimple. There, in the shade of the last tree, she squatted and removed a radio from the box. It was a battered device, stolen years back from the dim storerooms of obsolete equipment at Eastbase, but it worked well enough for her purposes.

She fiddled with the dials and antenna, checked her watch, and toggled on the recorder. When the signal came in clear, she applied her ear to the built-in speaker, turned the volume down low, and eavesdropped on the clandestine frequency she had discovered by accident the year before.

". . . until three or four," the speaker whispered. "Sector twenty-eight, path B's been scheduled. Proceeding slowly because of extra load."

The set squawked and chittered before another voice answered. "Standard or special?"

"Special, and caution. Pick the most reliable for this. Nothing can be allowed to go wrong."

"Alibis?"

"Simple disappearance, no clues."

"Three hundred nine–four Brown out," the second voice said, and the first one also signed off and cut the connection.

Quellan rocked back on her hams, turned off the machine, and sat staring at it for a moment before she packed it into its case and returned it to the car.

Three hundred nine–four—that would be Stover at Eastbase. And the other speaker was, undoubtedly, Haecker, broadcasting from his offices at Tyler's. Sector twenty-eight, Path B identified the route she had scheduled for and the one which, as far as the Company was concerned, she was currently on. She reran the conversation mentally as she stripped and rolled into her sleep-sack, and felt proud of her decision to take the alternate route to the base. She dispelled any remaining tension by glancing at the sleeping off-worlders in an almost proprietary way. If they were big enough to make Haecker want them out, they were big enough to be worth Quellan's time. She remained skeptical of Sutak's insistence that he only wanted to explore the ruins at Tashik, but if he wanted to keep his cover, for a while at least, that was fine with her.

She tucked the sack more closely around her shoulder and decided that for once in her life, she might have made the right choice.

ALIN'S JOURNAL

I woke up three-quarters out of my bag, pouring sweat, and sore all over from the lumpy ground on which I lay. Sat up, kunckling sleep from my eyes, and looked around.

Toyon was sleeping completely out of his bag, one arm tucked under his head. I could just see Quellan's head on the far side of the jeep where she too slept. It took a while to spot Haapati, but I finally saw him curled into a hollow of grass, his barrel chest moving rhythmically.

It was oppressively hot, despite the shade of the trees, and sunlight shafted so thickly through the branches that it obscured what lay behind it. Listening hard, I could hear the swift hum of invisible insects, but they did not bother me, although Haapati, in his sleep, swatted at the thick fur of his shoulder with one hand. Last night's annoyance rose again; I stood and crossed to the Hannin's hollow, carefully skirting the spring, half-seaming my suit as I went. I had seen the Hannin, during the bustle and rush of yesterday evening, standing by the governor's recently planted bed of *R. supplex*, doing something furtive and deliberate while the plants withered and drooped, one by one. When I reached him the plants were dead, and he had refused to acknowledge, let alone answer, my question about it. It irked me.

The Hannin lay on his side, broad back toward me. I stopped and contemplated him for a moment, then grimaced in self-disgust. Of course, if the plant-killing was so important to him that he would stop in the middle of last night's rush to do it, then naturally he wouldn't tell me about it just because I asked, and the more I prodded, the more he would withdraw. Still, there had been something ritualistic about Haapati's movements, something so set and determined that I couldn't help being curious.

I walked softly around the hollow to see his face, and was startled to find his eyes open. He seemed to stare through me, through the grass and trees, and his fierce concentration sent an involuntary shiver down my neck. So unwavering were his eyes in his pale saffron face that I almost thought him dead, but his hand came up and slapped at a buzzing on his thigh, without disturbing that long-range glare, and a sense of the absolute alienness of him hit me, a physical blow. I stepped back and it took all my will-power not to break and run, but to retreat slowly and deliberately from his side of the spring.

My sleeping husband, in contrast, seemed like a beloved pillar of the universe, but I didn't wake him. Why should I, if not for reassurance? And if for reassurance, then I would have to tell him about Haapati's sudden, terrifying otherness, and I couldn't cope with the triumph of his comfort.

The spring formed a small, soggy pool that emptied into a respectable stream. I followed the water through the trees until it dropped to flow through a tumble of boulders. Scrambling over them, I found an unexpected basin of water, fed by two or three subsidiary streams that chuckled up from the rocks. Deep and about ten meters across at its fore, the pool's far end spilled over a lip of rock to form a small bog, and the fierce sunlight sucked moisture from it, to the accompanying whine of darting insects. The pool itself, though, was in shade, and before I'd consciously made a decision, I was unseaming my sweat-soaked clingsuit. I tossed it over a bush, kicked out of my boots, and ventured into the water.

Cool, soft, and the underwater ripples of my passing pressed against my thighs as I walked into the pool's center. The water was barely deep enough to float my breasts, and my feet trod cool patches of moss over boulders. I folded my legs and sank to the bottom, feeling my hair lifting about my face, then surfaced and floated on my back. I closed my eyes to the dappled canopy of tree overhead; my ears, underwater, heard only the lapping of tiny waves on the rocky edges of the pool. Tension drained; anticipation and its sister vice, memory, retreated, and I floated at peace.

Then a liter of water fell on my face and I came up, sputtering, to find Toyon close to me in the water, his hand raised for another splash and a wicked grin on his face. He lifted a cautionary finger to his lips, jerking his head back toward the clearing where Quellan slept.

"Where are your clothes?" As he turned to point, I walloped the water at him, ducked back to avoid the tidal wave of his reprisal, splashed again, and he slid a leg around mine while I was otherwise occupied and tumbled me. I came up blowing water.

"No fair," I gasped. "You've got the reach on me."

"How's this, then?" He stepped closer, loose hair tumbling red around freckled shoulders, eyes sparkling, and I reached for him, wrapped my arms around his neck. He lifted me higher as we kissed, I swung my legs about his waist and, with the special grace he always seems to find on these occasions, he carried me out of the pool and we lay on the springy ground near his unruly pile of clothes. His body felt solidly and delightfully human over, under, and within my own.

We swam again in the pool later, in no hurry to leave this one spot of coolness in the savannah. And we talked, of the business we had left behind, of managers, of home, of gardens, of my new enterprise in West Wing, of a symphony we heard before leaving Alta Morena. Of Hoep-Hanninah, of Rhodes, of Quellan.

"What were you asking the Hannin last night?" he said. He sat in the shallows, water lapping around his waist.

"About the prayer plants, the new bed Rhodes set in."

"New bed?"

"Oh, I guess I didn't have time to tell you." I sketched the hunting of the *supplex*, Rhodes's planting of same, and Haapati's mysterious killing of the plants.

"I guess I was too rushed to think last night," I said. "It seemed, when Haapati spoke Standard to me, that we'd established some sort of link, some breakthrough, but I suppose I was wrong."

"Well, you've only been around him a short while," Toyon remarked. "Maybe you're expecting too much of yourself."

I smiled at him, surprised and pleased, and leaned over to kiss his shoulder. "Maybe. I'll tell you one thing I expect, though, and that's clean clothes. I'm damned if I'm going to crawl into those things again."

"Right. Let's raid the car."

"Check. You prance, I'll slink, and if Haapati wakes up we can shimmy at him."

Toyon smothered a laugh. "We must look awful to him."

I hid my surprise at this sudden observation, and we bundled our clothes under our arms and walked quietly into the camp. We managed, with difficulty, to locate our sacks of clothing in the general confusion, and changed.

"I need the shovel," Toyon whispered. "Where do you think . . ."

"Under the seat. I'll get it."

I reached under the seat, but my groping fingers scraped on a number of metallic-feeling cylinders. Opening the side door, I lay on the floor and peered under the seats.

The shovel wasn't there. Instead, I saw one long rifle and a pistol, and boxes which I suspected carried ammunition, resting quietly and treacherously in shade. Turning my head, I saw the shovel hanging from spring-clamps under the instrument panel.

"Found it?" Toyon whispered.

I brought out the shovel slowly and handed it to him in silence. When he was out of sight, I made sure Quellan was still asleep, removed the weapons and boxes from the car, and carried them up the rise after my husband.

He was tamping earth over a small hole as I reached him, and his eyes widened at the sight of my burden.

"Where did you get those?"

"Hush. They were under the seat."

He took the rifle, looked it over, balanced it in his hands, performed various actions on the barrel, the grip, the trigger, and parts for which I had no name. "This is damned near ancient," he said. "I don't think they've made these things for, oh, two or three centuries at least. Good condition, though."

"Well, it won't be for long. Give me the shovel."

"Alin, what are you doing?"

"*Hush.* You know damned well there's a law about weapons on Level Four planets. And there's nothing in the Hoep-Hanninah charter abridging that law."

"Jesus, Molly Do-Good strikes again," he said, still grasping the rifle. "Can't you just ignore them? After all, we don't know why Quellan keeps them."

"That doesn't matter. Think, Toyon, do you realize what would happen if the Hanninah found these in the car?"

"Who says they're going to find them?"

"Right. With a Hannin right in the car with us. Sure. Haapati says what's that and you say, oh, just licorice. Sure."

"At the rate he's going, Haapati wouldn't say anything if we were about to be eaten by wild porodin."

"They're herbivores. Damn it, Toyon, he can just as easily wait until we're around a tribe, and tell

74

them. Or tell Rhodes, or someone in charge at East-base."

"You think so?"

"I don't know, and that ought to worry you." He still looked skeptical, so I said the one thing I knew would convince him. "You get us kicked off now, Toyon, and you'll never see Hoep-Tashik. Ever."

Reluctantly, he handed me the rifle. "All right. But I don't want to know anything about it, and if Quellan finds out . . ."

"Yes?"

"I don't know anything." He turned and away marched through the trees. I felt the peace and pleasure of our hour by the pool slipping away, sighed, and began digging a hole in the baked ground.

TOYON'S JOURNAL

"This is as far as we go," Quellan said. She nosed the ground-car toward a copse that grew on the side of the rocky defile we had been following upwards, since midnight, and flipped the switch. In the sudden silence, the pops and squeaks of the cooling engine were startlingly loud.

"What?" This from Alin, again in the back seat among the luggage.

"This is it. Eastbase is over that ridge, there, about two or three kilometers. We're slightly east of it now."

"Aren't you going on in?"

Quellan turned to me, brushing hanks of hair from her cheeks and tucking them neatly behind her ears. "No. And before you try to, maybe we'd better have a talk."

I turned to Alin, frowning, but she shrugged and clambered from the car, stood stretching herself. Around us, the edges of the narrow canyon paled upward toward the dawn light, although we were still in deep shadow. A faint smell of dust. Two or three stars left in a peach-colored sky.

"I don't think I understand," I began. "You were going to give us a lift . . ."

"And so I did. But before we go any further, maybe you ought to come clear with me, okay? I'm not too interested in risking my neck for bloody nothing."

"I still don't understand," I repeated. "Risking your neck? How? The road to Eastbase is safe, isn't it?"

"Is it?" She included both of us in her glance.

"Oh, come on, Quellan," Alin said. "Don't read us the script. Just what's on your mind?"

"I've been waiting for you to tell me. I've taken you this far, and if you let me in on your game, maybe I can take you the rest of the way, to whatever it is you're after. My help for a cut, that's reasonable, isn't it?"

"A cut of what?" I yelled. "We're going to Tashik, I told you that before. I want to see the ruins, Alin wants to study the Hanninah, what the hell kind of cut do you expect from that?"

"Ah, shit." Quellan swung herself out of the car, reached under the instrument panel and pulled out a battered box, which she opened to reveal a radio. "Listen, I'm in on the game. I heard about it last night over the line from Tyler's. You want to pretend with everyone else, go ahead, but I've got the gaff."

"Alin, can you figure out what she's saying?"

Alin shook her head, and together we watched Quellan connect various leads on the radio. Haapati, still in the car, was superbly oblivious to everything.

"I picked up a transmission last night," Quellan said, holding a crystal between thumb and forefinger. "This is it. Listen." She slipped the crystal into the slot.

". . . *most likely* . . . *proceeding slowly because of extra load* . . ."

"*Standard or special?*"

"Standard, and caution. Pick the most reliable for this, nothing can be allowed to go wrong."

"Alibis and excuses?"

"Simple disappearance. No clues . . ."

Quellan popped the crystal from the slot and carefully placed it in a keep-sack. "Well?" she said.

"Well, what? What's all that supposed to mean?"

She sighed, crossed her arms, leaned back against the cooling car. "Sector twenty-eight, Path B is the one we should have been on last night, except that I took a different route without notifying the Pool. If we were on it, we'd all be neatly tucked under grass blankets by now. For some reason, Haecker wants you two wiped, and since I'm with you, probably me too. Now it's up to you to tell me why."

"Of all the damn fool, stupid tricks," I said, trying not to bellow. "I don't believe any of that crap, faked crystal or anything. Shit, woman——"

"Toyon," Alin said, touched my arm. I flapped my hands with disgust and moved away from her.

"Look," Alin said to Quellan, "maybe that crystal isn't faked."

"Maybe!"

"Let me finish. So we suppose that Haecker, or whoever it was, has had some misunderstanding. Take us to Eastbase and I'll call him up and explain. It's probably just confusion, shouldn't take more than a few minutes . . ."

"Great mother," Quellan said. "You know what's going to happen the minute you stick your head in Eastbase?" She made a very suggestive noise in her throat.

"Prove it," Alin said.

Quellan consulted her archaic watch, then gestured to the radio. "In ten minutes, Haecker's going to com Eastbase again. He always does, this time of day. Private frequency, but still, probably thinks he's got the whole planet so tight he can piddle anything he wants. Look, I won't touch the set, *you* turn it on, tune it. See what he has to say. It ought to be good."

"Toyon?"

So I lifted the radio, stripped it of its case and prodded through the works. It all seemed clean, no hidden crystals, no auxiliary 'corder hidden beyond the first one; a bit old-fashioned, but nothing out of the ordinary.

"Okay, what's the frequency?"

She told me and I set the dial, turned it on, and we sat in silence, consulting our timepieces. Haapati came out of the car, lumbered about for a bit, then settled a meter or so from us, but well within hearing distance.

The opening squawk of transmission startled us. We leaned forward, and I boosted the volume.

"Three hundred nine–four Brown, clear me?"

"Clear and ready."

"About last night?"

Brown, whoever it was, seemed nervous. "Tracked Path B from the base to Tyler's and back, and didn't find a thing."

"You didn't look hard enough."

"Double-checked, with scopes. Not a thing down there."

There was a long silence.

"Tyler's?"

"Shut up."

More silence, decorated with chitterings and static.

"All right, they took another route in. Take five of the offs, check the base in all directions, and check it good. I don't want them showing up, understand?"

"Sir."

"You know what's going to happen if they show up in one piece?"

"Yeah."

"I don't mean just GalFed, Stover. I mean from me."

"Yes sir."

"All right. Do it."

"Three hundred nine–four Brown out."

"Out."

I listened to the static for a while before killing the set.

"See?" Quellan said finally. "Now why don't you come clear?"

"We have," said Alin. "I can't figure . . . Toyon?"

I shook my head, still both confused and angry. Who the hell did they think I was? Damn it, I could buy their petty planet and each of their asses, individually . . . and then I remembered how far away Alta Morena was.

"There's got to be some reason," Quellan said.

"Let me think." Alin stood and paced about for a bit, kicked the side of the ground-car, returned, stared speculatively at Quellan for a moment, paced some more, squatted beside me again.

"How long do you think it'll take for this Stover person to round up a search party?"

" 'Bout half an hour. Off-duties are scattered all over the base."

"And how long after that to find us?"

Quellan shrugged. "No idea. Maybe immediately, maybe not for a day, if we just sit and wait for it. It's pretty rocky around the base, and after what Haecker said, they're going to be damned thorough."

"All right. First thing is, you're positive that we can't get this straightened up? Call Tyler's from somewhere, something like that?"

Quellan grimaced. "Listen. Three years ago someone was pilfering from stock at base, small stuff, crap. Stover set up a light trap, you know what they are?"

"Yeah," I said. "Spring-triggered lasers, intensity varies. No big thing."

"Not the way Stover set it up. One by one, and when they took the guy out he had second degrees over eighty percent. Didn't take him out until Haecker arrived special from Tyler's to see the show. The two of them took him in one of the med-rooms, Haecker watching with this pie grin on his face and Stover doing the magic. Five hours. The guy lived, barely."

"How do you know all this?" Alin asked.

"I took him in and I brought him out, and Haecker had that grin frozen over his mug like permanent, barely sitting still in his chair. Stover's hands were messy. You want to try going into Eastbase?"

"So how do we get out of here?"

"You going to get clear?"

"Let's not go into that again," Alin said. "The only thing I can think of that makes any sense is that Haecker's up to something not so clear himself, and he's afraid we might find it."

Quellan frowned and nodded. "He's up to something, him and Stover. Okay, that makes sense."

"So maybe he thinks we're spies, or God knows what. The important thing is, we've got to move before we're found. Toyon?"

"Yeah," I said, my head still busy with little pictures of seven-intensity laser cages.

"Me, too?" Quellan said.

"I'm no Haecker," Alin said, grinning. "If you're not safe at Eastbase, or Tyler's, then you've got no choice but to come, and we've no choice but to take you. Besides, I have the feeling we'll need you along, since we can't get route information at Eastbase now. Deal?"

Quellan considered a moment, then stuck out her hand.

"Okay. I still don't know what your game is, but I'll string."

The two women shook hands on it.

"And now we drive off into the sunset?" I asked.

"Not in this thing," Quellan said, kicking the ground-car. "Fuel's almost up, and no way to get more. Besides, I can't get it over mountains."

"So we walk to Tashik, carrying our gear?" I couldn't help the sarcasm. Seeing my wife and Quellan busy striking deals and making plans grated.

"No. Remember the porodin? Right. And there's sure to be an encampment near by, we can hitch with the Hanninah. Here's where the ape starts earning his keep."

We turned to stare at Haapati and, to my surprise, he gazed back at us and solemnly nodded.

NOTES FROM THE
GOVERNOR'S WASTEBASKET

1) Into garden this A.M., sifted through bed of *R. supplex* in hopes of finding live plant. No luck. However, found packet wrapped in yellow kitchen preservative buried @17 mm. Contains dried pollen of some type. Suspect Haapati either dropped it accidentally or left it on purpose—connection between H. and death of plants? If deliberately left, why? Have put in safe, will analyze tonight. *Not to mention to L.H.*

2) Remember to get hopper tuned—call Kapl.

3) [On a printout sheet] GLFD 49QY to RH/HP-HH 6690-FJI-9; 22-48. Ref #997SK Qry. GLFD-sec check clear T. Sutak A. Kennerin HB Alta Morena, Clnce A-ML-9. [Underneath, in a scrawl of green ink] Good!

4) A tri-card, bottle-shaped, crumpled. View of trees and river. Note in black type: "Many happy returns. Leo Haecker."

5) An overlay map of the continent of Hoep-Hanninah, transparencies in chronological order through eighteen months. Each transparency bears groupings of small, tentlike symbols; the earliest transparencies show a wide scattering of these symbols, but over the course of months a definite northward progression is apparent. Three tent-symbols, however, remain consistently in place, and they are circled in green ink on each transparency.

6) Why not hoppers?

7) H. Weiss in company of L.H. today, fourth time in week. J. Stover with L.H., bimonthly visit. Port records show Weiss to Xanadu bimonthly, dates just after J.S. visits. Connection—what?

8) Pollen checks out. Chem. struct. next.
9) 3 liters tak
   1 kilo greens—whatever's in
   4 kilo beef—real this time, maybe?
   10 eggs
   2 kilo loaf bread, whole-grain
   butter—as much as poss.
   misc. vegs in season
Kapl, could you *please* remember the cleaning solution this time?

                —H. S-P. Rhodes, Gov.

Chapter 4

ALIN'S JOURNAL

Quellan drove us to the lip of a ravine and parked in the dense sunlight. Without speaking, we clambered forth and began off-loading some of the sacks and boxes: Toyon's tools, my cubes and kits, food, and a crate of the supplement pills that would allow us to eat native foods without danger. Quellan removed the radio, groped beneath the seat, and came up empty-handed.

If she had given in to fury, shouted, raged, cursed, I could have handled it. But she simply asked, and listened in silence to my explanation. And turned to help move the sacks away from the car. Toyon kept his head down, well out of it, and Quellan ignored him as she ignored me.

When we had moved the sacks a sufficient distance away, she backed the car downslope, let it scream through the gears as she aimed it toward the ravine, and waited until the last possible moment before leaping from the already-tilting vehicle. It upended almost immediately, slid through the browned grasses, danced ponderously around and over bushes, and finally stopped against a large tree three-quarters of the way down.

"Sweet mother," Quellan said. "Look at that."

We had left a number of sacks in the ground-car, Quellan claiming that our pursuers would be more likely to believe we'd crashed if some of our belongings were left behind. One brown package, not one of ours, had slipped from its stays and flown forward to crash against the hot bonnet of the car. A thin liquid seeped from it and, as it touched the metal of the bonnet, it hissed.

"That's the package that came off the ship with us," I said, forgetting for a moment my discomfort over the weapons. "I noticed the packaging. But that's not a medicine, is it?"

"What it is is dangerous, damn it," Quellan muttered. "You'd think that they'd tell me when, shit. Look, if we don't get out of there before the searchers arrive . . ."

"Some sort of acid," Toyon said. The bonnet of the car looked corroded where the liquid touched it.

"Come on, move it," Quellan barked. "You want to get our asses fried?" We shouldered our sacks and she bullied us upcountry, cursing under her breath as we stumbled under our awkward loads. Grasses died out; we moved through parched bushes, parched rocks, until no vegetation grew around us. The heat had no direction, simply pervaded the atmosphere as though it were tangible, material, something to be fought against for every step, every breath, and the glare was painful. Directly ahead of me on the narrow path, Haapati plodded along, carrying his load as though it were no more than one of Rhodes's trays of seedlings. Thick back, long arms, thick legs, damned incongruous waist pouch slapping at his hip, yet all the proportions were right, and his dark brown pelt sheeted white in the hard light. Ahead of the Hannin, Toyon moved ponderously around the boulders, head down, concentrating on his steps. Heat shimmered between us, I could not read his posture. During a brief rest in the shade of a stony overhang, he grinned suddenly at me, and I was at a loss to understand. Enjoying? Comforting? Gloating? What? The heat addled my brains, and I stared stupidly at him until the grin disappeared and he turned away from me.

Quellan bullied and pushed us onward, exasperated,

running with sweat, cursing. By noon, she led us to a deep cave halfway up a rocky, pebble-strewn slope, and we sank to the cool floor. Hiss and rattle of breath drawn by dry throats, slosh of the canteen, the sound of low-flying aircars.

"If they've got trackers, they'll find us no matter where we are," Toyon said, glancing at the light-curtained mouth of the cave.

"They don't," Quellan said. "I've checked it. They've got spitfires, light-cannon, side-arms, that sort of thing. They'll be carrying all of it. But for finding us, just hands and eyes and common sense. That's probably enough." She rolled over onto her back, stretched thoroughly. "Kennerin, you keep a lookout. Wake me up quick and fast if you see anything and don't show yourself. All we can do is hide. I'm going to get some sleep. Sutak, you'd better do the same thing, we're going to steal stink-beasts tonight, you and me. Need the rest. Oh, Kennerin? Make sure the ape doesn't get away, okay?"

She didn't wait for my reply, simply turned on her side and tucked an arm under her head. Toyon too lay down, without looking at me, and within moments they both slept. Haapati curled motionless in an angle of the wall, eyes glazed again, and I turned away and squatted just within the mouth of the cave. I glanced around at the heat-dancing rocks and sky. I had received orders. I would obey orders. My head hurt.

Spitfires. Light-cannon. Side-arms. That sort of thing. An aircar buzzed overhead, and when it had passed I found that my lungs ached with the holding of breath. A light breeze rattled pebble upon pebble on the dry slope and I started, almost cried out. Light-cannon, to melt the entire hillside. Spitfires, which did.

The bleached slope quivered, reversed shade and light, flipped again. I closed my eyes, opened them, fought dizziness, scrabbled after shreds of rationality. Held a stone in my hand.

I had never been tracked before, never had people

85

looking specifically for me, looking specifically to kill me. Kill me? I was frozen in this one small, dead-ended cave, so terrifyingly exposed on its gradual hill-side, with a stupid rock in my hand. If they come tramping up here, up that slope, hiding behind boulders, looking for me to kill me, I've nothing to stop them with, at all, at all. Hands? Feet? Nails? On Hagan's World they fight with elbows and shoulders, and they kill people there. Knees? Ankles? How could it even matter? Find the cave, aim large monstrosities upslope, and kill me without seeing my face. My own fault, my own damned fault. I shook, shivered, sweat turned cold and clammy and the rock dropped from my palm, ice and fire in my belly, and the need to run was so overpowering that I could not move. Fear. Terror. Fear. This is what it's like. Fear.

"Here," Quellan said, put the canteen to my lips. Gradually the shaking stopped, terror receded. I tried to speak an apology, for the fear, for the weapons, but she shook her head and pointed toward the back of the cave. I lay in darkness while she squatted by the cave mouth, a figure of black etched in light. Turned over. Haapati's distant eyes stared through me, and I squirmed until Toyon lay between us. One by one by one, I turned off the programs in my head, but still could not sleep.

At sunset we left the cave and dodged through the long shadows of boulders with bundles on our backs. Quellan led us in a large, northerly tending circle around Eastbase, then left Haapati and me in a dust-filled ravine while she and Toyon went to steal the porodin. Haapati and I were supposed to find the location of the nearest Hanninah tribe, or, rather, he was supposed to find it, and I was supposed to get him to tell me. A moving tribe, Quellan had insisted. Not the local Eastbase tribe. Before I could ask her to clarify, she and my husband slid into the dusk.

"Where do you think the tribes are?" I whispered to him in Standard, turning my back to Eastbase. He looked blank, so I dragged the phrasebook from a pocket and tried it in Hanninee, with no better luck. I rephrased, tried to correct my pronunciation, asked it in simple Standard, court Standard, and many different ways in Hanninee, and in the midst of this Haapati lay on the ground, eyes open, and achieved the same rigid nonpresence I had seen in him beside the spring on the savannah, or in the cave that day. I cursed him as loudly as I dared, shook his arm, waved my hands before those staring eyes, and he would not move.

The fear began to return. Toyon gone, Quellan gone, Haapati in some alien other place, and I alone in the night, straining eyes and ears for my husband's return, while images of death played through my mind. Then, abruptly, I shook myself out of the alien mood and turned my back on the entranced Hannin. There would be a wait; very well, I was prepared to wait. There would be danger; very well, I would prepare myself for danger. Immediately the oppressiveness of the night lifted, the uncharacteristic gloom vanished, and I began repacking the sacks, making the loads more compact, more easily manageable. Calm and rationality, yes, and when I heard the rattle of guns from the base I simply crouched lower and continued working. Whatever happened, I would be prepared.

THE GOVERNOR TAKES A STAND

"And here's your report," Haecker said, dropping a crystal on the governor's cluttered desk. Rhodes stared at the object with distaste.

"Go ahead, play it." Haecker reclined his pudgy body in the governor's deeply upholstered chair and clasped his hands loosely before his belly. Abruptly, Rhodes leaned over the desk, popped the crystal into a decoder and activated the machine.

Stover to Tyler's, report 7-10, 1900 hours, 42-16A. Supply car hasn't come in yet, can you confirm departure?

Tyler's to Stover, confirm departure Quellan in one supply car, carrying three passengers, Tyler's 1700 hours, 42-13. Scheduled sector 28, path B, ETA Eastbase 1700 hours, 42-16. Have you instituted search?

Stover to Tyler's. We'll give her another six hours. Stover out.

Tyler's out.

"So?" Rhodes demanded.

"So, they obviously haven't made it to Eastbase."

"Hadn't," the governor corrected. "That was last night's report."

Haecker removed the crystal and held it between thumb and forefinger, letting the clear morning light rainbow through it.

"Well, it's not enough," Rhodes said. "I'm supposed to follow up on these things. I can't just tell GalFed that two Terrans disappeared on planet and that's it." The governor ran long fingers through his hair, displacing the smoothly combed locks. "Besides . . ."

"Yes?"

"Besides, I don't believe you." The governor straightened his back, twitched at the badges of office on his shoulder, but could not meet the planet manager's eyes. Haecker seemed vastly amused.

"Is that so? Perhaps you'd like to talk to Eastbase yourself? After all, a Governor's got certain responsibilities, has to confirm things, right? We certainly don't want anything out of order."

Rhodes nodded suspiciously. "Get out of my chair, then, I'll com it myself."

Haecker moved from the chair and perched on the edge of the desk as Rhodes bent his angular body to the cushions and reached for the comset. He carefully imprinted the codes into the machine, and the line opened almost immediately.

"Eastbase, this is Governor Rhodes in Tyler's. I want to talk to Jaerek Stover immediately."

"Sure. Hold clear, Guv."

Rhodes glowered at the tittering speaker.

"Stover here. How can I help you, Governor?" The voice was strong, businesslike, clear.

"You've a missing supply car, I hear."

"That's right, the regular monthly run."

"Two visiting Terrans were aboard, in my jurisdiction. Have you found them yet?"

"In a manner of speaking, Governor." Stover's voice seemed almost apologetic. "It seems that our driver took an unscheduled route, sector 29 Alternate. Probably thought it would be cooler that way."

"And?"

"We discovered the supply car down a ravine this morning, about twenty kilometers from the base. It looks as though they had an accident."

"Accident? Are there any—have you found the bodies?"

"No," Stover said, but Rhodes' surprised relief was short-lived. "We haven't cleared the wreckage yet. It's fairly inaccessible. We're bringing in equipment now."

"I see. Well. Tell me, Mr. Stover, in your opinion, this driver, Quellan I believe, is she competent?"

"Competent, sir? I thought so."

"Ah. This is the first time she's not followed orders?"

"Not exactly, but this is the first time it's something major. She's a cypher, Governor, just one of many. Could have been anybody."

"One of many, Mr. Stover?"

"I'll be honest, Governor. There are plenty of Company workers who would have accepted a bribe to take your Terrans . . ."

"Mr. Stover, that is speculation. What I want is facts. Has she been driving ground-cars for long?"

"She's been running the supplies for three turns now, air and ground. But I don't see what you're getting at, Governor."

89

"Bear with me. Has she driven the alternate route before?"

"Let me check. I think, yes, seven or eight times. It's allowed during the hot months, the perishables have more of a chance that way."

"Ah. And, despite her competence and knowledge of the route, she managed to drive into a ravine?"

"She was overloaded. The cars aren't built to carry that much."

"Well, thank you for your time, Mr. Stover. Oh, and one thing further."

"Sir?"

"When you remove the bodies, I want them shipped to Tyler's ASAP. GalFed expense. Is that understood, Mr. Stover?"

A long pause. "I'll have to check with the Company," Stover said finally.

"That won't be necessary. Mr. Haecker is here with me, and I'm sure he'll authorize it, won't you, Leo?"

"You heard the governor, Stover," Haecker snapped.

"Yes sir. Eastbase out."

The connection was broken before Rhodes could sign off, but the governor smiled slightly as he turned to the planet manager.

"No bodies, Mr. Haecker?"

"I don't understand you, Rhodes." Haecker rose and stood by the window, and his usual sarcastic jollity vanished. "You're not beginning to feel suicidal, are you?"

"By no means." Rhodes slounced lower in his chair, hands clenched in his pockets. "But I do have certain requisites to fulfill, you do understand? And if they aren't fulfilled then GalFed gets very interested."

"Not if you handle things correctly. And you will handle things correctly, won't you? An investigation now would harm you much more than me."

The governor's hands clenched still more tightly, bunching the fabric of his tunic. "Mr. Haecker, you have discovered certain unfortunate things about me and my past. Things you have been using to blackmail me since I was posted to this planet. Very well, the fault is half mine, for I went along with you. Still, I'm not a quick man, Mr. Haecker, but I do eventually arrive."

"Arrive?" Haecker leaned against the window, but his fingers beat a tense tattoo against his thigh. "I'm afraid that I too may be somewhat slow. I have certain information about you, true. And should you not, let us say, cooperate, I will release that information to the appropriate authorities. And then you, Governor Rhodes, will be relieved of your post, drummed out of the service, refused your pension, and be left destitute and disgraced. A terrible fate, certainly. I fail to see where that gives you any power over me."

Rhodes took a deep breath. "There's more than simply accounting irregularities that you want covered. I'm not entirely sure what the details are, but I'm sure enough to have post-played a crystal to GalFed Sector, ready to go the minute I decide to send it."

"And?"

"I don't believe that Sutak and Kennerin are dead, but I do think you'll try to kill them. I don't know just who or what they actually are, but if I do not receive proof positive that they're alive, if I even begin to suspect that you've killed them, then GalFed's going to be sending a team to Hoep-Hanninah, Mr. Haecker, as soon as I blip that crystal. And when they arrive, they're going to be asking one question." Rhodes leaned across his desk. "Mr. Haecker, what has IDC, and what have you, been doing to the Hanninah?"

Leo Haecker began to laugh. He leaned weakly against the wall and guffawed, slapped his thighs, shook his head, wiped tears from his eyes. Rhodes, startled, sat back and stared.

"Governor, I'm glad you're around, just for the amusement of you. I honestly didn't think you had it in you, but you do surprise me, indeed you do. What have we been doing . . ." and, still laughing, Haecker left the room. His voice echoed in the hallway and down the stairs, but ceased as he reached the outer room. Rhodes, at the office window, watched the planet manager march to his elegant air-car, slam the door behind him, and fling the machine into the air toward Tyler's.

Rhodes frowned, plucked at his tunic, then raised a hand to his lips and gnawed thoughtfully on his nails.

TOYON'S JOURNAL

"Where's Quellan?" Alin demanded. I waved a hand upwards to the porod whose's guide-rope I held, too exhausted to speak. Alin scrambled awkwardly up the back of the beast and climbed over the high sides of the canopied platform that hung precariously on the animal's back.

"Good lord," she said. "Here, help me get her down."

I shook my head, and summoned breath. "No, we haven't got time. Have to load, get going, they're following us."

"Then throw me the med-kit and get moving," she said curtly. "When was she hit?"

"Hour ago, around. Couldn't do anything."

"Come on, get me that damned kit, hurry up."

I started upward in foggy resentment, then found the kit, lobbed it up to her and began dragging sacks to the porodin. Every muscle ached, my head throbbed and, if I could, I would have hidden somewhere to shake for a few hours. I had followed Quellan to the base, to the enclosure for the porodin, helped her dismantle the broad wooden gate, and waited while she strung three porodin one to the other and tied them to the fence. Then she had rushed, flapping and beating through the herd until the huge beasts panicked and fled through the open gate. The noise had brought further noise from a nearby hut, angry voices, a few

92

misdirected shots which, although probably intended to stop the fleeing porodin, only terrified them the more. I wove through ponderous legs to the three tied beasts, and as I reached Quellan she took one of the shots in her left shoulder and slumped over without a sound. I didn't think the Terrans knew they'd hit anyone, or, indeed, that the stampede was anything other than self-induced, but I nonetheless flung Quellan's still body atop the lead porod, grabbed the guide-rope and tugged the stupid animals through the broken gate and away from the base. I followed the stampede for a kilometer or so, running quickly, then doubled around and followed the path Quellan and I had taken into the base. If they bothered to look, they'd find human blood on the trampled dirt of the enclosure, they'd find the opened gate with no breaks in it, they'd find the three diverging tracks of the beasts.

I turned to the pile of sacks, and discovered that Haapati had somehow induced the porodin to kneel, and was flinging items into their platforms so fast that his body was a moving blur. By the time I shook myself free of the mood, he had finished stowing the sacks and motioned for me to mount the second porod with what I almost took to be impatience.

Alin knelt up in the platform, pushed back curtains, glanced at me. "She's all right, a flesh wound, just shock now. Haapati!"

The ape turned to her.

"The others won't follow us to a Hanninah camp, I think. Can you find us one, can you take us there?" She added a phrase in Hanninee, and the dark alien immediately hoisted himself onto the neck of the lead porod and delivered three sharp whacks to the beast with his heels, and the elephantine creatures stood and lumbered off across the broken ground. Swaying, jolting, pitching; Alin bent to pad Quellan's body with sacks, then lay down out of sight. I clung to the side of the platform and stared out at the night. The porod smelled acrid, dense; the moons threw conflicting shadows on the ground, and the stars were unfamiliar and cold. As far as I could tell, Haapati was leading us northward, and I felt a sudden, fierce exaltation. Now, finally, now we moved toward Tashik, away from obstacles, blockages, stupidities, misunderstandings. Now the real journey began.

I woke to morning and stillness, hauled myself up, and peered over the side of the platform. During my sleep, we had entered the forest, and were halted beside a broad, shallow river which we had evidently just crossed. Haapati and Alin had lowered Quellan to the ground, stripped her, and Alin was carefully bathing her while Haapati cradled Quellan's head and injured shoulder in his broad arms. She looked startlingly small and pale, the stitches standing out bluntly on her shoulder.

"How is she?" I called, and Alin raised her head to me.

"Doing better," she said, bent again to her task. I felt left out, and scrambled from the beast's broad back. As I approached, Quellan opened her eyes.

"Doing better," she said, and grinned weakly. "Never thought I'd be nursemaided by an ape, but it does pretty well, friend. You got us away in one piece, uh?"

"I'm not completely incompetent," I said. "How does the shoulder feel?"

"Terrible."

"I'm afraid you got jounced around a bit while I got us away from the base."

"Luckily, it didn't do any great harm," Alin said, standing to wring water from a cloth. "A millimeter or so lower and things would really have been bad." She lifted a clean clingsuit, unseamed it, and Haapati lifted Quellan from the grass and maneuvered her legs into the suit without disturbing the lie of her head and shoulders.

"Hey, I can dress my own damned self," Quellan protested.

Alin shook her head and continued sliding the fabric up Quellan's lean and muscled body. "No. You try too much, you'll end up with a fever, or worse. Lie still."

Alin's Tones of Authority voice, used, for once, on someone other than me. Quellan grumbled but let them finish dressing her. Haapati carried her to the kneeling porod and lay her in the platform, turned, gestured.

"Onward," Alin said wearily. "You want to ride with Quellan now? I've got to get some sleep before we get there."

"Get where?"

"A Hanninah camp. Haapati's taking us there."

"Haapati? Are you sure that's where he's taking us?"

"Yes. I trust him."

"You trust him! How the hell . . ."

"Can you suggest anyone else?" she said coldly.

Quellan? No, even if Quellan were not wounded, she didn't know the northlands. And what was unfamiliar to her was complete terra incognita to us. The Company blocked us to the rear, while before us stretched forest, jungle, and mountains in which we would be completely lost without a competent guide. No, Alin was right, we would have to travel with Haapati, with the Hanninah. I shrugged an acceptance, but was not reconciled.

Two days later jungle began to close in on us, and still Haapati led us to the north. High jungle, air still clear, maybe 24°C, the ground covered with low shrubs, the trees not yet forming canopies overhead. I again rode with Quellan, who now sat, leaning back in her nest of sacks. Haapati had, without consultation, changed the order of the porodin, so that he rode on the neck of the lead beast. Quellan and I came next, and Alin sat rocking in the third platform, dictating into her omnipresent cubes. Quellan slept, as she always did when we rode together; it was only when Alin shared her palanquin that she woke to my wife's ministrations. The shoulder was healing rapidly, thanks both to Alin's skill and Quellan's own natural health.

Sometimes Alin slid from her beast, ran forward, and swung up to the platform with Haapati. Lithe, lean, quick, brown, but I hated the sight, hated watching wife and alien together, as they sat side by side and talked, framed by jungle. What did they find to talk about? I could see Haapati's mouth moving, saw the flicker of Alin's fingers on her recording cubes; she gestured as she spoke, but the Hannin gestured not at all. How had they attained this familiarity, this conversation? I could not remember a turning point, a definite change from Haapati's previous sullen silences to this reserved but ready communication. Did they talk about the route? About the jungle? About Quellan? About me?

I asked her once, as we changed places on the middle porod, but she shrugged my question aside.

"I'm still learning the language, really," she said, sliding fingers over Quellan's face to feel her temperature. Quellan stirred gently under her touch.

"But *what* do you talk about?"

"This and that, nothing important."

Quellan woke and smiled lazily. "Hullo, angel of mercy," she said, and I left the two women smiling at each other, Alin's fingers still curved on Quellan's cheek.

Instead of retreating to the third beast, though, I ran forward and climbed up beside Haapati. The route sloped downward, and it took me a moment to settle myself securely. Haapati didn't even look at me.

"Well, how's it going?" I asked. The ape gave me the cold-silence treatment. I tried again.

"You think we'll be there soon?"

Haapati lifted his arm and pointed ahead of us. Squinting, I could barely make out smudges of un-junglelike colors through the open avenues. "Is that the camp?"

As though in answer, Haapati kicked the porod into a slightly faster lumber, and I turned back.

"Alin! The camp! Ahead!"

"Yes, I know," she shouted. "Haapati told me."

Damn.

THE CONTENTS OF A CUBE

No. 18. Haapati is seventeen years old, and fairly young. Let's see, the Hoep-Hanninah year is 1.8 Terran Norm, so that makes Haapati, what, thirty- thirty-one? Thereabouts. A junior member of the tribe. He explained it this way: at the second turning (year), a Hannin begins to walk. At about the same time, speech comes in. At the tenth turning, the male Hannin enters puberty (for the female it seems to center around the ninth turning, but this is something I'll have to check on later). At the fifteenth turning, a Hannin is considered to be an adult. This was as far as he went, and I could get no information from him concerning the typical life span of the Hanninah. Still, there is enough here to conjure with. Why, for example, the extended infancy? It argues a high degree of species development, this long period of growth and learning. As far as I know, we've yet to discover an intelligent species of quick maturity—the more intelligent the species, generally, the longer the span of infancy. Still, this is just a rule of thumb. I'm not prepared to say that the Hanninah have achieved greater mental development than, say, Terrans. Question of planetary conditions, too. I wonder how long the gestation period is? With luck I'll get more information when we finally reach a tribe.

No. 19. Haapati refuses absolutely to tell me about those trances he enters. I pushed a bit, then dropped the subject. Taboo? Or does he not know? Or what? This isn't the only thing he won't talk about: his mating before his service with Rhodes, the death of his mate (if she was his mate, this is open to conjecture); the death of the prayer plants. Et cetera. Still, if gleanings are all that's offered, gleanings are all I'll get, and I try to accept that with such grace as I can muster. At least until we reach a tribe.

No. 20. How did Haapati know where to find a tribe? As far as I can tell, he made a beeline from Eastbase, and he hasn't diverged from it. Is it simply a matter of knowledge, that at this time of year there will be a tribe or tribes heading in this direction, on this route? I asked him today, and he said "Because that is where they are," which is no answer at all. Again, when I tried to press the point, he retreated to silence.

No. 21. My language skills are increasing. Today Haapati and I conversed, off and on, all afternoon, and all in Hanninee. I originally thought that I would have to use him as an interpreter, but I'm optimistic enough of my progress by now to feel confident about speaking to other Hanninah on my own. I don't remember ever learning a language as quickly as this one. Structurally, it's a complicated tongue, grammar convoluted, and meanings dependent on intonation and rhythm, pitch, that sort of thing. Toyon claims that the language is complete gibberish to him, yet he speaks more languages than I do. Quellan knows a pidgin-Hanninee, and has trouble enough with that. When I have time, I'll have to consider this more closely, but right now I'll remain grateful for, and unquestioning of, the gift.

No. 22. The spells of dizziness have faded, and only appear now in the midst of disturbing dreams. I ran some tests on myself, but nothing showed up, so I suspect it's merely tension and anticipation. And heat.

QUELLAN AMONG THE APES

The porodin were left grazing at the outer edge of the camp, while the three Terrans and the Hannin walked through the circle of goods toward the innermost clearing. Quellan had insisted on walking alone, but after a few steps accepted the support of Sutak's shoulder; Kennerin and the ape strode on ahead, the ape impassive as always, but Kennerin eager, almost running toward the sagging curve of huts. Sutak, too, seemed eager, not so much for the encampment as to keep up with his wife, and Quellan fought off his offers to carry her and thus double their speed. She would get to camp under her own power or not at all.

Tens of them, twenties of them, more apes than she'd seen in any one place during her entire tenure on Hoep-Hanninah. Most of them had already gathered around Kennerin and Haapati, but moved aside to let Sutak and her through. Quellan stared at them, willing herself to calmness, but grateful for the strength of Sutak's muscled arm. Haapati stared impassively before him; Kennerin, from her calm, dark face, gazed with an impelling interest at the Hanninah. Sutak glowered. And although the Hanninah gathered and stared, Quellan could not detect the smallest flicker of interest among them.

Soon an old maroon-sashed male moved through the Hanninah and faced Haapati. They made a series of ritual gestures at each other, and the old one began to speak, his voice rising and falling in the cadences of that musical language that seemed so unlike its speakers. Haapati answered, the old one orated again, then Haapati lifted an arm to Kennerin, orated; moved to Sutak, spoke some more, and finally delivered a long harangue with his arm raised to Quellan. She stood more rigidly, felt small crawlings down her spine, and the wound in her shoulder twinged fiercely. The orations, punctuated by protracted silences, stretched on, and her legs began to give way.

"Don't sit," Kennerin whispered. Sutak moved his arm more securely about Quellan's waist, pulled her body to his and supported both of them. She rested her head on his shoulder and let waves of dizziness spill over her. The old Hannin approached, prodded her shoulder with one gnarled, hairy finger, and she slumped to the ground.

She awoke in the semidarkness of a hut. Sutak lifted her head and held a canteen to her lips, and she drank the cool water gratefully.

"So?" she asked.

"We're going with them," Sutak said, and she strained to interpret the emotions in his voice. They eluded her.

"Where?"

"North, they say. Or, Alin says they say. They're leaving in a day or two."

"Day after tomorrow." Kennerin entered the hut. "I think they may be able to take us all the way there, over the mountains, maybe to the city itself."

Haapati entered the hut behind her, his arms full of sacks. He placed them on the packed dirt floor, then squatted beside them.

Quellan struggled upward, and Kennerin leaned forward to slip a cushion behind her.

"All the way to what?" Quellan asked.

"To Tashik, of course."

"What's at Tashik?"

Sutak grimaced. "Ruins. We told you. The city."

"Oh, shit. We're hauling it across this damned planet, surrounded by apes, stealing stink-beasts, getting shot at, all that crap, just 'cause you want to look at a bunch of dead buildings? Come on, Sutak, you might as well clear with me."

Sutak and Kennerin exchanged glances. Sutak shrugged, Kennerin laughed, Quellan glowered.

"You've got to admit," Kennerin said to her husband, "it's a pretty raw deal. Quellan ties in with us expecting something worthwhile, robs in our behalf, gets shot, and all she gets for it is dead buildings. Not nice."

Kennerin, smiling, leaned over and brushed hair from Quellan's forehead. "Here, look, when we leave we'll take you with us. If Toyon hasn't got a place in the company for you, I'll find one, okay? Believe me, you won't regret it."

"I regret it already," Quellan growled, but the cool palm felt good on her skin.

Sutak stood suddenly, almost hitting his head against the low ceiling of the hut; shoved hands in pockets and stalked about angrily. "I suppose you're going to find a place for Haapati, too," he said bitterly. Quellan frowned in surprise, but Kennerin removed her hand, watched her husband coldly.

"Are you objecting?"

"No, don't mind me, just forget the whole thing." He paused at the hut's door, turned to speak, then made a helpless gesture with his hand and stooped outside. Kennerin half rose to follow, and he turned and shouted into the hut. "God damn it, I'm not going to share! Not with her, not with the ape, not with anything, you understand?" And disappeared into the sunlight again.

"Share what?" Quellan demanded eagerly, but Kennerin calmed her with a hand.

"Me," she said quietly, then turned to smile at the fielder. "Nothing terribly valuable. Just me."

Haapati rose swiftly from his corner, hands clenched tight, lips drawn back, eyes staring at Kennerin. She cried something to him in Hanninee, he made a tense gesture and almost ran from the hut. Kennerin jumped up and followed him out, leaving Quellan confused and angry in the thatched gloom.

THE IMAGINARY CITIES OF TOYON SUTAK

And we wait. And we wait. Quellan tells me that
dark conspiracies are afoot on this planet, although
she doesn't know what they are. Sunlight slides through
the door of the hut, slicing colors in the dirt. Quellan
tells me that much is to be made, that fortunes are
to be had, that the figurative streets are lined with
mythological gold, know we but where to look. The
camp around us is silent, save for the ponderous movements of the porodin, save for the shriek of a bird.
Quellan tells me that we are pursued by blood-thirsty
demons, hideous and unstoppable, and she points to
the wound in her shoulder as confirmation. I do not
believe her. A shot to stop fleeing porodin, a stray
bullet, nothing more. There has been confusion, there
has been misunderstanding, I will clear it up when
I emerge. Demons? Fortunes? Conspiracies? I am
Toyon Sutak, I am a man of business, of practicality,
of wealth. I do not believe her.

Alin my wife burns in cold fury. She tells me that
I have caused her pet alien to flee from the camp,
that she does not know where he has gone. She re-
peats the story Rhodes told us, so long ago, and I
cannot make sense of it. Dead Hannin, live Hannin,
Haapati stained with red. Did I cause that, too?
She stands in the fading sunlight, damp of face,
hair matted, brown eyes chipped from agate and hard
against me, nor can I even touch that chocolate skin.
She shares the hut with Quellan, while I lie under the
canopy of night and count unfamiliar stars. At times
I hear my distant wife bringing water to the wounded,
but otherwise the camp is thick with silence.

How long have I been on this planet? How long
working northward? Tomorrow begins yet another
leg of this millipede journey, and nothing is clear
except that we move circuitously northwards, slowly,

toward my waiting ruins. Hoep-Tashik. Terraces broad as fields, choked with vines, upon which skitter small sleek mammals of passing strangeness. Endless flights of stairs curving and recurving about lofty turrets, helices of steps with worn edges and dusty rails. Fountains, upon whose dried surfaces cling small scrubby flowers, blooming amid the broken stones of fallen statues. Statues of what? Statues of whom? A shattered stone hand with tapered fingers, clinging to a scattering of small weeds; a statue with missing eyes. Alleyways, streets, avenues, roads, paths, drives, concourses, promenades, rows, esplanades, walks, courts, quadrangles, yards, passages, mansions, mews, stables, tenements, castles, huts, palaces. Brick, mortar, stone, plaster, shale, wood, tile, clay, marble, onyx, alabaster. An arch of crystal bridge, ending abruptly before its conclusion, and the fallen stones below glitter in the light. Listening to the antique echoes of caged birds, brilliant as sunsets, the warm-rock melodies of household lizards and snakes, the passing of slim brown legs through shafts of sunlight, the slap of slender feet on stone floors long since piled to dust. City, city, city, all of the rare, all of the unexpected, waiting in brilliance under a burning desert sun.

We moved northward, we proceed, we advance toward mystery. We persevere. And I shall walk at last through dusty wonders, learning the stones, hearing the stones, owning the stones by fiat of desire, by the rights of love. And she will be without question mine. At last. Without question. Mine.

A QUICK SKETCH OF AN EVIL MAN

Jaerek Stover broke the connection with Tyler's, drank a glass of water and tugged briefly at the gold ring that dangled from one malformed ear. Considered options, gains, and losses. Smiled briefly, a flattening of already tight lips. Reviewed.

Haecker had been surprised that the wreckage of the ground-car had yielded no bodies, but the surprise seemed almost gratified, as though he now knew the measure of those he tracked. Had heard in silence of the theft of the porodin and said, simply, "Get them."

Get them. Of course. Stover did not bother to think of the implications of that small phrase, the penalties for failure. Stolid, thorough, dependable, one of his greatest virtues was an absolute lack of imagination. He worked on evidence and solid conjecture, honing himself until he moved from goal to goal free of the encumbrances of emotion. And even his violence was flavored with an implacable practicality.

Get them. Himself, of course. And Christ, without question. Who else? Torres? Kilzer? Holmes? Holmes. By hopper to the edge of company territory, with one stop at tamecamp for pickup and any information available; then, perforce, on foot, for this time there would be no waiting Hanninah to show the way. General equipment and light arms, it shouldn't take anything more powerful than compact coldarms, a skitterbomb or two, nothing fancy, proven stuff. Light stuff. Holmes, he remembered, preferred knives. He pushed himself away from the desk and moved out of his stark office into the afternoon light of Eastbase.

The base chattered and hummed around him as he strode through it. Mining machines clattered into the mills, their holds crammed with precious ores, with unextracted minerals, with semiprecious stones. Beyond the mills, the machines of the extractors thumped and sang, battering delicate scents from evening twin-suckers and yellow, orchidlike lililingers, productive of essences that fetched a year's wages per ounce in the perfume markets of Holman's. Here the hydroponic gardens, here the storage sheds for the pelts and skins, here, too, the carefully maintained laboratories where specimens of the life of Hoep-Hanninah were prepared and shipped to the Federation's great universities, to Dyaan, to Kroeber, to Tassent, to

Greaves, for the Company recognized its social responsibilities, yes, along with its economic ones.

Chist, at Stover's signal, emerged from the vats of the ore crusher. Dirty, huge, his tools enveloped in enormous hands. Thick black hair shorn short and covered with a helmet. Eyes impossibly small above the impossible expanse of jaw and cheek. He filled space, prevented the sight of anything else within view by virtue of his incredible bulk, yet of the two men, Stover, small, wiry, hard, seemed the more dangerous. They spoke briefly, Chist nodded once, and Stover returned to the sunlight.

Holmes was harder to find, but Stover eventually located her at the controls of a micrometer, carefully slicing the heart of a winged leafhopper. Long, delicate fingers, long delicate face; a cat-woman, silent, quick. She listened, asked a question, returned with calmness to her work. Stover watched the economic precision of her movements and nodded once, reaffirming his choice.

A stop at Supplies for the more innocuous items he would need, a second stop in the double-locked vault below for the weapons, which he carried out disguised as specimen boxes. He directed the loaded floater to the hidden vault in his office, folded the floater and filed it. He glanced at his chronometer; four hours to sunset, five until they left. Smiling, he passed a fingertip through a light-beam on the comset, and a few moments later a young boy entered the room.

"Close the door, Jer," Stover said, and smiled. "Come here." He sat comfortably, looking up at the tall child. "I'm going away, Jer. Tonight."

"For a long time?"

"It all depends. Do you want me to go?"

"I'm not to demand," the boy said stiffly. "I am only to accept."

"Good. Very good. You learn quickly, Jer. I may not have to punish you again. Take your shirt off."

The boy unseamed his light shirt and let it fall to the floor behind him.

"Turn around."

Stover ran a finger over the angry red stripes that crossed the boy's back. "Did it hurt very much?"

"Yes," the boy whispered.

"Ah. Turn." Stover cupped the boy's genitals through the thin cloth, smiled. "And what shall I do to you, Jer? Tell me. In detail."

The boy stood trembling, legs slightly apart, hips canted forward. Spoke. Breathed raggedly. Moistened his lips. Spoke. Stover fingered the boy's crotch, eyebrows raised in mock surprise.

"You want it, Jer? Tell me."

"I am not to demand," the boy gasped. Stover's fingers tightened.

"Do you want it?"

"Yes. Oh, yes."

"Then beg," said Jaerek Stover.

Chapter 5

ALIN'S JOURNAL

It must be the heat. We entered deep jungle two days ago, endless days, and I am divorced from my mind, my words are jumbled and obscure, and new, and alien.

Heat. Thick, pervasive heat that turns the jungle around the caravan to jelly, and the thick scent in the air must be dissolved vegetation. The porod rumbles along below me, pushing its heavy legs through air that must be as hard to walk through as it is to breathe. Things don't rot in this heat, they can't. They must melt, instantly, the moment full growth is achieved. Boil back to angry molecules that juggle and push and rush against each other, molten trees and quivering jelly-earth down there below me. I lean over the edge of the platform, half convinced that the porod doesn't exist after all, that nothing but the impenetrable viscousness of the air keeps me from tumbling to the ground and being sucked into the fluidity of the jungle.

Colors, though. Shake this mound of flesh and flit like that, there, the bright flash of pure red through green trees, pulse of orange looped about branches, startling against the pallid flesh color of the bark. And always the changing greens, in streaks and bunches, coils and ropes. The wall of the jungle breaks, gives me a view of an alcove festooned with varicolored creepers, of a dank tarn fairly moving with steaming

107

life, of unexpected avenues through the dense under-growth, avenues unnatural in their height, in their directness, and infinitely more inviting than the tunnel through which we ride. But they don't run north, none of them, at all. I look forward, hoping for some sign of a break in the jungle, although I know that we are barely halfway to the river that is today's goal. Nothing, of course, except jungle, rot, fluidity, death, beauty.

Ahead, the rump of Toyon's beast plods mechani-cally along, thump-sway, thump-sway, thump, just enough out of sync with the thump-sway of my own mount to be disturbing. Toyon's platform sways in sequence. One of his hands, draped over the high side of the platform, sways also. The curtains of the palanquin are open, but the hand is all that's visible; he's probably asleep, sprawled over the carpets and pillows, bathed in sweat, and snoring. The heat forbids any sharp emotions, any anger, any hatred, but a dull, sullen, dizzy resentment blends with it very well. Bas-tard. Bastard. Obsessed, narrow-visioned. Jealous. Clinging. Smooth. Pale. Grasping. Where has Haapati gone? It's his fault, his fault, he lumbers into my soul and suffocates me. I hate him. *Hate him.* Kill him. Kill.

Toyon?

Toyon?

The jungle darkens suddenly and sheets of rain descend. I shiver in fear, grope for my mind, and it slips, it slips. The rain falls curtainlike, no different from the constant, humid nonrain except that the world suddenly shrinks to the sides of my platform and gives me no glimpse of caravan, Toyon, or even the slender neck-stalk of the mountain that carries me. With sight gone, the other senses take over, and the stench chokes. I sprawl under the canopy, water crawls over my body like hot worms. My mind is sticky.

Toyon?

BESIDE A THREE-FACED RIVER

The ponderous swaying had ceased, the taste of the air had undergone a subtle change, heaviness gone. Quellan raised herself slowly, pushed back the curtains of her palanquin, and looked around. They had stopped beside a wide river, whose far banks were smudges of greeny-black over the rushing brown water. Just upstream, the riverbed constricted until the waters shouted and foamed, white against the white of rocks, and just downstream the banks seemed to disappear entirely, so that the main current of the river ran swift and deep, while the sides spread out as a dank swamp from which rose tendrils of mist and the twisted, long-rooted trunks of fleshy jungle trees. The tribe had halted in the patch of dry ground between swamp and rapids, and were constructing their usual bull's-eye camp. Turning, Quellan saw Toyon shaking his head sleepily, knuckling his eyes, and beyond him Alin scrambling from the back of her porod. The river cut a channel through the jungle from east to west, and it was along this channel that the sun cast its last rays, bathing the scene in amber.

Quellan rotated her shoulder slowly and grimaced. Before Alin could reach her, she grasped the side of the platform and swung herself to the dry ground, straightened, then tapped the porod's neck firmly with her knuckles. Obediently, the kneeling beast stood and began grazing on the small grasses.

"How's the shoulder?" Alin asked as she approached.

"Better. You do a good job with the med-kit."

"You do a good job getting shot. A bit lower and . . ."

"Yeah, well, it's better."

Alin's quick fingers unseamed the shirt, lifted the

dressings, and probed the wound. Quellan suffered the inspection in silence.

"There's no infection, and the stitches are holding. Just don't overdo anything, okay? Next time, wait for help before leaving the platform."

"Look, I made it out on my own all right, didn't I? I've got one good arm and I've got sense."

Alin raised an eyebrow, shrugged the shrug that Toyon copied so often. "Okay. Just making sure."

"I know. I just get antsy when I can't do it all myself."

"Do we eat with the apes, or what?" Toyon's voice was uninflected, flat, still heavy with sleep.

"If one of them understood Standard, others might," Alin said curtly. "You ought to remember that."

"I'm just sleepy is all. Hungry, too"

"So wake up and get fed. I've got the pills somewhere . . ." She probed in her hip pouch and produced three supplement pills. They each swallowed one without comment, then Alin led the way into the camp.

The central fire burned hot and bright within the hastily built walls of the firepit, but the air was too warm for the Terrans to venture close to it. Quellan and Toyon stood by the side of a hut as Alin approached the elder and waited while he finished some business with another Hannin. Quellan looked about the circle, curious.

She had spent most of the previous two days asleep, and in her waking periods only vaguely aware of Alin and Toyon moving around her—of the Hanninah, she had little recollection. And here they were, maybe fifty or sixty of them, moving about the circle intent upon their own business. Older ones and younger ones, males and females, pleated sashes in all shades and colors, gleaming knife-hilts. Yellow faces, bellies, palms, but the shades of yellow varied as much as did the shades of pelt, from light brown through dark brown to intensities of black, and the oldest one, the elder, had patches of pale fur amid the thinning hair of his chest. Nursing females, the only ones with apparent breasts, and four of those. Children. A low murmur of voices. Activities across the circle, where, it seemed, a meal was in preparation. Slicing, stirring, cooking, patting, but no matter what the activity or inactivity, each Hannin moved completely self-contained, and the knife-hilts thrust through their sashes caught and carried the gleam of light.

The elder finished his business, and Alin addressed him haltingly in Hanninee. To Quellan's surprise, the elder delivered himself of a long speech in reply, replete with gestures. Quellan, straining, could hear passing words and phrases: "guest of our travels," "hospitality," "given freely."

"I think we're going to be fed gratis," she whispered to Toyon.

"Fed what?" he whispered back. Quellan spread the fingers of one hand and teetered them, a manual shrug.

"Did you understand any of that?" Alin asked when she returned.

"Little bit, I'm no linguist," Quellan said. "Dinner's in the works, right?"

"Right. Soon, I'd guess. Toyon, listen, whatever they feed us, eat it, will you? Please?"

The two exchanged a glance, Alin's not quite pleading, and Toyon smiled. "Sure. I'll behave."

"Good. We're to sit beside the elder, me on his right, you on his left, Quellan next to you. I think the food goes clockwise from him, so you'll get served second. Don't eat until the bowl gets back to him, and then wait for him to start."

"Rhodes's phrasebook?" Toyon asked.

"A great blessing," Alin said with sudden dry humor, and they advanced toward the firepit.

The adults of the tribe were already seated, and the Terrans sat in the spaces left for them. The children brought bowls and heavy platters, and deposited them before the elder. They then brought cups of yellow liquid, which they set before each of the Hanninah—the cups given to the Terrans, though, contained only water. The old one waited until the children, too, were seated before lifting the first bowl, removing some of the contents to the heavy wooden plate before him, and handing the bowl to Toyon. Quellan restrained her curiosity until Toyon passed the bowl to her, glanced at the yellowish stew within, and stoically scooped a small handful onto her plate. The next platter held a fried, breadlike cake, the one after seemed to be sauced vegetation, and the final one held condiments which, in imitation of the elder, the Terrans sprinkled atop the yellow stew. Waiting for all the food to go around, Quellan leaned forward and sniffed at the contents of her plate. The smell was alien, cued no analogies, but was not repulsive. She waited, ambivalent, for the eating to start.

At last, and after a few brief remarks, the elder raised a morsel to his lips, and Quellan slowly dipped her fingers to the plate. Raising a lump of yellow-coated something, she eyed it suspiciously, brought it to her mouth, and licked quickly. Licked again. Nibbled. Then stuck the entire lump in her mouth and chewed enthusiastically, grinning and bobbing her head toward the still reluctant Toyon. Meat, fresh meat, probably killed during the day's trek. Sweet and flavorsome, but the sauce surrounding it was rich, surprising, highly spiced. Hot. Sweat broke out on her forehead, and she flipped the cake of bread into a spoon and used it to shovel more of the stew into her mouth. The vegetables, too, were sauced, blending deliciously with the stew; the condiments sent sweet, contrasting tangs through her mouth. She elbowed Toyon, waved the loaded bread, and sputtered her approval.

It was only then that she noticed the silence of the camp. The Hanninah were eating calmly, without enthusiasm, as though eating were a dreary duty to be finished deliberately and without pleasure. Quellan choked on the meat and calmed herself as she felt the chill of their silence settle around her. She reached again for the stew and finished the meal in uneasy silence, trying to ignore the spicy incandescence of the sauces.

As soon as the meal ended, the children rose again, cleared away the platters, bowls, and plates, and took them downstream to wash them in a clear pool. The adults too cleaned themselves by the river. Quellan, sticky from the day's heat, would have immersed herself in the rushing waters, but Alin held her back, shook her head, and nodded at the elder, who stood straight by the riverbank, arms raised an impossible distance over his head. In the swathe of sky above the river, a few stars appeared.

"*Aan akera*," the elder intoned.

"*Aan akera mahali*," the tribe responded, in the same emotionless tones.

"*Aan akera teyehi aan.*"

"*Aan akera aan.*"

"What is it?" Toyon whispered, but Alin shushed him. The three stood transfixed as the monotone of phrase and response droned on, building a subtle syllabic rhythm.

"*Ahmali takena ahmali teke.*"

"*Enteka entep.*"

"*Entep akera akera aan.*"

"*Ahmali. Ahmali teyehi.*"

The Hanninah swayed slightly with the intonation, arms straight at their sides, all seemingly relaxed except for the elder. He, rigid, arms extended, turned slowly to face the three Terrans, and during the next lines of the ritual the entire tribe turned too. Quellan felt a sudden tightening in her stomach and reached for Toyon's arm. But when she glanced at Alin, she found her swaying, too, in counterpoint to the swaying natives.

"*Eka. Eka. Eka matre.*"

"*Aan.*"

"*Aan eka, eka akera.*"

"*Akera aan.*"

The elder lowered one arm, fingers curving slightly,

toward the Terrans. Quellan and Toyon shrank back, but Alin, entranced, extended her arm toward the elder and stepped forward.

"Alin! Stop!" Toyon lunged toward her. But she was moving rapidly, and his fingers missed the curve of her dangling arm. He stood frozen, watching her as she paced away from him. Quellan grabbed his arm, pulled him back; his breath came ragged, eyes glazed, and Quellan found her wounded shoulder throbbing in time to the thundering of her heart. Still Alin walked, until she stood beside the elder and their upraised hands met, finger to finger, above their heads. Quellan noticed that the elder's sixth finger had nothing to touch, and she stifled a hysterical giggle.

Now the tribe moved downstream, solemn, still chanting, parting to flow around the two rigid Terrans. As the last of them passed, Toyon broke from his spell and swung around, staring after them.

"Alin! Alin!"

"Shut up," Quellan hissed. "They don't kill people. She's all right. For the love of God shut the hell up!"

Toyon stared at her. "She's with them, in that swamp, she's gone with them . . ."

"She's all right. They won't hurt her, that's not the way they are."

"She's . . ." and he shuddered so strongly that Quellan's hand was thrown from his arm. He turned and stumbled toward the camp.

"Toyon, where're you . . ." But he didn't stop, and Quellan watched him go without further words. Slowly, as though against her will, she moved downstream toward the swamp.

As she reached the first twisted trees, she saw movement ahead and ducked into shadows. The young of the tribe came slowly forth, and walked away toward the camp. She waited until they passed, then, drawn by the low sound of voices, she crept forward, the muddy water sucking at her boots. The sun was completely down, but a pale phosphorescence from the water gave the swamp an eerie, dreamlike glow, and in the glow she saw, three meters before her, a Hannin roped to the trunk of a tree with thick jungle vines. The Hannin faced away from her, and she slipped forward silently, clinging to the darker shadows.

Here, the trees formed a rough circle. Facing each other across the glowing waters, the Hanninah stood each tied to a tree, and Alin, too, stood roped, her face bleached in the light, eyes huge pools of shadow, and her mouth continued to repeat the words of the chant. Faster, it seemed, higher, more forceful, making the air dense with its rhythms. Quellan groped for the knife lying between boot-top and calf and began to move around the outer periphery of the circle toward Alin, when she was frozen by a scream of such intensity that she almost fell, clutched a tree, stared in terror at the circle. Again the scream, and she saw Alin straining against the vine bindings, mouth open, in a posture of agony. Quellan tried to push herself forward but was riveted by another scream, this one from a Hannin. Another, and another, until the chant shattered into voices of pain, yearning, hatred, ecstasy, passion; death-shrieks and the shrieks of conception, the screams of birth and the screams of giving birth. Quellan stood rigid and terrified as the Hanninah vocalized every emotion they never showed, until the swamp shook and ran with the piercing cries, until she found herself screaming in response, hands gouging into the tree, the searing pain of her shoulder forgotten. Again, scream. And again. And again. And again.

And a silence so sudden that she did not know if she had passed out, if the screaming had, indeed, ever happened at all. Raising her head from her hands, she saw the Hanninah slumped against the ropes, some bleeding from the cuts of the vines, some swaying with the motion of their breathing. She pulled herself upright against the tree, rubbed her brow, passed her hand over her thighs and sides, touched her shoulder and was almost reassured by the answering twinge of

115

pain. Her legs were clammy with swamp water, her boots soaked. She breathed deeply, moved forward and saw Alin slumped against her bindings. Swiftly, now, Quellan moved around the circle, sliced Alin's vines and, grunting softly with pain, slung the unconscious woman over her shoulder. Stumbling, almost blinded with mingled hair and sweat, she carried the woman from the swamp and into the moon-shadowed firmness of the camp.

BETWEEN CHAOS

As limp as fish. As limp as chewed grass, with all the heart taken out. Quellan carefully arranged the flaccid limbs, pushed a pillow under the dark, frizzy head, pawed clumsily through the med-kit. Dizziness came and passed in waves, and she cursed steadily under her breath. Stuff for broken bones and broken stomachs and broken skin and shredded muscles, but nothing for whatever it was that kept Alin so dreadfully still.

"Let her sleep it off, then," Quellan muttered, stood, groped to the door of the hut. She waited for another wave of dizziness to pass, noticed distantly that her shoulder felt warm and sticky. In the thin dawn light, she found Toyon squatting by the side of his porod, head buried in his arms. She kicked him.

"Come on, get it up, come on, wake up, you bastard, ass moving, come on."

"What?" Toyon lifted his dirt-streaked face to her.

"Come on, gotta take care, damned shoulder's open. Alin's in the hut, come on, you goddamned crapeater, you've got to take care of us." And kicked him again, feebly, before the dizziness approached and took her away with it.

A dense filtering of sunlight through thatch and doorway, and an equally dense silence. Quellan sat

116

carefully, feeling the clean dressings on her shoulder.

"Alin? Toyon?"

She heard a rustling behind her, and turned so swiftly that her shoulder burned. The elder of the tribe squatted easily by the side of the hut, knees up, arms resting on them. He watched her calmly, appraisingly, and Quellan repressed a sudden shiver.

"Where's Alin?" she asked, then haltingly repeated the question in Hanninee. The elder nodded toward the door and made no effort to help her as she struggled to her feet. Tired, yes, and weak, but her head was clear.

"Take me there," she said, neither command nor question, and again the elder nodded, but this time as though in decision. He rose and preceded her from the hut.

Either late morning or early afternoon, she could not tell which. And apes all over, many more than the night before. She stared at them, the congregations surrounding the firepit, the stolid leaners against huts, the passing shadows between the further rings of the camp. The elder led her to a hut on the far side of the circle and left her there. She glanced around once more, then ducked inside.

Toyon lay on his side, awake, one hand holding the hand of his still sleeping wife. Quellan knelt on her other side, placed fingers on her neck and felt the strong pulse, saw the rise and fall of breasts and the flickering of dreaming eyes beneath the closed lids. Sleeping. Just sleeping.

"How's your shoulder?" Toyon whispered.

"Not bad. Did you have to fix the stitches?"

"I got you numbed, then the old ape came in and worked you over. I watched, but I had to take care of Alin."

"I'm glad you finally remembered." Quellan flexed her shoulder carefully.

"What the hell . . ."

"Calm down, Sutak. She's all right, I'm all right, little thanks to you." They stared at each other over

117

Alin's sprawled body. "What would have happened if I was too hurt to move, last night?" Quellan's voice was easy, simply wondering. "And Alin got hypnotized, and went off with the apes? Would you have gone in after her?"

"I was sick, the heat, feverish. Besides, why the hell did you do that? You were still down, no condition, you didn't have to." Toyon's eyes narrowed. "Why, Quellan? What's Alin to you?"

"Sutak, you've got a filthy mind." Quellan reached forward, brushed a coil of hair from Alin's face. "She helped. That's what keeps us alive, see? Helping. I couldn't *not* go after her, understand?"

"I helped you," he muttered. "When you were shot, I helped."

"Yeah, and if you need help, I'll come. But I don't keep score, Sutak."

Sutak nodded reluctantly, and Quellan relaxed. "You got anything to eat in here?"

"No. I haven't asked."

She stepped outside the hut, pulled the proper phrases from her memory, and asked the nearest ape, in Hanninee, for food and drink. A few minutes later, platters and bowls were set within the hut.

Cold cakes and hot tea. They ate in silence, setting aside a share for Alin when she woke up, but she showed no signs of doing so. The numbness in Quellan's shoulder began to wear off, and Toyon gave her another dose of the anesthetic. The snout chilled her skin. Quellan glanced at the sky from the door.

"Afternoon."

"Yeah. The old one said that we make the river crossing tomorrow."

"Any idea how?"

"I guess we'll find out. You want some more tea?"

"Thanks."

The hut faced west, and long streaks of amber sunlight groped further into the darkness.

"Why're you here, Sutak? I mean the desert, the ruins, what's so important?"

118

He talked, and the sunlight darkened toward night. Platters and bowls were brought to them again, and again they ate.

"Me, I just work. One place to another, moving around. Been with IDC about ten years now, I'm getting itchy. I'm gonna make it big someday, wait and see. Not filthyrotten, not any great thing, just enough to lay by, quit the drudge. Break out. You know what happens to old Company workers? They've got a planet, call it Sunset or something dumb like that, full of little square houses and little square parks and little square activities, and that's where they retire you. Saves 'em money that way, not paying out pensions, they bring in stuff and take stuff out, another fucking monopoly. Can't see myself kicking it off with fish and townies, playing four-D Spingle and seeing the meds once a day. Not me."

"Yeah. I guess, except for Tashik, I've got everything I want."

"Everything?" Quellan asked, and Toyon flushed, shrugged. Together they glanced at Alin. She made a small twitch in her sleep, rolled on her side, and her breathing steadied again. Toyon rested his hand on Alin's forearm, and Quellan stared at it.

"Funny contrast, you two," she said, and Toyon glanced up sharply.

"What do you mean by that?"

"Colors. You sort of orangy, freckled, all that, and her so dark. Don't think I've ever seen anyone that dark, sort of caramel color."

"Yeah. They did it deliberately."

"Um?"

"The Kennerins, they're all that way. Bunch of centuries back, they were dirt farmers on a place called Aerie, settled by some Terran, Cauc type, brought his wife and kids along and bought the mudball. What were they? Eurasians? Alin told me once, but I forgot. Near 'Bama, you know about them?"

Quellan shook her head.

"New Terra movement, and it went sour. Most of

119

the darker folk left, and most of them ended up on Aerie. Engineers, doctors, physicists, the whole works, brought it all with them. Except the Kennerins owned the whole planet, and in the course of the settling, the Kennerins made a bushel. Smart folk, took in the brighter of the emigrants, married them to family, set up a regular dynasty. Made it a point of pride not to marry too far from the color, sort of a flag. All kinds of flak when Alin and I married. Her parents were dead by then, but she's got half a dozen siblings who raised a stink, until they found out we didn't want kids, and after that they didn't offer to sell me off anymore. Not that they're polite, just not violent."

"And you married the color and the bushel, um?"

Toyon glared at her. "Listen, you, I made it up on my own, the hard way. When I married Alin I had half of West Wing, and she had the other half, and still her company was only grossing two or three over what mine was. And that's not too damned much."

"Hey, calm down, friend. I believe you."

"That's more than her damned family did. They held a confab in that castle on Alta Morena, Alin's place, her planet, but they all got together for it, invaded the place, damn near locked us up in the north wing for a month while they bitched and moaned and screamed. Had a tag on me so thorough that it took nine months to complete."

"Would she have passed you up if they'd vetoed it?"

"No. We talked about it a lot, and she'd have gone ahead and done it anyway. Life would just have been noisier, is all. They can't touch me now, of course. Between us we've got all of West Wing shipping so tied up you can't take a shit in space without hitting one of our ships."

"Big as IDC?"

"Not our end, by itself, even with our companies combined. But you take the whole family, all the property, all the growing planets and mining operations, the soft industries, and we'd probably swallow IDC and never know what we ate."

"Sweet mother. And I thought you'd be interested in the life and fortunes of a two-bit fielder."

Toyon smiled and was about to speak when Alin stirred more violently. Faintly, from the direction of the river, came the sound of chanting voices. Alin twitched again, moaned, and they lay their hands on her, sat listening to the incomprehensible ritual, stared at each other until it was far too dark to see.

THE CONTENTS OF A CUBE – 2

No. 30. The sashes are definitely symbolic, in color, of age and status within the tribe. Up to what I think is the thirteenth turning for a female, the fifteenth for a male, the young wear sashes of undyed material, rough and awkward. At thirteen, or fifteen, the plain sashes are replaced with pale yellow ones, at about twenty the color darkens to gold, and thereafter progresses through the spectrum until, with the elder, the sash is of a deep maroon. There seems to be a considerable age gap between the elder and the wearers of bright red sashes, the seconds-in-command, if "command" is a proper word to apply to this ragged group. This age gap is something I will have to research more carefully; as of now, I have no data, and no theories. The sashes are also symbols of acceptance, along with their age-symbolism and their simple, practical functions as pleated pockets. In any event, Haapati did not wear a sash, nor did he carry a knife. Instead, that omnipresent little dark-brown bag hung continuously at his hip, either a mockery of his Terran masters or a symbol of their power over him, I can't tell which. I wonder where he is, what he's doing, where he's going, why he left. Whether he wears a sash again. Or a knife.

No. 31. The knives. I asked the elder here about them, but received no satisfactory answer. The hilts are common, stowed in large skin bundles amid the piles of goods, but the blades are carefully hidden away. I've had another chance to examine them at close range, and am willing to swear that they're machined, and well machined at that. I wish I could get my hands on one for just an hour, run an analysis on it, identify the machining. It's possible that they are Company-supplied, but if so, what did the Hanninah use before? The knives seem so ingrained into their culture that I find it hard to believe that they were only recently introduced. Oddly enough, though, the need to study the knives is not urgent, I can work up little enthusiasm for some good old-fashioned steal-and-see ethnology. Have the feeling that, if I just leave it all alone, I'll learn the entire story eventually. And that, by the time I learn it, it won't matter.

No. 32. The dizziness lessens and increases, and seems to have become a standard part of my life. It's not bothersome, though. When it comes over me, I simply lie down and sleep until it goes away, although when I awaken my eyes are always dry and reddened, and my body tense.

No. 33. I spent a good part of this afternoon watching Quellan, and cannot shake the feeling that she is deeper than I think, or than she lets on to be. A something about the eyes, an observance, a sense of covered irony that belies her simple image. Yes, yes, I believe she's all that she says she is, that what she wants is what she says she wants, but still have the feeling that there is a certain saving grace to her rough clumsiness, and I begin to be very glad that she is along.

No. 34. Tonight, at dinner, they set before me a cup of their yellow wine, although Toyon and Quellan still received water. I felt flattered, accepting this as a mark of favor, of acceptance. The drink was harsh and bitter, but I drank it all, unwilling to reject the gift. I will not mention this to Toyon, though—he too easily misunderstands.

TOYON'S JOURNAL

Alin was up at sunrise, dressed, striding about the camp as though she had not spent the last twenty-some hours in a deathly sleep, as though this above all was the place where she belonged. Quellan and I took longer about it and staggered out only when Alin called us to breakfast. The Hanninah began dismembering the hut as soon as we emerged. Quellan tired, more quiet than usual, and I still ashamed of myself, still twisting within to find an honorable out; but Alin, ah, Alin my wife. Fresh. Active. Chattering at the elder who, to my amazement, listened to her, occasionally spoke, actually conversed with my incredible wife.

The camp slowly collapsed around us, the firepit was kicked back to dirt, the porodin loaded and lined up facing downstream. Most of the Hanninah walked, we three rode to the point two kilometers from the camp where the river broadened even further, into a swampy ford.

"It's easy until almost the middle," Alin shouted to us from her beast. "Then it gets violent. Remember to hold on."

I nodded and turned to shout it to Quellan. But she had heard, waved her good arm, and began wedging herself firmly into the platform. She roped herself to the posts of the canopy, using, from what I could see, hitches that could be opened in an instant, in case the beast tumbled and she had to get free. I considered her preparations apprehensively, wondered if I should take some of my own, then saw that Alin was sitting free and easy above her mount, arms gesturing to the elder who rode with her.

The swamp, if possible, stank even worse than the jungle behind us. Great bubbles of gas rose and farted with each step of the porod—an evil, sulpherous, rotten scent. The Hanninah, of course, didn't react one way or the other, although Quellan and I and, eventually, even Alin, wrapped cloth around our faces to filter the stink. Peering ahead, I could see the two porodin beyond Alin's, each carrying a load of goods. The first one reached the deep channel of the river, and two of the walking Hanninah scurried aboard, while a third one scrambled forward to sit on the porod's arching neck. Prods, grunts, flailings, and the porod most unhappily slipped into the deep water and began flailing with mighty legs. Between its kicks and the swift current, it scrambled to swamp about fifteen meters downstream, stood still while its passengers rearranged themselves, then plodded toward the jungle. By now the second porod had begun the crossing, with a bit more difficulty, and when I looked again Alin's mount stepped into the river.

Tilted, righted itself, plowed across the waters with the elder perched on its neck. Alin clung to the sides of the platform, and even at this distance I could see her pale knuckles, her strained face. Halfway across, the porod began tilting again, and I shouted, my belly a knot of ice. Two or three loose packages tumbled from the platform and were swept away, but Alin held on and the beast regained its balance, completed the crossing, and clambered to the swamp bank. Alin turned to wave at me, and I waved back, weakly.

A young, yellow-sashed Hannin scrambled up the side of my porod and seated herself astride its neck, her mud-caked, hairy legs grasping the porod firmly and guiding it toward the channel. I dug fingers, toes, knees, elbows, even belly into the platform and peered over the rim. Our entry was smooth, no tilting, no loss of balance, and the platform seemed to ripple as the porod pumped its legs. The current swirled around us, white water of our own creation. The Hannin grunted, slapped the porod's head, and suddenly we were tilting, tilting, tilting. I shouted, rolled away from the tilt, trying to right the porod with the weight of my body; the flat head whipped toward me, and suddenly the young Hannin was flung upstream. A thin scream broke from her mouth, almost lost in the roaring of the waters, and she landed hard, about seven meters from me. Without thinking, I grabbed the scramble-rope, threw myself over the porod's side, and reached wildly for the Hannin. My fingers just missed her and she slammed against the porod's side. In that instant, I grabbed her ankle, dragged her to me, pushed her up into the platform and scrambled up myself. The porod, gazing around stupidly, had stopped swimming, and we were floating rapidly downstream. I crawled up the scaly neck, slid my legs around behind its head and, slapping, kicking, shouting, cursing, got it started toward the bank again. I was still shouting and kicking when I realized that we were on the semisolid ground of the swamp, and I leaned forward, resting on the porod's head. It cocked both eyes upward at me, each one the size of my palm. I pushed myself up, peered around until I saw Alin's beast in the distance, aimed my porod in that direction and got it going again. When I looked around, the Hannin I had saved sat upright on the platform, gazing stolidly at me.

There were no other incidents to the crossing. As soon as we reached the other porodin, the young Hannin slipped away and another came to take her place. I crawled into the platform, and when Alin appeared I was too exhausted to feel exaltation at her fussing and worry. She got me into a clean suit, praising me; even Quellan appeared briefly, butting her porod up against mine.

"I lost the damned radio," she said grumpily.

125

"That's too bad." I waited for some words of commendation from her, but she frowned fiercely at me.

"And you lost a couple of sacks, some of your clothes, I think. Maybe a bundle of tools."

"I was too busy to notice," I replied shortly.

"I think they went out of their way to give us a scare," she announced. I refused to reply, and she grinned suddenly. "All right, you did a good job, Sutak. I'm impressed."

I thanked her rather stiffly, and still grinning, she moved away. Alin, too, was smiling rather broadly, and I flipped over on my side and fell asleep.

We camped that evening in higher jungle, less dense and less humid than before. Again we were given a hut together, but this time the atmosphere was one of friendliness and, at least while around Alin and Quellan, I felt somewhat the hero. Just before we joined the dinner circle, though, the young Hannin appeared at the door of the hut and, facing me, made a long speech that ended with her handing me her knife, hilt forward.

"What?"

"She says that you saved her life," Alin said. "She says that you witnessed her shame, and therefore you must carry the knife until you have deemed her shame to be ended."

"Her what? She was thrown, she couldn't help it, that's not shameful."

Alin spoke to the Hannin, then turned to me again. "You heard her scream, she says."

"That's shameful? Didn't she hear all my screaming and shouting? I can't take her damned knife, Alin. Tell her so."

"You have to. If you don't, she'll have to leave the camp. As it is, she can't eat until she gets her knife back, and she can't get her knife back until she's overcome the shame. And that's for you to decide."

"Crap. Just tell her she's forgiven, or whatever, and make her put that thing away."

Alin dug into her pouch and produced one of her cubes, activated it and pressed it to her ear.

"No, there's no verbal forgiveness possible," she said after a while. "You have to think up something for her to do, something to show that she's stoic."

"Says who?"

"Ke'empah, the elder. He told me about it yesterday, when I asked about Haapati."

The Hannin continued to stare at me. "Ask her what her name is," I said.

"Taleti," Alin said after a moment of conversation.

"Listen, tell Taleti that on my world, the words of forgiveness are more important than . . ."

"No, Toyon. This is *her* world, and you've got to do it her way."

"Shit." I turned away from them, stalked to where Quellan sat rubbing her shoulder and listening, then stalked back. "Now I've got to worry about the spiritual health of apes. Damn it, Alin, you come up with something."

She shook her head. I sat, hands around my face. "What did your damned elder say about all of this? On the cube?"

"Something physical. Something painful."

"Yeah? Then what about Haapati?"

"The person affected by his shame was dead," Alin said quietly. "The only option was banishment, and that's worse than anything else."

I stared at Taleti. I didn't want to give her pain, didn't want to involve myself with her or her people's rites at all, yet if I didn't give her a "punishment," a penance, real enough, her shame would be multiplied, and it would be even more my fault. Reluctantly, I gave in to the responsibility.

"Tell her that I'll take her knife," I said slowly. "Tell her that she has to, to burn her hand. Water and fire. Is that enough?"

Alin stared at me, then nodded. "Yes. Yes, that's enough." She turned to speak to Taleti. The words sounded too melodic, too fluid, to mean what they did.

Taleti extended the knife to me again, and I took it awkwardly, thrust it into my belt, and followed her out of the hut.

Chapter 6

RHODES SALLIES FORTH

Governor Rhodes stood before his reflector and plucked unhappily at the black clingsuit. He looked, he decided, like an animated bannister, all rails and poles stuck together somewhere in the middle, probably with rusty nails and failing glue. His head and hands appeared white against the dark fabric; not an elegant whiteness consistent with his profession, but the white of damp plaster. His silver hair, though— at least his hair was properly combed and floated smoothly over his brow. The governor drew black gloves over his fingers, considered applying dark creams to his face, settled instead for a clinging two-way that covered his entire head and translated him, quite suddenly, from human to alien, from grotesque to the almost terrifying. Rhodes peered at his image in the reflector, grinned, flapped his arms in something approaching a menacing manner, and was delighted.

He shouldered a dark pouch and palmed off the lights of the dressing room before stealthily opening the curtains and peering out across the dark grounds. The moons hid behind thick clouds, and only a sprinkling of stars appeared at the horizon. Unseasonable weather, damp, almost cold, but suited to his purposes. He moved warily through the dressing room, down the dark stairwell and to the back door of the rambling house, where he spent some three minutes peering suspiciously around the shadowed garden. Nothing moved. Cautiously, the governor came down the steps, closed the door quietly but firmly behind him, and crept around the side of the house toward the drive. As he passed the empty car port, he sneered under the black mask. Let them try to keep the governor locked up. Just let them. GalFed didn't pick its representatives for their stupidity, as certain parties would soon discover. Yes.

Of course, the loss of his hopper was annoying, if nothing else. Kapl had apologized for the mistake made during normal repairs, the slip of a wrench at the wrong time that had caused a small nut to eat its way through the overhead generators, the centrifugal pump lines, and out the stabilizers. Four months to get the necessary parts, Kapl said. The Company itself was out of parts, Kapl said, and therefore couldn't sell them to the governor or the governor's mechanic. Such a shame.

Shame, indeed. Rhodes scampered across the open drive, stalked into and through a grove of trees; *Kapliana robustus*, to be exact. Last time he'd name anything after that incompetent idiot, and perhaps he might even change what names he had bestowed. He hadn't, after all, sent in the paper to the *Journal of ExtraTerrestrial Flora* yet, so there was plenty of time. He'd do it. First thing when he got back. Absolutely. Besides, he strongly suspected Kapl of being in Haecker's pay, and that was not only unfair, it was against regulations. Of course, Rhodes had gone against regulations himself. But he was making it up, doing something about it. Had done something about it, had planted the code at GalFed Transmissions that would, unless he personally revoked it in five days, key his suspicions about Haecker and the Hanninah straight to GalFed Security. Rhodes was pleased, and frightened, at this bold stroke. So much like a romance, some intergalactic agency thriller, that he was almost embarrassed. But some things needed doing, he assured himself as he threaded his way parallel to the main road and ten meters from it. Besides, when he came back he'd revoke the key. And if he didn't come back, well then, if he didn't come back it wouldn't matter to him anymore anyway, would it? No. Throw caution to the winds. Act tempestuously. Perhaps, thought the governor as he approached the grounds of Haecker's private mansion, perhaps I should have applied for Security at the very beginning, instead of going the diplomatic route. After all, I seem to have a calling.

Haecker, he knew, had an elaborate alarm system spread about his property, something to do with wires in the ground, infrared beams and other devices too devious for the governor to comprehend. Rhodes had no illusions about his ability to fool the system, and knew that he would have to rely on speed and surprise. Skirting the low hedge that marked the boundaries of Haecker's property, he moved about the house until he was within three feet of the Landing area. He peered over a bush and saw the planet manager's new air-car sitting in the middle of a cleared area. Someone had thrown a tarp over the machine to ward off the threatened rain, but had not thought to batten the air-car to the ground; the only things keeping it in place were two small cables running from either end of the elongated machine to eye-hooks embedded in the plasteel landing pad. The governor crouched behind a bush, removed the pack from his back, and extracted a thin laser torch, then shrugged the pouch back over his shoulders and peered over the bush again. No one in sight. Haecker obviously thought so much of his security system that he didn't think a separate enclosure for his pride and joy of a car was necessary. Mr. Haecker, Rhodes decided, would be very surprised. Very surprised indeed.

Well, no help for it, now or never. The governor flexed his knees, then took the bushes in one long-legged bound and tore across the plasteel pavement to the car, snapped on the torch and was already shearing through the aft line when the lights flashed on and alarms began to scream. He rushed to the front of the machine and sliced the bow line, heaved at the tarp. As soon as the cockpit emerged from the fabric, he vaulted into it, slammed the toggles into position, rammed the engines on and gave the machine no time to warm before shoving the lifters into position. The car shuddered, strained, bucked, and lifted from the pad just as shapes poured from the door of Haecker's house.

The governor almost put his feet through the floorboards in his anxiety, his legs straining as he urged the air-car out of the range of fire. One or two bolts zinged by, but the car was still bucking enough so that the shafts of light and lumps of metal kept missing the machine, and they soon ceased. Of course, Haecker wouldn't want his pretty machine ruined, if it could be helped. Rhodes risked a peep downward, and saw the shapes milling in the light below—could even pick out Haecker standing by a cut mooring line and staring up, hands planted on thick hips. Rhodes repressed the urge to shout something derogatory, instead goosed the air-car higher and sent it winging toward Eastbase. The lights of Tyler's vanished behind him, and he took off the two-way, threw it to the floor, stretched his long arms over his head and, giving in to an ungovernable urge, crowed with triumph. There were GalFed citizens in trouble out there, and their governor, at risk of life and limb, rode to the rescue. Just let anyone try to get in his way. They'd see that GalFed chose its servants well. Haecker was nothing, Stover less. He'd get the entire mess straightened out and be back at Tyler's in plenty of time to revoke the key. Still, did he really want to be an unsung hero? Could he not, perhaps, leak the tiniest bit of the story? Without implicating himself? Rhodes settled himself back to consider the question as the air-car hummed over the rolling plains.

OF FIRE AND A BURNING

Again a circle of Hanninah, again silence, again a slanting evening light conflicting with the flames in the pit. Toyon followed Taleti into the center of the circle, her knife sticking out of his belt, and together they stopped before the firepit, facing the elder. Quellan slipped into a gap in the circle and stood watching while Alin walked a pace into the circle and stopped.

Toyon looked grim, and determined. He slipped the knife from his belt, held it before him, and spoke.

"Taleti was thrown from a porod during today's crossing, and I heard her scream," he said flatly. He paused while Alin translated, then continued. "It is my place to give her penance for this. I have decided that she should hold fire in her hand." Again the pause, again Alin's clear voice being melodic in a foreign tongue. "Does this meet with the approval of the elder?"

Ke'empah nodded. Toyon turned to face Taleti, and Quellan saw the strained tightness of his jaw. "Do it," he said to her, but the tone of command approached a quiver.

She turned and dipped her hand to the fire, brought forth a burning coal and held it out to Toyon. She stared at him, face still impassive, but her arm began to shake and a smell of singed flesh charred the air.

Beads of sweat appeared on Toyon's face, and his hands slowly clenched around the knife. "That's enough," he whispered, but Taleti didn't drop the coal. Her body was shaking now, firelight danced from her brown pelt, but her gaze held steady.

"That's enough!" And when still she didn't move, he swung his arm and knocked the coal from her hand. The coal fell and rolled toward the elder, and Taleti walked toward the circle. But Toyon ran after her, grabbed her arm, and half marched, half carried her back to the hut. Quellan shook herself swiftly and followed.

"Stupid fucking apes," Toyon muttered as he pawed through the med-kit, one hand still gripping the Hannin. "Dumb stupid crazy goddamned idiots, have to go through with it, no sense, damn it." He slathered Taleti's palm with ointments, muttering, cursing, eyes damp and rimming with red. Slapped a skinsheath over the burn. "Take your knife, go on, take it, you've done your stupid penance, you've gone and made a big hit, you can take it and get the hell out!"

He threw the knife on the ground and stumbled into the hut. Taleti slowly bent and picked up the knife with her unburned hand, shoved it into her sash, stood as Quellan brushed by her and entered the hut. Toyon lay curled in a corner, and after one brief glance, she backed out of the hut and prevented Alin from entering.

"Why not?" Alin demanded.

"He's got to be alone for a while," Quellan said. "He wouldn't want you in there now."

"And how the hell do *you* know?"

Quellan breathed deeply and wiped sweat from her face. "How many people got burned out there?" she asked. Alin looked at her oddly, but turned away from the hut. The two women moved toward the ring of goods, not speaking, not touching.

"What about Taleti?" Alin said as they reached the edge of the circle.

"She'll take care of herself."

Alin sighed. "I ought to be recording Ke'empah. He's willing to talk, he's almost garrulous, comparatively. A gold mine. I ought to . . ."

"That really hits, doesn't it?" Quellan said after a pause.

"What?"

"That business there. Tie yourself to a tree and scream, sure, go ahead, no one gets hurt much, pick up a sore throat, so what. But that, that's different, isn't it? That's hard to take."

134

Alin sat with her back to a pile of pelts. "It's not just screaming, Quellan. It's . . . there was something to it, something big. Important. And that—that ceremony that Toyon did, they've got a reason for it, I'm sure. I should be recording Ke'empah."

"So go ahead. There's plenty of time before nightfall."

"I don't think I could, right now. I don't know."

Quellan squatted beside her, staring at the porodin and beyond them at the thick ridge of jungle.

"I blew it," Alin said softly. "I didn't even know it, but I was playing with them. Interesting natives. Quaint. Busy being the amateur ethnologist. God help me, I was worse than Toyon. The Rituals and Rites of the Fascinating Aborigines. Lord, Quellan, who do I think I am?"

"I don't know, friend. Maybe you're different now."

"Maybe I am." Alin stood. "I'd better get back. You think Toyon could use company now?"

"Sure. But not me."

Alin smiled suddenly, tightly, and moved away toward the huts. Quellan stretched against the pile of pelts and watched the darkening sky until dinnertime.

ALIN'S JOURNAL

I woke before dawn, raised from dreams by the liquid notes of a kula bird in the jungle. Lovely, to be awakened thus by melody. Ke'empah tried to point the bird out to me yesterday, but it was hidden by the jungle, its presence betrayed only by the pouring of crystal sound. A bird of omen, the Hanninah believe. An ambiguous harbinger, of what, of what? They hesitate to say, they hedge their bets, and thus the kula bird prophesies whatever comes next, very neatly. Trills and runs, high pure notes that cascade down the scale and rise hesitantly once again. I kept my eyes closed, blocking out the hut, Quellan, Toyon, all the now-sleeping problems, and lived through my ears. And listening, I was suddenly overcome with homesickness, all the more bewildering for having no cause—nothing in the fresh morning reflected Aerie to me, yet I lay drowned under unexpected longings for things decades past. Not the cries of tropic, invisible birds on an alien planet, but the harsh caws and cackles of swooping hrathlings as they wake in the morning and search out their prey on sharp, sky-circling wings. The shining cold of winter mornings, a bleak gray shoulder of mountain supporting a rising orange sun; the air so cold and clean that each breath is a revelation, a wine, a scourging tonic for the soul. Huge, brown-winged hrathlings, so graceful in flight and so terrifyingly clumsy on the ground that, the first time Kale and Pera took me to them, I cried and clung to Pera's long winter coat, afraid to voice my terror, afraid to advance. But Kale hefted me in his arms and brought me into the nest, held me with one fur-clad forearm as he mounted a bird and we soared far above the isolated valley of our home, over the stone mountains, over a limitless wonder of blue that Kale told me was the sea. That flight, and flights later, up the stone flanks at the break of spring to discover small, secret blossoms hidden in the rock; down to other valleys, more temperate climates, other farm-holds, distant towns, and even more distant, the smudge of Aerie's one city. The moment I saw that distant place I wanted it, wanted to walk its streets, explore it, learn it, but Kale laughed and said there was plenty of time yet, the city would wait. And it did, it did, until that cold, crystal day when I discovered that Kale and Pera were not mine at all, that another family and another life waited for me in some unimaginably distant sector, that I was old enough, that I would have to go. Kennerins were always raised on Aerie, whence they once had come. I hadn't known that. Kennerins always left for their owner-ship planets, for their careful education, for their empire. I hadn't known that. But they had raised me

136

well, these sudden strangers, and when I mounted the hrathling for my final, solo flight away from them, I neither cried nor pleaded, and they became two specks of darkness against the gray mountain, left childless once again in their high home.

Dark, intense people who looked like me. Sultry, angular house spread over cliff and beach and meadow and forest, a castle of a house, a city within one set of walls. Servants and slaves and workers and managers and holders and entertainers and cleaners and sewers and makers and destroyers, all centering on me. One year, and from there to Dyaan, and back to Alta Morena when the dark, intense people died suddenly, distantly, quietly, leaving me an unwanted empire, ships, planets, people, oh, more than anything, people. To work, putting aside dreams, and to Toyon, and to marriage, and to tension, and finally to this small island beleaguered by a world of ocean. To the kula bird singing foreign euphonies from the boughs of a samisu tree.

Kale and Pera. Rare smiles of great worth. Long, narrow fingers fixing scrapes and wounds; great clouds of smoky hair to hide in when the world crept in too close. Slow, easy voice in the light of a firewall, thick warm arms and a deep, almost inaudible laugh. Pera and Kale. Lying in my sleep-sack I was overcome with longing, with grief; twenty years skittered away and I was lost and abandoned and filled with stories I didn't want to believe. Aerie and hrathlings were world enough for me, and I was a fool for not going home again. I wriggled completely into the warm sack and cried in darkness.

Then Toyon rose grumbling from the bag next to mine, Quellan made snuffling noises, the Hanninah outside moved in morning ritual, and I rubbed my face dry, unsealed the bag, pushed myself out and stood. Already the air had begun to heat up.

ALIN'S JOURNAL

We are rising now. The jungle has thinned, the air seems less clogged, and occasionally a strong breeze brings us clear air from the north. Quellan claims it's cooler than usual, claims we should be steamed through, but it feels hot enough to me. I still feel disconnected, uneasy, my mind crowded with memories that I try to push away before they interfere with the pacings of the day.

This morning, as Toyon clambered aboard his porod, the young Hannin Taleti appeared silently beside him and swung herself up to the neck of his beast, and there she sits, her burned hand cradled in her lap, oblivious of Toyon's attempts to get her down. She makes him wildly nervous; were I not feeling so disconnected it would amuse me to see his plight. He doesn't understand what she wants—well, neither do I, but the fuss doesn't seem worth it. She sits silently and guides the beast, rarely turning to look at my confused and glowering husband, while he comes tearing over at every opportunity to ask me what in hell is going on. Quellan, that surprising and many-leveled woman, watches it all with calm interest, and if any of us approaches the answer, it's probably her. Between these episodes of demand and doubt, I sit quietly while my mind goes back and forth, back and forth, as though testing, tasting, evaluating, exploring memories and emotions, and I am powerless both to stop this and to wish to stop this.

In the dense sections of the jungle the trees perch on their toes, thick trunks ending three or four meters up and myriad flesh-colored aerial roots reaching down squeamishly to touch the soggy ground. Here, they have overcome their fastidiousness and thunk solidly into the earth, roots prudishly hidden amid the duff. The choking vines, too, lose a certain intensity, and

138

they appear here as symbiotes rather than parasites. Altogether a more tame and acceptable place, but jungle still. I'm not sure I appreciate the change.

Ke'empah too, it seems to me, has been acting strangely. Has somehow, today, lost that detached quality that colored even our more detailed conversations. He sits with me on occasion, and I automatically finger the cubes, record our mingled voices, then he is gone again, from one beast in our caravan to another, back to his own, over to mine. Expectation? Anticipation? He is restless, most emphatically restless, but when he lifts his head to stare, it is back along our path, rather than before us.

We stop at noon, briefly, to allow the porodin to drink at a clear stream which they quickly muddy with their great flat feet. The Hanninah wander about, nibbling at foodstuffs, relieving themselves, rearranging piles of goods, and we, too, pace the forest floor. Taleti and Toyon stand under a tree, she offering him bites of the dried travel food stashed in her capacious sash, he nibbling dutifully and trying to hide his puzzled glances. When they finish, he changes the dressing on her burned hand. She watches stolidly. Quellan, casual as any Hannin, squats behind a bush, then rises to wander about the forest, flexing and pulling her shoulder into a more limber quickness. The porodin are finished, we climb each to our own beast and line up. Across the stream, on through the rising avenues. I think I will sleep.

But my sleep was interrupted. In midafternoon, there was some commotion at the back of the caravan, and soon two Hanninah sprinted toward Ke'empah's beast at the front of the line. Within moments they returned with the elder. He paused beside my still-moving beast and lifted his saffron face to me.

"Come," he said, and I immediately checked to make sure I had an adequate supply of fresh cubes, and slithered down the clamber-rope to sprint after him.

"Hey, what's going on?" Toyon called as I passed.

"Don't know yet. Tell you later," I yelled without pausing. Ke'empah, for all his grizzled pelt and ancient face, set a furious pace.

The last porod was kneeling, but as soon as we swung aboard the beast rose and lumbered after the caravan. The platform was crowded with eight or nine Hanninah, and lying in the midst of them, on a thin reed stretcher, was an old female. They parted to let me approach, and I sucked in my breath with shock. Her entire back was burned and singed, hair and much flesh charred away. I plunged my hand into the pouch, pulled out the med-kit and, falling to my knees, passed the clensor over her back.

"Who did this?" I asked in Hanninee. "What happened to her?"

"Your elder from the base burned her," Ke'empah said. "One of your people. Four days ago."

"At Eastbase? And she ran all the way here?"

"She had to come. Her time was ready."

Salve. Skinsheaths. I hesitated over the antishocks, then administered one of the least specific, monitored her carefully while it took effect and assured myself that it would not harm her alien physiology. Ke'empah waited until I was finished, then said, "You were not called here for that."

"I was—Then why did you have me come? Why didn't you stop me?"

"It's fitting that you should try to repair what your people have done."

"My people? They're not my people. I don't know who did this. I'm—I'm sickened at what's been done, but I'm not responsible."

Ke'empah stared down at the now-sleeping female. "She is elder of a tribe near your base," he said without looking at me. "Her tribe has been there many turnings without moving, and it was necessary that they be there. But her time for the north journey came, and your elder of the base did this to her, because he did not want her to go. Also he burned her daughter's

140

daughter, and a child. Four days ago." He glanced up at me. "To move the will through force, is this not the way of your people?"

"Too often," I admitted uncomfortably. "But we are not all alike. The man who did this . . ."

"Your mate forced the end of Taleti's penance. Is this not the same thing?"

"But he was trying to spare her pain," I explained. "He used force as a mercy, because his words couldn't help her."

"Yet he used force."

"So did you," I snapped. "That entire penance ritual, that was pure Hanninee, we have no ceremonies that demand suffering in penance for a natural action."

"None?"

Discomfort again. "We're a very large race, and among us we believe many different things, and we act different ways."

"Yet what one can do, many can do, is this not so?"

"No, not that way! I couldn't do this, what was done to this elder. My mate couldn't, the woman who travels with us couldn't. This is repugnant to us, we loathe the man who did this as much as you do."

"Loathe?" said Ke'empah. "We do not loathe him. Come, it is time to go."

He swung over the side of the moving beast without giving me time to reply, and I grabbed the scramble-rope and followed him.

"She will die," he said as we walked past the slow-moving porodin.

"I think not. She is sleeping, and her responses seemed good to me."

"She is a Hannin, you are a Terran," he said without rancor. "She will die. She is irreplaceable. Her tribe will suffer in her absence."

"But she's absent from it now. Isn't that as much as dying?"

"No, she's with them as long as she lives. But when she dies, then they have no elder whatsoever, and then they will suffer."

"Surely there's another old one in her tribe . . ."

"No," he said again, and that flat negative began to grate on my nerves. "She is irreplaceable. I am irreplaceable. As is the elder of each tribe. There are no other elders."

And that was all he would say, despite my prodding, until we reached my porod. I turned to grasp the scramble-rope, then said to the Hannin, "Ke'empah, if it is permitted to ask, how old are you?"

And I swear that the old Hannin twinkled, that some small spark of mischief appeared in his flat black eyes. "Very old," he said solemnly. "Oh, very, very old." And moved swiftly up the line.

As soon as I gained the platform, Toyon and Quellan ran forward and scrambled up beside me. I told them, in detail, what had just happened, and what had been said. Toyon looked disturbed, and Quellan looked completely sick.

"Stover's after us." She drew in her shoulders protectively, and her lips tightened. "The 'elder' at East-base, that has to be Stover. He went to tamecamp to find out if we'd been through, to pick up whatever it is that he picks up there, it must have happened then. Four days ago would be the day after we stole the porodin. Yeah. Stover."

"Tamecamp? Picks up what? Slow down, Quellan, take it easy. One thing at a time."

Quellan shook off Toyon's hand and huddled into herself a bit more tightly.

"Tamecamp's a place Stover set up about six months after they made Eastbase. He found a tribe of Han-ninah and forced them to stay in one place. Doesn't let anyone out there unless they go with him, and then it's only two or three picked people."

"But he can't do that," I protested. "It's against the Charter. Hasn't anyone told Rhodes?"

Quellan shrugged her good shoulder. "IDC's not about to tell, if they even know, officially. If the Han-ninah haven't said anything, maybe they don't give a crap."

142

"They care, I think," I said. "Remember what Ke'empah said about that wounded woman. But why wouldn't they complain?" No one had an answer to that.

"What about this stuff he picks up?" Toyon asked. "What stuff?"

"Damned if I know. Something, comes in tiny plasteen sacks, I got a look at them once. Company sacks. I think that's what Stover and Haecker have got going, something to do with tamecamp and the sacks, but I don't know what. Something illegal. Hell, I wasn't in on it. What does it even matter? Stover's tailing us, and he'll catch up. It won't be pretty."

"He wouldn't attack us in the middle of the tribe," I said. "Would he?"

"You ever take a crap?" Quellan demanded. "Take a walk before dinner? Swim? And besides, what makes you think the Hanninah would object? They don't complain about tamecamp, do they? The old ape talked about your people burning that old woman, right? So what makes you think that Stover can't come marching in here, fry us like bacon, and march on out again, and no one even to say peep?"

"Wait a minute," I said slowly. "If Stover's that violent, he'd probably *not* stop at hurting the Hanninah to get to us. So we're a liability; if we weren't here, the Hanninah wouldn't be in danger."

"Brilliant," said Quellan. "If we weren't here, *we* wouldn't be in danger, either. So?"

"So I'm going to ask Ke'empah if he wants us to leave," I said resolutely, and Toyon gaped at me.

"You mean you want us to go through the jungle alone?" he said. "Without a guide or anything? Listen, we don't even have proof that this Stover character is after us at all, just this burned Hannin and Quellan making up stories to scare herself."

"Me what?" Quellan shouted.

"Well, you don't, do you?"

"Don't what, you stupid fish?"

I flapped my hands wearily and, unnoticed in their

143

wrangling, slid from the porod and found Ke'empah near the front of the caravan. He listened solemnly to my offer to leave and refused to allow it.

"You are the guest of our travels," he intoned. "You have joined your path to ours, and we travel together because that time has come to us."

I shook my head, unwilling to unravel all of this. "No, listen. We are a danger to you, this elder is following us and will kill you to kill us. For your own safety, we must leave."

"We do not wish you to go."

"But the safety . . ."

"Would you," he said suddenly, "would you use violence to evade violence?"

"I don't understand you."

"Understanding is not necessary. Our times have merged, and we travel together."

"You don't want us to go? You're quite sure?"

"I have said it." He turned to face forward, effectively terminating the conversation, and I took myself and my confusion back to my porod. Quellan and Toyon fell silent as I clambered up the rope.

"Well?" Quellan demanded.

"He says we're not to go, he doesn't seem to give a damn for Stover or anything else one way or another, and I think he'd get very angry if we left."

"See?" Toyon said triumphantly to Quellan. "I told you that you were going overboard. The old man wouldn't have us stay if he thought there was any danger."

"That's not what he said . . ." I tried to say, but Quellan turned to the side of the platform, grabbed the rope, said, "Bullshit" very emphatically, and swung down. Toyon shrugged, patted my arm, said, "It's going to be all right, she'll see," and disappeared himself. I sighed, lay on the cushions, and fought the increasing dizziness.

TOYON'S JOURNAL

Jungle still, although through the broken limbs above I can see the lofty spread of mountains, and Taleti has told me in the somewhat sign language we have developed that we begin the ascent tomorrow. No huts tonight, the clearing is barely big enough for the assembled porodin, and we sleep in hammocks and nets strung between the thick-fleshed trees. Vines, trunks, hammocks, all pale and dancing in the light of the firepit.

The clearing isn't big enough for a dinner circle either, so tonight we fend for ourselves. Ke'empah has taken charge of feeding Quellan and Alin; they sit, one on either side of him, before the fire, and Quellan has still not learned to hide her enthusiasm for this spicy, incandescent fare. Alin eats with precision, quietly, and reaches for her cup often. Ke'empah refills it again and again. Taleti feeds me, bringing me dried fruits and vegetables, strips of spiced dried meats, cooling drafts of spring water and swift nips of tak, shared from a skin flask. And although there are many, many Hanninah around us, we nonetheless seem to sit in a sphere of absolute privacy, of uncomfortable intimacy. She passes food, gives me water, accepts what I give back to her, lets me tend to her hand, and if I am not entirely at ease, there is at the least a companionship to this sharing. I wondered, during the day, whether she accompanies me under orders from Ke'empah, but, during this evening meal, have decided that she simply likes me. If this is not true, I'm not sure that I wish to know it.

The burned Hannin lies in a hammock of woven vines covered with moist branches, and someone feeds her by hand. I wonder if she finds it comforting, this disinterested care she gets from her own kind? I wonder if she even feels the need for comfort? I wonder if she feels at all? I want to ask Taleti, draw her out, discover her opinions, but the barrier of language lies between us. It's not the type of thing I would ask Alin to translate, this sudden, floating curiosity of mine. Taleti sips the tak and passes it, I sip and pass it back. Alin says Taleti is barely postpubescent, that she is too young to be mated and too old to be child-related to specific parents. That, in any event, her parents are with another tribe, for it is the custom for the young, after puberty, to seek acceptance in an unrelated group. I wonder why. I wish I could ask. I am somewhat glad that I can't.

Taleti's pelt, in the firelight, is an auburn brown, and glows.

Dinner ends, the fire is allowed to die, the Hanninah seek their beds. Taleti has strung hers on the trees next to mine. She slips into it, turns slowly, closes her eyes, and soon her flat chest rises and falls with the rhythms of sleep. How odd that she has no breasts. How odd that none of the female Hanninah have breasts, except those nursing young, and then they have four. I wish I could ask.

Quellan, too, sleeps, and the only light comes from Alin's glower and my own, as we sit on opposite sides of this small clearing. She bends over her data-cubes, probably listening to the sibilant noises of Hanninee recorded during today's trek. She stirs as I watch, but it's not to look at me; her hand rises in that habitual manner to her face and she tugs at a puff of hair, then tucks it back behind her ear. One leg stretched out beneath the collapsible work table, the other braced against a thin leg of the stool, foot skewed at an angle, childishly, and I feel a sudden wave of desire for her, for the cool brown length of her body and the softness of her breasts and, even more, for the workings of her mind, the pulsings of her emotions, all the small, infinitely important things about her that I can never hope to touch or taste. But if I thread my way to her through this populated darkness, she will raise those disconnected, friendly

146

eyes to me, she will talk in the unfamiliar, almost emotionless cadences that have changed her voice. Dark-haired wife in a pool of light across darkness, and it is as though she were further from me than ever before, as though the untouchable quality of her that I have lived with for so long has been transmuted from the merely unfamiliar to the absolutely alien. I do not understand. I would be afraid to ask.

Now she does lift her head toward me, meets my eyes, smiles a smile whose meaning I can't fathom, and I find myself smiling back with the strained politeness of someone at a party given by friends of friends of friends. I look down at my work table, make great pretense of busyness. Soon she fingers her table into its compact and tiny traveling mode, rises, stretches, calls something in Hanninee into the darkness, and climbs into her hammock. The light winks out, and I am the only actor left on the stage to amuse the apes. This will not do, not at all. Rise, fold my own table into the messy package it always becomes, head toward the hammock. Douse the light before stripping. But, before I clamber into my hammock, I find myself leaning out in the night to pass a hand over Taleti's sleeping head, and I cannot tell why.

ALIN'S JOURNAL

Out of the jungle, into a forest of hardwoods, grasses, low green bushes. No kula birds here, but other unidentified ones that dip through the meadows, gray and brown and blue. One or two unexpected clouds in the sky. Rising, but still far enough from the mountains to see them. Impressive, bald-headed, huge, fanged, formidable. Ke'empah assures me that there is a way up, but I'm not entirely sure I believe him. Ramparts at the edge of the continent. End of the world.

The old Hannin, the burned one, rides in my palanquin now. She lies on her stomach and is unconscious most of the time. When she wakens, her mug-face made a caricature by pain, I feed her, or one of the Hanninah helps her relieve herself. She babbles and moans in her sleep, and makes no sense. Gainings, losings, returnings. Something she lost, will lose, or is losing. Ke'empah listens during the times he is here, nods as though she makes perfect sense to him. Perhaps, to him, she does.

Toyon refuses to ride with me. Rides with Taleti, both of them waving their arms at each other. Gestures replace words, yes, but she seems so eager, so un-Hanninah, arms milling about her head, back swaying. Slender back. Flash of yellow fingers. Toyon's face so pink in contrast, hair so red. Could Toyon have burned someone? Could I? Could Ke'empah? The old one groans and dithers. Quellan rides alone, glancing often behind us. Won't ride with me. Says she's leery of the sight of blood, but there's a sardonic twist to her lips when she speaks. She mentions pursuing Terrans. She observes Toyon and his mascot. Slips from her mount to explore the forest. Collects sticks and stones, pitches them casually at the trees from her swaying mount. Cowards, both of them. Irresponsible Terrans. Care nothing about a dying woman. Running from reality. Useless. Fools.

The old one falls into a deep sleep midway through the morning, and I nap, wake to find the caravan stopped for a resting. Jungle far below, recedes farther as we move again. By evening we're high enough so the mountains aren't visible any more, but they exist, their presence is unmistakable. The old one is restless and thrashes about. They take her from my palanquin at evening and set her in a nest of moist leaves then cradle the leaves in a hammock of vines. No huts on this steep ground. No trees for hammocks, other than the small grove where the old woman lies. Tonight we sleep on the open ground, and the wind from the peaks is cold.

There are more of us now, many cramped dinner

circles, great vats of yellow stew, great bowls of bitter yellow wine. Toyon and Taleti observe ritual silence, Quellan stuffs the food greedily. No yellow wine for them. Pink. Pink. Pale. Hairless. There's a woman dying in the grove and I'm feeling so dizzy. So terribly, terribly dizzy .

QUELLAN ATTENDS A WAKE

Quellan looked up from a handful of stew to see Alin staring blankly toward the fire, as did all the Hanninah in the circle. Eyes opened wide and without motion, faces so calm as to be supernatural. She shivered involuntarily, lowered the food, and glanced about. Toyon gazed at Taleti, a small frown creasing his forehead. He picked up her limp hand, waved his fingers before her face and hummed softly to her. He looked puzzled but not concerned, not until he glanced about the circle and saw Alin. He stood abruptly and moved through the circle toward his wife, and dropped on his knees before her. Quellan followed.

Alin stared through her husband as though he were so much air.

"Alin? Alin? Wake up, love, come on. Alin?"

"Hush," Quellan said, holding his upper arm. "Don't startle her."

"Startle! Alin?"

He laid a palm along Alin's cheek and pushed her face gently to the side, but as soon as he removed his hand her face swung forward again. "What's going on?" he demanded, turning to Quellan. "What have they done to her?"

Quellan shrugged and was about to reply when, without warning, the tribe stood and moved toward the small grove. Alin moved with them. They walked so swiftly that Toyon was still gaping, Quellan still about to speak, by the time the tribe entered the woods. The two Terrans plunged after them.

149

The Hanninah, facing the center of the grove, squatted in close-set rows, and Quellan, craning over them, saw a form lying still and stretched, caught a glimpse of wrinkled yellow face, a bit of burned back.

"The old one's dead, I think," she said quietly.

"Where's Alin? I don't see her, where's Alin?"

Quellan stared, saw her, tried to turn and discovered squatting Hanninah surrounding her, pressing against her legs and staring blankly before them. More Hanninah entered the grove and squatted in turn, until no portion of earth was visible. Toyon silently and furiously pushed his way through the Hanninah toward his wife.

The pressure was so great that Quellan began to lose her balance. She took one involuntary step; then another, moving through the lake of dark fur, sidling carefully, filled with a deep silence, a foreboding beyond words. Firelight flickered on the outermost trunks, and the last slanting rays of the sun cast a diffused glow over the grove. For a moment she heard a pulsing in the silence, moving to the beat of her heart, then the quiet deepened even beyond that. Step. Slide. Step. Turn. Slide. Toyon moved furiously ahead of her, thrusting aside the squatting forms, bullying his way through, but Quellan soon ceased to watch. The silence entered her lungs, filled her stomach, and she moved with purposeless caution.

When the chanting came it grew from the silence, delicate sounds that separated into four-part rhythms, laced with an incomprehensible keening. Alin's clear voice wove tortured arabesques around the structured emptiness, the sounds a saint might make after assuming sins but before assuming grace, and Quellan's careful stepping took on the cadences of dance.

Then abruptly Quellan stood still, closed her eyes, clenched her fists at her sides. Jaw rigid, she fought against the enchantment, fought against the fear. She concentrated on controlling the terror, establishing possession of her body, possession of her mind. The

150

Hanninah swayed about her and chanted more loudly, but she locked her knees, spread her legs, withstood the pressure, then slowly opened her eyes again and stared into a sea of alien beings. Rid herself of repulsion, of fear, of any noises in her head, and paced toward the meadow, plowing a straight line through the tribes. She broke free at last and slumped against a tree. The chanting rose and fell, twisted and turned, inexorable, unhurried, under Alin's agonized soprano. Toyon now straddled the body of the dead Hannin, struggling to reach his unreachable wife.

"Quellan!" he bellowed over the voices. "Quellan! Help me!"

She pulled herself upright. "Walk," she called to him, then more loudly, "Walk! Don't stop! Don't listen! Walk out!"

He pushed one more step through the Hanninah, caught his wife by the arms and hoisted her clear of the ground, up to and over his shoulder. The chanting changed pitch, and Quellan groped at her waist for the weapon which wasn't there, but the Hanninah did not move, nor did Alin cease chanting as Toyon plunged through the tribes, ignoring the limbs on which he stepped. As he passed Quellan he grasped her wrist and pulled her after him.

"We're getting the hell out," he said grimly. "Now. Tonight. Where's our gear?"

"Hold it." Quellan jerked her arm away, ran in front of him and blocked his path. "Just where do you think we can go?"

"Back to Eastbase, back to Tyler's, get off this damned planet."

"Right, and walk smack into Stover and get killed. You want that?"

"You're paranoid, we've got to get Alin away from this."

"But not that way."

Toyon glowered. Alin had not ceased her soprano keening. "Look, at least let's get to the beasts, okay?"

Quellan stepped away and they moved toward the

porodin. As they reached them, Toyon sat and cradled his wife in his arms, called her name again and again, but the chanting did not falter. Quellan gathered armloads of cushions and cloths and rigged a tent three meters from the outer, rough-edged ring of the camp. She lit a glower as Toyon placed Alin within, then dropped on her knees.

"Great mother, I can barely feel a pulse," she muttered.

"Can't you make her stop singing?"

"Don't dare. Can't give her a tranq, don't dare try an upper. Maybe some water, something that isn't chemical. Wash her face. Something. Can you get me some——"

She broke off and stared at Taleti, who stood at the makeshift opening of the tent with a bowl of water in her hands.

"What do you want?" Quellan asked in broken Hanninee. Taleti answered.

"What's she saying?" Toyon demanded.

"She says it wasn't necessary to take Alin, but that she, Taleti, can help us. I think that's what she means. Get the water from her."

Taleti knelt beside them as they bathed Alin's face, slapped her cheeks and wrists, tried to make her walk, all to no effect. Eventually they let her lie, eyes staring, the intense untuneful mourning pouring from her throat. They each huddled at separate ends of the tent, staring at Alin in the weak glow of the lamp.

Toward daybreak, when Alin's voice was a harsh and painful caw, her eyes flickered and she turned her head toward Quellan.

"You were almost with us," she said.

"No," Quellan said firmly. "No."

"And you took me away," Alin said to Toyon. "You pulled to the deep, you fight against. There is no clarity here. No help."

"You'd better get some sleep," Quellan said. "It's been a hard night."

"Only to those, and she is dead for us, for we have

152

done it and you feel no clarity. Oh, but oh, I could hear all the voices, all the voices, all . . ."

The voice was tortured, dry crackling, and Quellan felt small, cold prickles up her spine.

"Go to sleep, Alin," Toyon crooned, and reached to cradle her head in his palms.

"Not! For touching! Not!" She twisted away, but could not lever herself up.

"It's all right, no one will touch you," Quellan said. Toyon dropped his hands, and Alin's eyes began to close. "Almost had you," she said sleepily. "Amid all the voices, all the singing voices, and you were almost there."

Chapter 7

RHODES AT EASTBASE

The governor sat still in the chair, legs sprawled negligently, hands at rest, trying to appear completely relaxed, nonchalant, unreadable. But he could not stop himself from darting suspicious glances around the room. Somewhere, he told himself, there would be a listener, something stuck into the walls, or under the uncomfortable bed, or even in the lumpy stuffing of the chair in which he sat. And he would not give them the satisfaction of peering at an agitated governor. They had had enough satisfaction from him already.

Since his arrival at Eastbase two nights before, he had found himself enmeshed in a web of Haecker's weaving, from which he could not extricate himself. The planet manager, it seemed, had informed the base's acting manager that Rhodes had stolen the air-car on a bet, was inspecting Eastbase on behalf of GalFed, was to be extended every hospitality and shown the entire operation. At length. Not only had Rhodes spent the day before being hustled from one crashingly boring operation to another, but he had, thanks to Haecker, acquired a reputation as something of a practical joker. Workers were constantly coming up to him, clapping huge and filthy hands on his shoulder, and bellowing their approval in his ear for his neat theft of Haecker's air-car, which was now under lock and key somewhere out of sight. Rhodes had demanded to see Jaerek Stover, and been told that the base's manager was unfortunately unavailable but would be back very soon; he had explained that he really must return to Tyler's, a joke is a joke but paperwork was piling up. Bureaucracies, you know. Yes. Indeed they did know, and showed him another dump, another plant, another colossally uninteresting detail of IDC's operations. Surrounded, all the while, by smiling, pleasant, very big people, who made certain that the governor never felt the pangs of loneliness. To the extent of offering him women, boys, even a Hannin, all of which the governor forcefully declined before retiring to what, it turned out, was a well locked and unescapable suite of rooms. Rhodes glanced again at the rug, decided that the listener was probably not there, and barely avoided gnashing his teeth.

The sound of knocking interrupted the governor's thoughts. He turned as casually as he was able and called an invitation to enter.

"Governor? I thought, if you have a moment, we might go over today's schedule during breakfast. . . ." A small, plump man with an easy smile pushed a food-laden floater before him. Various clip-cubes dangled from his belt, and the stub of an imprinter poked from the neck of his worksuit. Dusty-looking face, thick hands. Acting manager. The governor donned one of his most diplomatic smiles.

"Thank you, Perez. You'll join me? I do so appreciate the time you've taken from your work to show me around, but I'll relieve you of your trouble, if you'll just get the air-car ready for me. So much to do back at Tyler's, don't you know."

"But governor, we've barely begun to cover the operational end, and haven't got to administration at all. Try some fruit? I'm sure you'll want a complete report for your evaluation."

"Ah, yes. Of course." Rhodes accepted a cup of tea, sniffed at the steam. "However, it's no problem to get back here, next month, say. Always have to keep in touch you know, finger on the pulse of the planet. Next month, certainly."

"But governor . . ."

"And perhaps Mr. Stover will be here then, do you think? I really do need to speak to him. For the evaluation, of course. You still don't, I'd imagine, know where he is, do you?"

"Didn't I mention? We're expecting him back today, this afternoon at the latest."

"Yes?" said Rhodes, leaning forward. "Indeed? Well, in that case, I really must speak to Mr. Stover, you understand. Perhaps I'll wait. But just until tonight, I simply can't spend another day away. Things to do, don't you know."

"Of course, I understand completely." Perez hauled out and displayed a smile full of teeth, rasped the cloth napkin over his hand, and stood. "Well, if you're ready, governor, perhaps we can start for the stamping inlets now."

"Of course, Mr. Perez." Rhodes wiped his fingers clean and, with a repressed sigh, followed the chubby man from the room. On any decently run planet, he merely would have called Security, and the entire problem would be taken care of in no time, the three missing Terrans found and returned to their proper places, Haecker and Stover made to show due respect to a servant of the government. On any decently run planet. But here, the governor thought, he *was* the government, the embodiment of the law, and it all rested on his shoulders. He gnawed briefly at his lower lip, considering the possible fates of his three missing Terrans, then pushed the worry aside. As soon as possible he would find and help them, of course. Yes. And in the meantime, he must remain calm and observant, as any good security agent would, unclouded by emotion. Self-contained. Dangerous. He sucked in his already concave belly and glowered around the sunlit base, then caught sight of the locked hanger where they kept Quellan's shattered ground-car. Immediately his confidence fled, and he gnawed at his lip again as he followed Perez toward the filthy stamping inlets.

INTIMATIONS OF MORTALITY

The tribes had started moving again at dawn, some riding porodin, many walking. Quellan stared over the side of her palanquin, amazed at the number of Hanninah on the trail. They stretched as far ahead as she could see, and as far behind; when the forest opened into meadow they spread in either direction, a dark mass dotted with the brightness of sashes and the gleam of knife-hilts.

Two porodin ahead, Quellan saw Ke'empah sitting upright in Alin's palanquin, back rigid. Runners approached, clambered up the rope, retreated again, a constant flow of messengers from every direction. Alin, Quellan knew, slept on rugs and cushions near the elder, limp and jouncing occasionally with the motion of the lumbering porod. Quellan turned her attention to Toyon, directly ahead of her. As always accompanied by Taleti, but today there seemed to be no conversation. The tall, red-headed man sat slumped against the back of the palanquin, shoulders bowed, hair escaping from the knotting of its club at his nape and straggling down his back. Taleti sat to the side, facing him, radiating a deep calm. Quellan watched her for a long time, trying to catch the gleam of shifting eyes, before she was convinced that the young Hannin's attention was riveted on Toyon. Alin remained out of sight, Ke'empah sat stolidly facing forward, and the marchers on either side were too far below to see into the palanquin. Reassured, Quellan slipped her capacious travel pouch from under the cushions, opened it, and began sorting through its contents.

One field knife, blade dulled, handle notched and scarred, and the secondary blade broken off at its

157

pivot. Three soft, transparent sacks of supplement pills. A coil of three-mil, quarter-weight rope, wound tightly about its cylinder, and within the cylinder an assortment of pitons and a small, collapsible mallet. She removed the mallet and pitons, spread them on the cushion before her, and ran her hands over their surfaces. She'd bought the kit years back, in a small shop in Playa Mujeres on Soledad, back before she'd joined IDC or come to Hoep-Hanninah. Back when she still had serious thoughts of a life spent in indolence on many planets, bumming about the galaxies. She'd begun a collection representative of all the things she planned to do, as soon as the wheel turned, as soon as some luck showed up. And, while waiting for the luck, the collection had disappeared bit by bit, into pawn shops, lost in games of chance, left through haste or carelessness as she moved from planet to planet, sector to sector. Now, all that remained was the untouched climbing kit, and she weighed each piece in her palm and frowned in contemplation before returning them to their cylinder and placing the kit beside knife and pills.

A very small med-kit: chemical clensor, basic antipains, stitchers, a few bandaging materials. A compass, set for a planet whose shameless abundance of magnetic poles was a galactic wonderment. Useless here, but he placed it, too, beside the other equipment. An expansible canteen. Two molecular sheets, expensive, stolen. Sunguard. A pair of nonagonal dice. Enough for two, taken all together? Yes, with some supplements, perhaps. Enough for two.

She groped in the pouch but nothing remained within. Then, after glancing about again quickly, she arranged and rearranged the items as though, placed in the proper pattern, they would present to her the way out, the answer, the path. Eventually she shrugged impatiently, shoved the articles back into the pouch, and bent to inspect the heels of her boots. She then unrolled her jacket and felt through its padding; removed her one spare suit and shook it out, gave it the same careful inspection she'd given boots and jacket. Flexed her arms, grimacing at the residual pain in her shoulder, worked at it grimly until it loosened. Then lay back, hands under head, and stared at the sky and passing branches above.

A commotion started far to the back, growing louder as it caught up with her, and she sat, looked back, then knelt and held to the side of the palanquin, shading her eyes with one hand. A new group of Hanninah made their way forward, and they seemed to be carrying objects over their shoulders or slung between them; it was only when they came abreast that she saw what they were carrying. She swung herself down, landing hard on the packed ground, and, followed the group to Alin's porod. They swarmed up, still burdened. After a moment of hesitation she followed.

Three burned bodies, one of them an infant, another a youth, but it was impossible, now, to tell the sex. An adult. She forced down nausea and looked at the panting Hanninah. Blank faces? She could not tell whether they were, indeed, as shocked as she, or whether her own turmoil painted emotions on their faces that were not there. One of the new Hanninah spoke at length, and Ke'empah listened, nodding at times, at other times gesturing and a phrase would be repeated. In an effort not to stare at the bodies, Quellan sought and found Alin, still lying asleep in a cushioned corner. Quellan sat beside her, brushed hair from her sleeping face, and stared back at Toyon, who continued to ride oblivious of the disturbance.

Ke'empah gestured sharply, stood, and climbed down from the porod. Within moments the other Hanninah had resumed their burdens and followed him down, leaving Quellan and Alin alone with one young male. He stared at them, then came over and squatted before Quellan, leaned over, and placed a hand on Alin's brow.

"I am Haapati," he said quietly in standard. "Am I not to be recognized?"

"Haapati?" Quellan stared, saw the familiar features somehow changed, charged. Certainly different, but in undefinable ways. "Where have you been? Why did you leave? Why did you come back?"

"It was time. Alin is very close now."

"Close to what? She's been screaming and yelling in the woods with your people, she's unconscious, barely has a pulse, she's probably forgotten who she is. Close to what, Haapati?"

"And you have come close to being close." He straightened suddenly. "I have come from the south, where there has been much burning. As you have seen. Much change. Time is moving fast."

"Who did that?" Quellan gestured to where the three dead Hanninah had rested.

"Your elder at Eastbase. The one who burned the elder who died here."

Quellan took Alin's limp hand in her own and stroked the brown fingers. "You make too many questions. Stover? Is it Stover?"

"Yes."

"Where?"

"Two days' running south. He moves with others, but they move quickly."

Quellan sat very still. "What happens if they catch us, Haapati? Will you defend us? Will Ke'empah defend us?"

"Ke'empah is an elder."

She glanced at him sharply. "And you?"

"I will wait here until Alin wakes up."

"Yeah? It's going to be a long time."

"I think not." He arranged himself on the pillows, knees high, arms resting on them, in that peculiar Hanninah squat that still looked so uncomfortable to Quellan. They rode in silence above the shuffle of feet and a low murmur of voices. After a time, she leaned back against the side of the platform, Alin's hand still cradled in her own, and watched the Hannin watching Alin. Surprising, how familiar he seemed, how suddenly and unexpectedly a relief. Familiar. Despite the deep red sash. Despite the flashing hilt of the knife. Despite, too, the changes in his face, which she defined, unsatisfactorily, as an animation, a sense of life different from his stony calm on the ride from Tyler's.

"Why do you talk now?" she asked, more to break the silence than anything else.

"There is need."

"Need?"

"It is now proper."

Another length of silence.

"How did you know about the old one, the elder that died? Were you there when Stover burned her? How did you hear about it? No one's left the tribe. Are there other runners, messengers?"

Haapati, as though in mockery, slid into his old blankness and remained silent.

"God damn it, you ape, how do you know where Stover is?"

"I have seen him. I was there when the burning happened."

"You've— How did it happen? Tell me."

The story was simple and brutal, despite Haapati's inflectionless recital. A small group, seven adults, three children, Haapati traveling with them for three days. Night rest in a place that seemed to be slightly to the east of the river encampment at which Ke'empah's tribe had stayed. Stover and two others invading the dinner circle, demanding information. Quellan made Haapati repeat his description of the other two Terrans until she was quite sure of one, Chist, the man-machine, and fairly sure of the other, either Kilzer or Holmes. A demand that turned into terrible games, three burned, one knifed. Holmes, then.

Haapati and the six remaining Hanninah had faded into the jungle until Stover and his crew tired of their sport, then had collected the bodies and moved swiftly north. The knife-killed woman had been swept away in the river, but they had borne the other three at a run until they reached Ke'empah's migrating tribes, and there they had laid the evidence.

Quellan put her hand on Alin's shoulder. "She can't take another of those—those wakes of yours. She'll die, she'll go crazy. She won't make it."

"She won't die," Haapati said.

"Crazy, then."

"No. But there will be no further wakes. We are too close now, time accelerates."

"What do you mean? Can't you make sense?"

Haapati slipped back to silence, and only stirred when Alin finally opened her eyes, just as the caravan came to rest for the night.

She looked around, bypassing Quellan as though the fielder were not there, and her gaze fastened on Haapati. She smiled.

"*Alen kemahni*," she whispered.

"*Alen kemek*," he replied.

"Alin?" Quellan said. "Alin, it's me, Quellan. How're you feeling? Can you hear me? Alin?"

"*Ahmen telteye*," Alin said to Haapati, and Quellan stood in fury, swung over the side of the platform and stalked back to her own beast. As she passed Toyon's porod, she hesitated, then climbed up to the platform.

"Hello. We're camped. Your wife's awake. That goddamned ape is back."

Toyon nodded. He and Taleti sat side by side, not touching, and he wore a look of calm.

"Stover's catching up with us, burning apes as he comes. Didn't you see them? When he makes it, they'll probably tie us up and give us to him, just to keep him off their backs. Understand?"

"Yes, of course."

"Sweet mother, Toyon, what's got into you?"

Toyon moved a hand gently. "She's very open, you know," he said without looking at Quellan. "She's very calm, very clear. Her hand's almost all healed. I'm going to take her to Alta Morena, give her some schooling, give her all the things she can't get here. I don't have any children, you know."

"Yeah? Well, it doesn't look to me like you've got one here, either. Damnation, your wife's going crazy and we're going to get offed any day now, can't you understand?"

"Calmly, Quellan. It'll get straightened out. As soon as we see Tashik, you can come with us. We'll all go home."

Quellan cursed savagely and slapped the porod's neck. Obediently, the beast knelt. She jumped off and stalked toward the woods, then paused and stormed back to the safety of her mount.

TOYON'S JOURNAL

And the wheel turned again, at some point that I missed during this long and confusing day. We are realigned, things once more have changed.

Quellan, it seems, has slid back to that roughness that she wore when we first started from Tyler's, as though she is hiding herself in a mask. Alin is reunited with Haapati and now ignores us, speaking only to him in Hanninee, ceaselessly. Is Quellan jealous of this? This evening, Quellan came to my wife with a bowl of yellow stew, as though making one final offering. Alin completely ignored her and continued talking to the Hanninah around her. Who now treat her as one of their own. Quellan stood angry and confused, then flung the bowl to the ground and stalked away.

Taleti continues quiet and close, and I have sliding memories of her tending to me during the day, memories that flash through the otherwise grayness to bring relief. Whatever it was that kept me so entirely subdued passed at sunset, leaving me relaxed and at ease with myself, far from the anger and disruption of last night. Shock? Retreat? Whatever it was, and I shall not worry about it, it has gone and I feel entire again. I shall see Tashik, and then we'll leave. Take Alin somewhere for help, if she hasn't pulled out of it herself by then. Take Taleti to Alta Morena and see that she gets a good education, see

163

that a place is made for her to grow and develop, for she is far too good for life on this primitive planet. And take Quellan, find her a job, if only in return for her help. Despite this nonsense about Stover and death.

"Here, come with me," Quellan said. I put down my cube and looked up at her.

"Where? Why?"

"Just come here, I want to show you something." She said it so stubbornly that, rather than argue, I rose and followed her. Taleti looked up from the small sack she had been playing with, nodded to me, and did not rise.

Quellan led me through the outer rings of the now huge camp and through trees. She walked with an alarmed quiet, and I followed in the same way, curious now. The underbrush thickened on either side of the path, then stopped abruptly at a shelf of rock. Quellan set the glower at full range and gestured.

Three dead Hanninah, lying side by side on the rock. Disfigured flesh and fur, burned and bubbled. The middle one was the same size as Taleti.

"Good God! What happened to them?"

Quellan's lips tightened. "I told you this afternoon, but you were out of your head somewhere. Stover got them, good old mythological Stover. That I made up to scare myself. He's catching up, Sutak. What're you planning to do about it?"

I backed away from the rock shelf, and we walked a few meters into the woods. The night wind was sharp and cold, and smelled of sharp, cold trees.

"Stover?" I said, far more softly than I'd intended.

"Yeah. The other side of the river, two days ago. There's something going on here, something he thinks we're after, and he's going to kill us over it whether he's right or not."

"And you want to find out what he's up to and cut yourself in?"

She flashed a look of hatred at me, then unclenched her hands. "No. Shit, Sutak, I just want to get the

164

hell out of here with my skin intact, and I'm damned if I can figure out how. The radio's gone, we can't head back to Tyler's alone, 'cause Stover would get us. And he'll follow us right over the mountains into the desert, if he can't get us here."

"You want a pitched battle, then? Get is over with now?" The sharpness of my voice surprised me, and she flushed.

"I don't want any fights, Sutak. Not with Stover, not with you, not with anybody. But if there's going to be one, we'd better get ready, and get all the help we can."

"The Hanninah?"

She shrugged. "I don't know if they would."

"Taleti might help us," I said. "I'm sure she would. But not Ke'empah, or Haapati."

"Or Alin," Quellan said bitterly.

"What? Of course she'll be with us, what in hell do you think she is?"

Quellan spat into the duff. "She's gone, Sutak. She doesn't give a damn about you or me anymore, and you'd better believe it."

"Damn it, Quellan, she's my wife!"

"Yeah?"

I barely stopped myself from hitting her. "My *wife*! What's got into you, damn it?" Something cold in the stomach, something with thorns in the mind. "Have you been—been with my wife, Quellan? *Have you*——"

"Shut up! You'll get the whole camp down on us. Shut up, for God's sake. No, I haven't been fucking your wife. But I've wanted to, Sutak." Her hand flickered to her boot-top and the knife appeared, gleaming in the dim light of the glower. Her voice was high and sharp. "You want to make something of it? You want to fight about that crazy ape-fucker back there? Or you figure you're even, she's got Haapati, you've got Taleti, is that it?"

And her face gleamed in the light, too, flickered before my eyes; my hands felt terribly empty, and the only thing I wanted in the world was her death. "I'm

165

going to kill you, Quellan," I said, and something zinged past my ear, thunked against a tree trunk. A knife, a Hanninah knife, hilt still quivering, blade bright. We stared at it, and the forest was suddenly very quiet. Quellan slowly lowered her arm, her knife dangling from her fingertips. I pulled the Hanninah knife from the tree and held it uncomfortably in my hand. Its hilt was still warm.

"We were going to kill . . ." Quellan whispered.

I shook my head, and the last anger fled. "Forget it, forget the whole thing. You didn't say it, I didn't feel it. Something else. Someone else."

She resheathed her knife. I hid the Hanninah knife under my suit-top and we walked carefully back to the camp. The glower in her hand swung shadows through the trees.

Taleti had spread out her sleeping robes and my sack, a meter apart, and was already asleep. I watched Quellan moving toward her own place. I glanced around and then, feeling ashamed, slipped my hand under the foot of Taleti's robes. Her knife was there, cool, innocent. I shoved the other knife under the foot of my own sack, stripped quickly, and slid in.

ALIN'S JOURNAL

I found myself here, worktable extended, perched on a stool rather than squatting on the ground, and this small cube glittering before me. It took me a long time to realize what it was, and a longer time to make sense of what I'm doing, speaking in an alien language, following the habits of another life. The camp is quiet and dark; Haapati lies sleeping a few meters from me, his shape dimly visible in the low light of my glower. Ke'empah is curled into his pile of pelts, a large hill of fur at the very edge of light.

The worktable is neat but scuffed, all the hinges tight, the edges straight, unlike . . . unlike whose?

166

Comparison? Someone has a worktable that . . . Toyon, yes, that's it. I can't see him now. He's gone walking in the night, and Quellan has gone walking in the night, and now I look out over an encampment filled entirely with Hanninah.

The phrase for "my own people" is *ka-mehi hanninah*.

This, I realize, is a very silly thing I am doing now. Sitting when I should be sleeping, talking when I should be dreaming. But I am not entirely of them, not yet. There are great and sudden silences, there are areas where their words go in one direction and my mind in another, and we fail completely to meet.

I said to Haapati, "Why did you leave us?"

"I did not leave all of you," he said.

"But you went alone, didn't you?"

"I went alone."

"And why did you leave us?"

"Not all of you." And after a number of questions, it appeared that he thought of it as leaving me, and me only. He said this using the formal mode, the style for significant utterings, the style Ke'empah uses to invoke the evening chant. Said it with such finality that I could not determine a way around or through his statement to what lay behind, and dropped the subject for something else.

"Where did you go after you left?"

"Many places."

"Where did you go first?"

"I went first toward the savannah."

And on, and on, but I seem to have gained an infinite patience, and the questions and answers built rhythmically until dinner.

He had gone to recover lost items, he said. His sash was one, his knife another, and there was a third thing he had lost at Tyler's and could not replace. He had found knife and sash where he had left them years ago, before he'd stepped into Rhodes's hopper and been taken to an alien life. The third thing he had lost he would not tell me about.

"Wasn't your sash faded?" I asked, looking at the bright red color around his waist.

"Yes."

"Did you get another one?"

"No."

"Did you redye the original one?"

"No."

It's like a child's game I used to play with Kale years ago; were my surrogate parents as often frustrated with the game as I am now?

"Were you happy at Tyler's?" I asked, and he could not comprehend the question.

Finally, just before the dinner circle formed, I asked again after the third lost thing, and he said, "There are things not to be spoken of, which cause *haahmin.*"

"*Haahmin?* I don't know the word."

He tried to explain it in Standard, then gave it up. "You have no words for it," he said.

"Tell me what it means, what it feels like," I said. "Perhaps there is a word, but you don't know it."

He stared at me then, his eyes going glazed, and I began to grimace with frustration at his retreat when an overwhelming sense of loss assailed me, panic and emptiness, sudden vertigo, sudden pain. I cried out, groped blindly in the dense air, and the feeling receded as quickly as it had come. Haapati held me, one arm around my shoulders, and again his eyes were wide, but this time with something approaching concern.

"Forgive," he said to me. "Forgive."

"Did you . . . was that you . . ."

"Your time is sooner than I thought," he said, then pulled away from me and, with an odd formality, ushered me toward the dinner circle, toward stew and amber wine.

I should have pried, poked, worried the questions in my mind, tried to make sense of this. There is something telepathic here, yes. They do this sort of thing on Ha Olam, but only in the Dark Caves, and only after intense hypnotism. I remember this now, and I remembered it during dinner, with a sense of detachment, a feeling that the questions are not necessary, that things should be accepted as they come. This is an alien mode to me, and perhaps yet another sign that I am closer to these dark, quiet people.

The camp is still this night, very dense, very quiet. They lie each upon a separate pelt, and not even the infants make a sound. It was not this way last night, no, nor the nights before, the camp is always buzzing with some small noise. But they are silent tonight, and I am captured by their quiet, caught unmoving for fear of breaking this absolute peace.

If Haapati touched my mind this night (see, ah see, they are not yet completely *ka-mehi hanninah*, I am still of an alien inquisitiveness), why have others not touched my mind?

During the death-wake there were voices in my head, there were tearings and singings and makings, yet I made them of myself, and rode the currents of my own creation. It was—they were—but the words now are Hanninee, and there are no translations. I heard all the voices, all the voices . . .

There is a stirring, as though of wind, and the Hanninah make their small night noises. It's time to sleep now, yes, it's time in consummation with darkness, and the silent amber is dissolved, I can move. I douse the glower and sit yet longer, watching the stars and patterns of cloud above, the dark places where the stars don't shine. I see Toyon and Quellan return from their night wanderings, walking stiff and apart from each other; they are the wrong colors, the wrong densities, the wrong sizes, but the shape of Toyon's back has a sweet familiarity. I want to go to him, to tell him of my nightly travels with the Hanninah, to bring him with me, but time is fully here and there is nothing now but sleep. So be it, then. I will fold my cube and fold my sticks and sink to the warm textures of the night. *Ke makera aanpali. Malyiti ann . . .*

IN WHICH THE GOVERNOR IS SURPRISED

"Grab him! Now! Fast!"

Rhodes spun around in the narrow room, and two clean-suited figures pinioned his arms, while a third quickly sprayed him with retaining foam until he was cocooned and immobile.

"What's going on! What's the— Damnation, let me go, get your hands— I'm the governor, damn it!"

"I'm so sorry, Governor," Perez said soothingly, and displayed many teeth behind the visor of his helmet. "It'll all be explained shortly. It's for your own good, believe me, sir. You'll be more comfortable in the hospital."

"Hospital! I demand——"

But his demands did no good. He was forcefully taken from the suit, hustled across the empty, dark main plaza of Eastbase and, within ten minutes, released into an isolation chamber at the base's hospital. The enveloping cocoon of foam dissolved as the door cycled shut behind him. On the other side of the thick windows, Perez removed the helmet of his clean-suit and smiled at the outraged governor.

"So sorry, Governor. There was a slight leakage at the radplant today, and I'm afraid you were exposed. Nothing serious, we trust, but for your own safety we thought we'd take precautions. I hope you understand."

"Understand! I understand that you were with me every blasted minute of the entire day, Perez. If there was a leak, then why aren't you in here with me?"

"You must be mistaken, Governor. You toured the storage dumps alone, remember?"

"Mr. Perez, I did not so much as defecate alone today. What's the——"

"I'm sure Mr. Haecker will be very pleased that you're being given the best available medical attention,

Governor. He'll be along as soon as he freshens up. I know you'll be glad to see him."

"I'll—— Perez! Damn it, Perez, come back here! This is your governor, damn it, *Perez*!"

The outer door clicked shut, and Rhodes kicked savagely at the floor-to-ceiling iso-window. The room was small and cool, its pale yellow walls unbroken by outer windows and supporting a number of monitors and life-support devices. To the right of the observation window, a door opened into a small, secure bathroom, and the door from the isolation chamber to the outer room was firmly shut an unopenable from the inside without a light-key. One high, narrow bed draped in crisp sheets, one straight-backed plasteel chair, a small table which connected, he suspected, with a shuttle-tube through which meals would come. If they came. When, after half an hour, no medical personnel appeared, he ceased his pacing and sat at the edge of the bed, willing himself to calmness.

An hour later, the outer door opened and Leo Haecker walked in, accompanied by Perez. The planet manager carefully closed the outer door, then cycled the inner door while Perez stood with light-gun ready, pointed at the governor. Rhodes sat very still until the two men were in the room and the door had cycled shut again.

"I trust you're enjoying the hospitality of Eastbase," Haecker said pleasantly as he settled into the chair. Perez leaned with his back against the door, the light-gun loosely holstered at his hip. Rhodes folded his arms across his narrow chest and remained silent.

"Such a pity about your accident today. The doctors tell me that they'll keep you under observation for a few weeks, and if all's well by that time, we'll get you right back to Tyler's."

Rhodes looked with hatred at Haecker's relaxed, chubby figure; at the pudgy fingers laced over the soft belly, the springy hair, the sarcastic, oily smile. He tightened his arms across his chest and glowered defiantly.

"Oh, that's not necessary, Governor. I'm here to talk with you. Our interests meet, you understand. We're both concerned that certain, ah, certain items remain within the family. I for reasons that are of no interest to you, and you because of the persuasion of your past. And I do believe that you've overlooked that. Must I keep reminding you?"

"That won't work, Haecker," Rhodes said, but despite his best efforts his voice quavered in a high register. "I don't care about your persuasion any more, understand? I have a job to do, and I'm going to do it."

"Am I saying that you should be derelict in your duty?" Haecker sounded shocked. "By no means, I'm simply trying to make things a little easier for you. You do see my point, don't you? And you won't make further problems, will you?"

Rhodes did not deign to answer, and Haecker heaved a sigh.

"All right, Governor, let me put it another way. You'll behave the way I want you to behave, because if you don't, your supply will be cut off."

Rhodes fought with himself for a moment, then curiosity won. "Supply of what?" he asked, and Haecker smiled with delight.

"Very good, Rhodes. Perez, give me the sack, please."

Perez reached into his capacious pouch and pulled out a small sack, which he handed to the planet manager. While Rhodes watched, Haecker pulled his chair to the table, opened the sack, and began removing objects from it while he talked.

"We've had discussions about you, Rhodes. Stover and I. My associate is a little more bloodthirsty than I am, and I was rather reluctant to follow most of his suggestions. However, I do believe now that he was right, at least in a number of things. And, since I'm nothing if not a magnanimous man, I readily admit my errors and move swiftly to correct them."

"Where's Stover now?" Rhodes demanded uneasily.

172

"My associate has gone to take care of some unfinished business," Haecker said. He lifted a hyposnout from the sack and took his time checking its seals. "A few illegal aliens. Oh, yes, I do like that. Illegal aliens, trespassing without permission on restricted Hanninah territory. Of course, he'll make every effort to bring them back without harming them."

"Of course," Rhodes said with as much sarcasm as he could muster. "I warn you, Haecker, if they're harmed, I'll——"

"You'll what? Pay attention, Governor, you're going to find this very interesting. Do you know what this is?" Haecker held up a small parcel, and with a start Rhodes recognized the packet he had found in his ravaged garden.

"You've gone through my rooms, damn——"

"Calm down, Governor. Now, you do recognize it, yes, but do you know what it is? I think not. It's pollen, Governor, from those cute little flowers you've been trying to raise, the prayer plants. *Rho—Rhodontia supplex*? I've no idea where you got this from, and to a great extent it doesn't matter. This yellow powder, Governor, is what I and my associates have been very carefully gathering for quite a while now. When mixed with a slight amount of hydrochloric acid and injected into a Terran bloodstream, it produces very powerful hallucinatory effects. Of course, you get some trips when the drug isn't treated, but, you see, the effects are so intensified with the HCl. And so very, very addictive. Perhaps the most addictive drug we've yet discovered. Which perfectly suits it for our purposes, of course." Haecker carefully measured a small amount of the powder into a beaker. "I have to credit my associate with the discovery of the potentiator. Stover's a slow man in many respects—slow between the ears, you understand—but not to be underestimated. Of course, most of the drug is sold offplanet, but we do keep some around. So kind of you, though, to bring your own supply. We have been running a bit short. A bit short on the HCl, too—that driver had the

173

latest shipment in the hold of her car. Such a mess."

"Where do you sell the—that drug?" Rhodes asked.

"Governor, you're invaluable. Think you might blackmail me, sauce for the goose? But I don't mind telling you—after you've sampled a bit of this, you're going to be too busy wanting more to make any trouble at all. We sell it on Xanadu, such a very open market, if you know the right people. We've a nice, docile messenger who gets it there without peeking, and gets a nice, fat bonus in return. Works splendidly. Keeps the association small and tidy." Haecker dissolved some of the powder in a small amount of liquid, added a minute drop of the hydrochloric acid, and stirred the mixture gently.

"And you steal the drug from the Hanninah."

"No. We persuade them to sell it to us."

"Sell it?"

"A semantic convenience, Governor. Until now, I've only known about the effects by hearsay."

Rhodes half rose from the bed, and Perez brandished the light-gun. The governor settled back uneasily.

"Haecker, you—you're a very evil man."

Haecker grinned. "Lovely, Rhodes. The question is, will you respond to the mere threat, or will I actually have to fill you with this?"

"I——"

"No, Stover's right. It's better to be absolutely sure. I'm told that the minimum amount is five cc's, and that's not much, is it?" Haecker filled the barrel of the hypo-snout and moved toward the governor. Rhodes shrank back on the bed, trying to make himself as small as possible.

"Ten cc's," Haecker said as he approached. "Just to make sure you're hooked indeed. Come now, Rhodes, give me your arm, we don't want to get violent, do we? Perez, put that damned thing down and take the governor's arm, will you?"

Perez shifted the gun to his left hand and reached around Haecker's side, and Rhodes kicked out suddenly, knocking the light-gun into the far corner of the room. He twisted from the bed and rammed his bony shoulder into Haecker's side as Perez leaped forward to grab at Rhodes. Haecker's arms windmilled and, off balance and in mid-shout, he rammed the snout of the hypo-gun into Perez's neck. Perez stiffened immediately as the strong drug washed his brain, and Rhodes grabbed the hypo from Haecker and shoved it against the planet manager's chest. Haecker's hands stopped halfway up, and Rhodes held the hypo tight until its continued clicking announced that it was empty; Haecker's face had relaxed to an expression of bug-eyed stupidity. Rhodes stepped back quickly, almost falling over the bed, and watched the planet manager topple to the floor. Haecker's limp arm brushed against Perez as he fell, and the chubby man half-twisted as he collapsed over the foot of the bed.

Rhodes dropped the hypogun, kicked it under the bed, then experimentally prodded Haecker with his toe. The planet manager's thighs were completely limp. Quickly, then, Rhodes found the discarded lightgun and stowed it under his belt before going gingerly through Haecker's hip pouch. A set of light-keys, miscellaneous bits of paper, a small bottle of sweets, various nonincriminating odds and ends. Rhodes replaced everything but the light-keys.

At the door to the chamber, Rhodes fumbled through the keys until he found the proper one, then stepped outside and closed the door firmly behind him. He peered once more through the thick window at the two recumbent forms within before turning off the lights in the observation chamber and carefully inspecting the corridor outside. Within a moment, he slid from the room, shut and locked the door, and tiptoed through the dimly lit hall. The hospital was quiet, and he easily avoided the two bright areas of activity.

The governor slipped through the shadows of Eastbase's streets, freezing at every slight noise, until he reached the hangar where Haecker's crimson air-car was stored. Except for the locked door, the hangar was unguarded. He lined up the light-keys and flickered through them quickly until, with a pneumatic sigh, the hangar door opened. He slithered inside, climbed into the air-car and, leaving it on its lowest and quietest setting, maneuvered it out of the hangar and into the clear night air.

"Mr. Haecker? Are you leaving?"

Rhodes panicked and slapped the accelerators, shot the air-car straight up, then beat the settings to a northerly heading and sped away from the base. He didn't begin shaking until the base was a distant speck behind him, and the first moon had set.

THE IMAGINARY CITIES OF TOYON SUTAK—#2

He finds himself in a salt-and-pepper place, a location compounded of black and white dots that never make gray, and no colors at all. He floats in the midst of this, suspended in a sameness on all sides; this does not puzzle him, or frighten him; he waits calmly for something to happen. Curious and tranquil, he experiments gently with his surroundings; he tries to grasp a handful of the black and white dots, but they elude him, seem to flee through his palm and fingers so that his clenched hand is always empty. He flexes his knees, he scratches his groin, he sees that he is still a mixture of red and pink and pale orange all down the length of himself of his naked body. He finds the contrast of himself and his surroundings vastly entertaining, and spends a small time watching the movements of his limbs against the Brownian movement of the dots.

Soon, though, the black dots sift downward and the white ones up. A landscape forms around him, an earth, a sky, and in the distance a maze of spires and arches. He begins to walk forward, but his feet do not touch the ground and he moves in place through the air. He grits his teeth, flails his arms, strains his

176

toes to the ground and cannot reach it; he tries to swim in air and does not move. His motions grow more erratic, more energetic until finally, exhausted, he floats quietly, and now the distant spires come toward him at a dignified pace. He watches with interest, with suspicion.

The city's paved periphery touches his toes, and there it stops. Again he tries to move forward, again he cannot do so. He reaches out, fingers barely caressing a difference in the air where the city lies, and this is as far as he can go.

Within the city there are colors; although he cannot perceive them, he knows that they exist. Spires and walkways and arches and windows hold deep, surprising hues, startling contrasts, amazing shadings of primary tones, and if he could only reach within the city he could see the colors. But no, and no, this is not possible. No.

Shapes move within the city, along the vertiginous walkways, among the crystal colonnades, and he watches hungrily. There are sounds and melodies within, speech and singing, but he can no more hear these than he can see the colors, although he closes his eyes and concentrates his being in his ears. Nothing. Nothing. He opens his eyes again.

There is a thick river through the city, and docks piled with incense and spices. There are flowering plants of wondrous scents, the aromas of distant cookings, the delicate perfumes of passing shapes. Globed and purple fruits hang along the paths, great platters of succulent dishes are borne through the air; he watches them pass, flails his legs, beats his arms against the sullen air, yells and shouts and curses, but the city's containment is not breached. He becomes a solid, angry, yearning battering against the invisible walls.

The city shimmers, there is a small and constant shifting, and as he watches with despair the city melts into the dance of black and white. Gone the spires, the scents, the flowers, the sounds, the moving shapes, the melodies, fruits, textures; he is left again alone in a formless place.

He bows his head, he buries his face in his arms. He is still weeping when he awakes.

OF STICKS AND STONES AND FIRE

She woke at dawn to a different kind of bustle, climbed from her sack and found the camp still in place, the Hanninah going about their morning business as though this were a permanent camp, not an overnight one. Wary and cautious, she dressed and walked toward the morning cook fires, and the Hanninah made way for her as she procured a cup of tea and a strip of bread. Alternately munching and sipping, she moved through the rings of the camp, looking for Toyon or Alin.

Even more Hanninah had arrived during the night, it seemed. Seven or eight camp circles, each as big as Ke'empah's, covered the meadow, and she saw the flickers of still other fires through the trees. The Hanninah seemed tense this morning, preoccupied. One or two of them, members of Ke'empah's original group, nodded briefly as she passed. She nodded in return and continued searching.

She found Toyon sitting alone by his porod, his small, wobbly worktable erected. Its surface was littered with cubes and work-blocks, and the imprinter in his hand moved from sheet to cube to cube to sheet. A small frown creased his pale forehead.

"Good morning," Quellan said hesitantly, and Toyon put down the imprinter. He returned her greeting warily and sat still, his shoulders tense, watching her.

"Where's Taleti?" she asked.

"Why do you want to know?"

"No. Please, Toyon, no more fights. I just asked to make conversation. Peace."

He searched her face, then relaxed. "Yeah, okay.

178

I had a bad night, and it's been a disturbing morning."

She hoisted herself atop a fur-covered sack, brought her feet up, and wrapped her arms around her knees. "What's happening out there?"

"I'm not sure. They seem to be getting ready for something, I don't know just what. Taleti tried to tell me, but I don't understand her well enough."

"Um. Where's Alin?"

Toyon gestured toward the inner circle. "In there, with Haapati and the old one. Has been all night, all morning. I saw her earlier, and she didn't seem to recognize me, just kept on talking with them in that damned chatter of theirs. She—she's got their look in her eyes, that uncaring, you know?"

"Yeah, I know."

"Come on, I want to show you something." Toyon stood and slapped the worktable into an untidy bundle, heaved it into the platform, and strode toward the north, while Quellan scrambled from her perch and followed him cautiously. But the big man did not hesitate, nor did he speak until they had cleared the first stand of trees.

"Taleti brought me along here this morning, just at dawn," he said. Quellan glanced around but saw nothing unusual; trees, underbrush, dirt, vines. Toyon strode on, then stopped abruptly and stared ahead of him.

"She didn't tell me what this place is, but she acted hesitant about it, as though I wasn't supposed to be here. I don't know why. It's not guarded, though. Look."

Quellan stepped around him and found herself at the lip of a huge stone amphitheater. Large shelves of rock spiraled down the conical pit and extended in dizzying perspective to a circular stage that seemed, in the distance, no larger than her thumbnail. Except for a large block of rough stone at the center of the stage, the rock of the amphitheater looked carefully worked from the base materials of the mountain, as though someone had found the natural depression and deliberately created this white, spiraling stone vortex. Quellan couldn't begin to guess how many Hanninah the amphitheater could hold. Extending northward from the circular stage were square monoliths, spaced at even intervals up the side of the amphitheater and creating a thin, triangular channel whose inner apex was the stone block on the stage, and whose third side reached out and over a mountain pass high above. Despite the freshness of the morning breeze, the theater baked and brooded in a heat of its own making, and no living thing grew within its bounds.

"What is it?" Quellan whispered.

Toyon shrugged. "I don't know, but I think it's the reason we're not moving today. They're up to something, and I don't like it."

"Up to what?"

Again he shrugged, and in silence they returned to the camp.

As they reached the edge of the woods, Toyon paused and placed his palm against the rough bark of a tree, then looked at Quellan, with a puzzled expression.

"I feel together today, you know? I was feeling foggy yesterday, and a bit the day before, as though I was moving through something thick. It's gone now, everything's lighter."

Quellan nodded slowly. "Me too. Something's changed. Maybe they're too busy to pay attention to us."

"What do you mean?"

"How the hell should I know what I mean? Yesterday everything went obsessed with me, I'd fasten on to one thing and everything else would disappear. Today I can see two things at once. I don't know what it is, but I don't trust anything, feeling bad or feeling good."

They moved forward again.

"What I was doing when you came up," Toyon said, "was making a list of places and people, a job for you, good schools for Taleti, the things I'll have to do once we get back. Someone for Alin. I've got a double handful of good psychs on payroll, but I don't know, maybe someone special. Doctors. But I keep thinking that maybe when we get away from this place, she won't need it anymore. It's being around all these Hanninah, you know?"

Quellan remained silent.

"I used to think that I could get in to her, just barely, at the right times, but the door was there, if I could only find it, approach it right. It happened sometimes, and it was like two people being one, as though we were so woven together that we'd never get pulled apart again. And when it would go, I always knew that there would be a way back in, eventually, that it would come around again after a while. Maybe that's why we fought so much, because when one thing's intense, the others have to be, too. But now it's like there's no doors at all, everything's closed off. Like she's been taken away from me, like she's dead, but I know I can bring her back, if I just try hard enough, if I take care of her right. If I can just get close to her again. And I've got to keep telling myself that, over and over again, every time I look at her and her eyes are somewhere else. It'll get better, when we get home again."

"What about Tashik?"

Toyon turned quickly and stared at her. "Why'd you say that?"

"That's why we're here, isn't it? Mysterious city in the north, ruins, all that."

"I don't know. I guess we're headed in that direction, at least we seem to be. So we'll see Tashik, probably. But look, if my only chance to get Alin away is before that, I'll take it, I'll have to take it. And if it doesn't come until we get to Tashik, then we'll see the city. I'll see the city. I guess."

" 'And this Survey speaker came and showed us holocubes, and a whole new world opened up . . .' " Quellan quoted softly.

Toyon shook his head. "Okay, I remember all that too. But there's something more important now."

Quellan observed him for a moment, then touched his shoulder and they moved forward again.

Taleti squatted by the porod, fingers busy shelling vegetables, and she nodded gravely to them as they came up, but her gaze fastened on Toyon. He reached forward and ran his fingers over her head, an automatic gesture of affection, and without changing expression she moved her head under his hand so that her cheek nestled in his palm. Quellan turned to go, then turned back.

"Listen, Toyon, do you still have that knife?" she asked in a low voice.

"From last night? Sure. Why?"

"Just don't let it go, okay."

"I wasn't planning to. You're going? Stick around for a while."

"No, thanks. I'm restless, I just want to walk around for a bit."

"If you see Alin, would you . . ."

"Would I what?"

He gestured aimlessly, smiled, shrugged. "I don't know."

She touched his arm, nodded, and walked into the camp. Hanninah moved purposefully, sorting and repacking their traveling sacks, shaking out robes and blankets stained with the dirt of migration, preparing enormous amounts of food, washing things in skin tubs of water laboriously brought from the river a kilometer to the west. The porodin were stripped of their platforms and stood about awkwardly, as though disturbed by the lack of weight on their broad backs. Hanninah swarmed around the platforms, reducing them to neat piles of timber and reed. Numerous small work fires sent up volleys of heat from almost invisible, sun-bleached flames. Pausing, observing, moving on, Quellan made her way toward the innermost circle.

Here the main fire pit of Ke'empah's tribe sent forth

thick waves of heat, and many Hanninah squatted before it, staring into its depths. Alin, too, sat immobile and staring, sweat pouring unnoticed down her face. An empty wooden cup lay on its side by her thigh. Haapati, beside her, looked up at Quellan as she hunkered down and touched Alin.

"Alin? Hey, Alin, it's me, Quellan."

Alin did not move. Quellan grasped her shoulder and shook it gently. "Alin, come on, pay attention. Hey, Alin, wake up."

When she still didn't respond, Quellan turned to Haapati. "What have you done to her, damn it?" she demanded. Haapati remained silent. Quellan snorted with disgust and walked away from the pit. She turned to look back when she reached the first huts, and Alin's body stood out sharp edged against the heat-shivering pit.

Noon approached, and she ate with a group of younger Hanninah near the eastern edge of the camp. They fed her, in silence, and otherwise ignored her; as soon as she finished eating she left. Reported briefly to Toyon her inability to communicate with his wife. Returned to her own porod and once again, but this time coolly and rationally, went through her small store of equipment, and layered everything into a small packing sack. The afternoon wore on, and the activity of the camp decreased. A chill evening wind rose. She glanced at her ancient chronometer, glanced at the sky, shrugged her jacket over her shoulders and made her way toward Toyon's porod.

"Dinnertime," he said as she came up. "You want to eat with Taleti and me?"

"Sure. Where is she?"

"Down at the river. Let's go get her." He stood and slipped into his jacket.

"It's still early," Quellan said. "She'll be back in time for dinner."

"She's been gone a long time, and she might need help carrying the water. You can stay here, if you want."

183

"No, I'll come along. The camp's beginning to scrape me."

"Yeah, something's going on. Come on, let's get there and back before dusk."

As they walked through the trees, Toyon spoke again of his plans for departure, his plans for life on Alta Morena, even laughing once when he considered the reaction of Alin's family to his importation of Taleti. Quellan, listening, allowed herself to believe that it would happen, they would leave Hoep-Hanninah intact, Alin would come out of her current insanity, Quellan herself would finally find a home and a job she could be comfortable in, and for the rest of her life. Toyon's confidence was contagious, the life he pictured took on a solid reality in her mind and so distracted her that when she saw the blooming of light at the riverbank, it took her completely by surprise. Then Toyon's shoulder crashed against her and brought them both down on the forest duff. She rolled from under him and assured herself that he wasn't hurt.

"What's——" he began.

"Shut up," she whispered fiercely. She wriggled forward on her stomach, feeling Toyon's body behind her, until one strand of bushes separated and concealed them from the riverbank. She parted the branches cautiously and peered through.

Jaerek Stover stood with his arms crossed across his chest, Holmes rocked on the balls of her feet and Chist calmly holstered his light-gun. Before them on the rocky bank lay a burned Hannin. Quellan felt Toyon moving up for a look, and she pushed him down roughly, fighting to keep him from seeing the riverbank. He looked at her face and his eyes widened, and one huge hand pushed her aside as he wriggled up beside her. Quellan turned to look at the riverbank again.

Holmes, knife in hand, reached down to the Hannin, who twitched fitfully. The Terran moved her hands swiftly, grinned as the Hannin's back arched in pain, and when she straightened she held a bloody hunk of flesh in her hand, Holmes lifted it to the fading light, and Quellan saw the flat, saffron skin and double nipple of a Hannin breast.

"Taleti!" Toyon's bellow roared down the bank, and in sudden panic the three Terrans turned and ran under the cover of an upright shelf of rock, while Toyon sped from the bushes, grabbed the burned Hannin in his arms, and slipped under a stone overhang. A bolt of light scorched the stone where the Hannin had rested, and Quellan forced herself deeper into the duff. Silence grew.

Then Toyon roared again, in fury and grief. A clattering came from Stover's hiding place, and Quellan lifted a rock, knelt, and hurled it as hard as she could. It banged against Stover's overhang, and the clattering stopped.

"Kennerin!" Quellan shouted. "Take that side and keep the apes down. Sutak! You got charged yet?"

She waited, sweating, for Toyon's reply.

"Yeah," he said finally, tightly. "The Hannin's dead. Stover, you coming out, or do we shred you there?"

Silence. Quellan made a quick decision and crawled until she was opposite Toyon's hiding place. He had already surveyed the area, and when he saw her he gestured toward a twisting, rock-filled ravine that might, with some luck, get him away from the river-bank without getting killed. Quellan nodded, gathered rocks to her, and wriggled back toward Stover, while Sutak cradled Taleti's body in his arms and moved down the ravine.

"Hey, Stover, you coming out? There're a lot of apes around here that would like to give you some of what you've been giving them. Or did you think they wouldn't object to getting roasted?" She threw a stone toward his rock, and heard a scrambling as it hit. She pitched three more, one on either side of his hiding place and one behind, and the scrambling ceased. She wished she could find out if there was a way out of his overhang, but didn't dare move too far from Toyon.

"Hey, Stover! You still beat and bugger little boys, or is Chist doing it for you now? I hear tell he likes to hurt you afterwards, when you're not expecting it. That so? Right, Chist?"

As soon as she heard Chist's growl, she pitched another stone, and the noise ceased. Glancing back, she saw Toyon halfway down the channel, burdened by Taleti's body and approaching the one exposed area of the route. She pitched four more rocks in quick succession and moved further from Toyon.

"Quellan!" Stover's voice called.

"What do you want, killer?"

"You let us out, we'll head back to the base. No more burning. Deal?"

"Are you kidding? I let you go and the Hanninah will do to me what they're going to do to you." She now aimed her rocks from the side, praying that their angle would convince Stover that he was indeed surrounded. Toyon passed the exposed place and moved swiftly through the rocks toward the forest.

"Quellan!"

"That's enough talk, Stover. Sooner or later, you're coming out. We can wait." She paused for a moment, until Toyon was well into the woods, then threw her remaining two rocks and wriggled backwards, caught up with Toyon. Together they ran through the trees toward the camp.

The dinner circle was completed, food being passed from hand to hand, when they broke into the circle. Trembling, Toyon laid Taleti's body on the mat before Ke'empah, smoothed her limbs, opened her sash and raised it to cover the hole in her chest. She stank of burned fur and burned flesh; death had loosened her sphincters and she smelled of that, too.

Haapati, Alin, and Ke'empah sat side by side. Alin ceremoniously drank a cup of yellow wine, set it down, and the three gazed calmly at the dead Hannin. It was to Haapati that Toyon spoke.

"Stover, from Eastbase, he's down at the river, he killed Taleti, they cut her, they cut— We've got to stop him. Now." Silence. "Listen, she's dead, don't you understand? They killed her, burned her and cut her, you've got to do something."

"There is nothing to be done," Haapati said evenly.

"Nothing!" Quellan shouted. "They're going to do it again, they're going to kill us, they're going to kill more of you! You've got to stop them."

"They move of their volition and our consent," Haapati said, and Toyon leaned forward and grabbed Alin's arms, dragged her to her feet.

"Alin, they'll listen to you, you've got to make them understand. They killed Taleti, they tortured her, Alin, please help us."

Alin looked slowly from her husband to Taleti's body, and her expression did not change. "Her time is," she said without inflection.

"Don't you care?" Toyon hissed.

"There is no caring," she said, and Toyon slapped her cheek. Her head jerked and a darker stain appeared under the dark skin of her face.

"You listen to me. She's dead, she's gone, and it hurt, every second hurt, and it's because of us, because of you and me, and more of them are going to die until they catch us and kill us. God damn it, you bitch, do you understand?" He was shaking her until her head whipped, and she suddenly closed her eyes, arched her back, and screamed. Ke'empah and Haapati leaped to their feet, pulled his hands away and grabbed Alin about the waist, but her screaming did not cease. Ke'empah raised his head and cried to the camp, and the Hanninah surged upwards with a fierce, shouting chant, turned, moved northward toward the amphitheater.

"No! You're going the wrong way!" Toyon shouted, and tried to grab Haapati's shoulder. The Hannin's free arm rose, clutching his knife, and Toyon released him, then snatched Taleti's body to his chest and sprinted around to face Alin. He shouted at her, pleaded, screamed, and all the time he moved backward, driven by the irresistible pressure of the moving Hanninah. Quellan stood frozen by the fire pit, hearing his screams and shouts above the terrifying chant, until his voice was drowned in the alien cries. She broke swiftly from her trance and, in blind panic, she rushed to her porod, grabbed her pack sack, and slapped it over her back as she ran east into the forest.

Chapter 8

A PAIR OF BURNED HANDS

She heard the mumbling first, ducked behind a tree then, listening intently, she moved forward toward the small, moonslit clearing. Peering around a trunk, she saw Toyon squatting in a small trench, hands busy, and beside him Taleti's body lay wrapped in her open sash and arranged carefully on the duff. He flung handfuls of dirt in the air, and muttered constantly.

"We bury our dead. Farmer folk, recycle everything. Back to the loam, work even after you're gone. Push up vegetables and forget the flowers. But she deserves flowers. Never had them, probably. Burned grasslands and bleak mountains and jungles filled with decay, she shouldn't decay, not my pretty one. How can I bury her here, with all these rocks so close under? She needs softness and quiet, not howling winds and cold stones. She raised her hands when they fired at her, she raised her hands, her hands are burned again, all gone, all down to the bone. My pretty child. My quiet, pretty child. My sweet and pretty . . ."

He slumped on his haunches and hid his face in his hands. Quellan stood uneasily in the shadow of the tree before moving into the clearing and squatting at his side. Toyon lifted his head and peered at her.

"I can't dig a grave here," he explained. "I tried, but there's not enough dirt, and the rocks won't move. So I can't dig a grave here."

"Leave her on the rocks with the others," Quellan said gently. "She's a Hannin, she would understand."

Toyon shook his head, then paused and reluctantly nodded. "With the others," he echoed, and gathered Taleti's body to him.

They laid her by the three Hanninah on the rocky, windswept ledge, and when they were done Toyon turned quickly and paced away through the forest. Quellan followed, ready to stop him, but the heavy man moved around the skirting of rock to the east. She lengthened her pace and caught up with him.

"You're not going back?" she asked. Toyon shook his head. "What about Alin?"

"What Alin?" he asked wearily. "There's a woman back there who thinks she's a Hannin, do you mean her?"

Quellan bit her lip. Together they clambered over the rough ground, and when they were far enough up the mountain, Quellan laid a hand on his arm.

"We'd better stay near here for the night," she said. "Stover's still around somewhere, and we've a better chance in the daylight. And the going's getting rougher."

Toyon allowed her to find them a shelter, watched while she spread the molecular sheets on the ground, then huddled into his sheet. She set the glower to heat but no light and crouched, wrapped in her own sheet, beside him.

"We'll get back to Tyler's and tell the governor," he said after a long time. "Get some federals in here and rescue her. Steal her back. They won't let her go, Quellan." He drew in on himself, arms wrapped tightly about his chest under the sheet. "They were holding her, but as though to steady her, as if she was something special to them, and she chanted and shouted and screamed and wept, and they all screamed and cried, louder and louder. The old one yelled words into it all, and they raised her up, high over their heads, and she was coming, Quellan, she was writhing and shouting, and I remember that so well but not

190

so much, Quellan, never half so much. And Haapati—Haapati stood beside her and he didn't touch her except with his eyes. Always his eyes. And he never shouted, not once, not one single time."

Toyon started to cry—long, shuddering sobs. Quellan watched him, not moving, until the bitterness washed from him, then she put her arms around him and crooned him to sleep. She eased him down, wrapped the sheet more tightly around him, then turned off the glower and sat staring at the mountain pass ahead.

CHANGES

He woke in the morning feeling coldly rational, acutely conscious of the pitted rock beneath him; the limpid quality of the morning light; the chill, scrubbed smell of the air; the slight, distant tittering of birds. Experimentally, he flexed his knees, glanced at Quellan still asleep in her sheet beside him, felt as though a grimy layer of skin had been removed from him, and his senses, in response, drank hungrily of the world around him. Yet the profusion of impression surrounded a curious sense of absence, a light, circular empty space within himself that he could not name. He stood carefully, as though the slightest movement would loft him into the pale blue sky and send him spinning and floating over the land.

The sleeping place Quellan had found was high up the flank of the mountain, and surrounded by white rocks considerably taller than himself, but with a west-facing gap to one side. He stood in the gap and saw, distantly and far below, the pallid lip of the amphitheater, already sending its banners of heated air into the sky. Beyond that he saw flashes of movement through the trees, as the Hanninah broke camp, and he squinted, trying to pick out the shape of his wife. The wind bent around the rocks and pushed him lightly, and he returned to his sheet, sat, and probed gingerly through his mind.

Taleti? A residual ache, a bitterness at waste and loss, but already something remembered from a different time, a different life, although the front of his jacket was still stained with her blood.

Hoep-Tashik? Alien, yes, and alluring, but lacking the flavor of obsession. Something a tourist might or might not make an effort to see, depending on how far out of the way it was.

Alin? Pain here, yes, immediate and hot, and he shied away from it, gnawed at its periphery, gradually approaching the core from its sides and back. Alin. But a different longing, this morning, a separate pain. His wife was down among the natives. Yes. She was in need of help, certainly psychological, probably medical; she would have to be rescued, returned, reintegrated, even if against her will. Of course, against her will. He remembered his fatuous plans of the day before, the fantastical pictures he had so carefully created, the imaginary lives he had meant to pursue; the visions seemed tawdry now, amateur and awkward, and carried none of the usual swift practicality of his mind. He remembered them with amazement, and remembered their shattering with grim determination. Alin would be rescued. Alin would be helped. This at least was certain, this, if nothing else, was sure.

What else, then? Pain and doubt, anger and determination, but where was that burning sense of betrayal, the outrage that had driven him · from the Hanninah the night before? His emotions seemed, in contrast to those of the night before, pale and weak, yet he recognized them as part of his normal mode; felt as though some intensifier had been intruded into his life, and had now withdrawn.

"Maybe they're too busy to pay attention to us," Quellan had said. Yesterday morning? Standing near the lips of that great stone mouth? Yes. Exactly. He felt as though, having been chewed and drained, he was now spit forth, left to move as he could, if he could, and the intense attention was directed else-where. He glanced through the stone gap of his shelter and felt suddenly cold.

Quellan woke slowly, humping and wriggling under the molecular sheet. She sat and pushed pale, tangled hair from her forehead, squinted around the stones, and finally glanced at Toyon warily, as though not sure what to expect. He couldn't smile, but he managed a cordial nod that cleared the uneasiness from her face. She stood and stretched slowly.

"First water," she said, still husky with sleep. "Then breakfast, then a place to crap. Then we can talk, all right?"

He nodded and together they searched the rocks until Toyon found a small spring. They drank and washed, swallowed supplement pills from Quellan's sack and, in awkward modesty, disappeared in different directions. When Toyon returned to the spring, he found Quellan busy running fingers through her tangled hair.

"Gets in my eyes," she muttered. "Grows too fast. Have you got a knife?"

He pulled the Hannin knife from his belt and handed it to her, and she examined it, grunted once, then set to work hacking at her hair. Strands littered the shoulders of her jacket and the ground.

"Last night you wanted to get back to Tyler's and call in the troops," she said as she worked. "That still your plan?"

"No, I don't think so." He settled back against the rocks. "There's Stover behind us, and even if we get past him . . ."

"Which won't be too easy, if I know him."

"Well, even if we could, it would take us, what, a month to get there? If we really push it? Traveling on foot?"

"Thereabouts."

"And that might be too late. For Alin, I mean."

Quellan put down the knife and watched him, her

193

half-cut hair making a lop-sided frame around her face. "So?"

"So the first thing to do is take care of Alin, get her away from the Hanninah before she— Well, soon."

"And then?"

"I don't know. Get her out, and if she can travel we can all try to get to Tyler's, somehow. And if she can't, I guess we'll have to think something up. Maybe one of us stay with her and the other go, or all of us wait until she can travel. Or something."

"Something. Depending on the supplement pills, and how long they last, and if we can steal some food or find some growing that won't poison us. And if Stover doesn't find us."

"Quellan, I told you I don't know. But we've got to get Alin before we do anything else."

"I'm not arguing." She picked up the knife and started hacking at her hair again. "I was planning to leave the camp yesterday, anyway. Before all of last night happened. I had everything all packed, enough for two."

"For two?"

"Not you, Sutak." She refused to look at him. "I thought I'd get Alin out somehow, leave you at the camp and hope that if Stover saw you there, he'd think we were all there. Get Alin back to Tyler's, call in the troops, something. Hell, look, I figured Alin needed help more than you did."

"And?"

"Well, I panicked last night. I didn't even think about you or Alin, just grabbed the pack and ran like hell. In circles, I guess, or I wouldn't have run into you. Creeping around in the bushes scared of the apes and scared of Stover and jumping every time I heard a noise. Couldn't even run away straight."

She finished her hair in silence and handed the knife to him. He slipped it under his belt, but made no effort to rise.

"Quellan? How're you feeling today?"

"Why?"

"Curious."

She frowned. "Light, sort of. Funny. Like something's missing."

He explained his early morning thoughts to her, and she listened, then cut him short.

"Okay, but I don't want to hear the rest of it, the part about the apes. We've got the same feeling. We've maybe got the same suspicions. You talk about it any more and I'll start running so hard toward Tyler's, you won't be able to see me go."

He rose slowly. "Does that mean you're coming with me to get Alin?"

"If you want me along. I've got nothing better to do," she said, but the joke didn't carry.

They returned to the sleeping place, and packed the camp, filled the canteen, policed the area.

"Any thoughts about getting her out?" Toyon asked when they had finished.

"Maybe. First, I don't think we can go back down there, get back in the tribes." She waited for his nod. "If that pass looks as rough and narrow as I think it is, they'll probably go through one tribe at a time, maybe one a day or so, starting from the big camp. I think we'd better go up a bit higher, find a place where the pass is narrow, and watch for her there. If she doesn't go through today, we can try to sneak into camp tonight and get her there. Otherwise we'll just have to follow her until we find a good place to get her out."

Toyon agreed, and they left the stone circle cautiously, keeping well into the rocks. But they encountered no sign of Stover or his crew, although below them they saw the first Hanninah tribe already well up the side of the mountain.

The rock sheets of the mountain's heights were here, shattered and heaped, and although the route was hazardous they found it possible to scramble up the rocks parallel to the clearly marked path. The pass followed the course of the river, and as it climbed higher the gorge narrowed and deepened, until the path clung precariously to its western edge, far below the top of the gorge yet high above the pounding, white-mantled water. They found a protected place facing a sharp bend in the trail, and they had barely settled themselves when the point-runners of the tribe jogged into view.

Each Hannin carried a large sack strapped to his back and shoulders, and Toyon realized that the porodin had been left behind. Of course, the ungainly monsters would never have been able to negotiate the slim path, the steep rises and descents; he found that he missed their huge, ill-smelling presence. But he soon forgot them as he searched each moving face for his wife.

After what seemed like hours, he grasped Quellan's arm and pointed. Two Hanninah jogged evenly around the bend, bearing between them a high-sided wooden stretcher. Squinting, Toyon could just see Alin's dark face cushioned against a pale rug. A pelt covered her body. A third Hannin, possibly Haapati, trotted beside the stretcher, one hand resting on its high side. From the distance, glanced at quickly, Alin looked like a slim, probably ill Hannin. Toyon turned to speak to Quellan, but she put a finger to his lips and shook her head, and together they watched the stretcher, then the rest of the tribe, file through and beyond the bend.

At last Quellan rose and stretched her legs, glanced at the sky and then at the river below.

"She looks like one of them now," Toyon said.

"Good, it'll be harder for Stover to find her."

"Well?"

She turned and spat down the gorge. "To Tashik, damn it."

"Yes. To Tashik. Yes."

UNEXPECTED ABSENCES

The Governor had recovered enough from his fright

196

to wonder what was happening to Haecker and Perez, and he entertained himself with speculation as the air-car hummed northward. It wasn't until just before sunrise that he realized how off course he was, and an hour after that hunger beset him. At first he tried to ignore it—a resourceful agent always manages to cope—then it actively annoyed him, and finally the clamoring of his stomach drove every thought but that of food from his head. He checked the sky around him automatically, a habit suddenly and firmly set in him on the night flight from the base, then set the car on automatic and ransacked the cabin. The food locker was empty, as was the cold-keep mounted behind the pilot's seat; he could find not a crumb in the entire cabin. Plagued by thoughts of hot tea and heaps of fresh breakfast cakes, the governor returned to his seat and scanned the land below him for anything that looked even vaguely edible.

When he saw the ragged circle of the Hanninah camp, he nosed the car down and sped toward it, landed as close to the outer ring as he could, and sprinted toward the huts. In his haste he almost collided with a young Hannin male. The governor grabbed the native by the shoulders and leaned forward.

"I'm very hungry," Rhodes said in execrable Hanninee. "I need food. Is there any food? I will pay for food, anything you want. I am very hungry."

The Hannin gently but forcibly removed the governor's hands from his shoulder, turned, and entered a hut. Rhodes wrapped his arms about his belly and almost danced with impatience, and when the Hannin reappeared with a bowl of cold tea and some equally cold strips of bread, the governor inelegantly devoured them, squatting in the dust. It was not until he had finished that he noticed the unnatural silence of the camp, the burned and broken huts, the fire pit devoid of flame. He glanced about in puzzlement. Three other Hanninah, all adults, sat staring at him from various points around the camp, and from within the hut came a single, piercing cry that was soon silenced; the Han-ninah turned toward the hut at the sound, but re-mained seated, tense. Rhodes rose awkwardly and bowed to the young Hannin.

"I am thankful for your hospitality," he said solemnly. "May the way treat you as kindly."

"You spoke of payment," the Hannin said, without returning the governor's courtesy. Rhodes groped about his clothing with growing despair.

"I have these," he offered finally, holding out the clasp of light-keys. The Hannin ignored them.

"There is a service you can perform."

"Ah yes, I see. And what would that be?"

The Hannin gestured to the hut and Rhodes fol-lowed him in the circular door. The shade within was intense, and it took him a moment to see the shape in the corner. A pregnant female, and then he saw that she was badly burned along her swollen belly and breasts, and down her thick thighs.

"My God," Rhodes whispered in Standard. The female groaned as a slow contraction moved her belly, and the governor realized that she was in labor. "I'll get the med-kit," he said quickly. "It's in the car, it won't take——"

"There is no need. She will give birth and she will die, there is no need for medications."

"But—but I can give her something to help, to stop the pain."

"She has little pain. She is being helped, but the child takes its time."

"Then I don't understand, you said you wanted a service."

The Hannin glanced at the female. "She is my mate," he said finally. "Your elder from the base came here, and he burned her, and he burned her mother's mother who was our elder, and he burned the child of my brother's mate. Our burned elder we have sent north, for her time was upon her, although she died before she reached the place of changes. Of the child there was nothing left to send."

Rhodes shuddered violently, unable to shake the vision of Stover stalking through the defenseless camp. "It must have been an accident," he said weakly. "A mistake . . ." and he thought of his three stray Terrans, somewhere to the north, being stalked by this same implacable killer. He turned swiftly toward the door of the hut. "I must leave, there's little time, I must——"

"But you owe us a service," the Hannin said, blocking his path.

"But my three, but—Sutak, and Alin, and there's so little——"

"Your Terrans are alive," the Hannin said. "They are living, they are well. My mate is dying."

"Then tell me what you want!"

"Sit with us," said the Hannin. "Until she is finished. In payment for your eating. Sit and bear witness with us."

"Sit with—" Rhodes stuttered. He stepped back a pace. "The Terrans are——"

"They are alive."

"But how do you know?" Rhodes demanded.

"Do we lie?"

"I don't know," Rhodes said miserably, and turned toward the laboring female as though she could explain, could excuse him, but she was lost in a distant world. "They killed a child?"

"Yes."

"And an old one? For no reason? Deliberately?"

"Your people have done many things deliberately to our people. Sit and bear witness."

Slowly the governor sank to the floor and took the female's hand tentatively in his own. The male too sat, and his eyes grew round and glazed; through the door of the dilapidated hut Rhodes could see the remaining Hanninah, gathered around the hut and staring in the same intense and fearsome way. The female's tortured breathing grew easier, and the governor suddenly felt as though he were alone.

He thought about the keyed message resting like a

bomb, ticking closer to the moment when Haecker and Stover and Rhodes himself would be pinned and spread on Security's inspection board, and he fidgeted, tempted to tiptoe from the hut while the Hanninah were entranced. Then the hand of the female, in response to a contraction, tightened about his own and he turned to look at her, at the salves heavy on her burned flesh, the charred and singed fur that, even in the dusky light of the hut, was of an amber-golden color. Thought of Stover burning, burning, and he thought of Haecker's blackmail, his pile of cubes and documents and dates. It seemed now the detritus of a small and paltry crime, compared to the horror of what Stover and Haecker had done, were doing, to the people under the governor's care. An illegal liaison, an illegitimate bending of regulations in aid of an illegitimate offspring, some pilfered funds, some doctored documents, a little theft; Rhodes remembered his terror at the time and his terror afterwards as something ridiculous, something faintly absurd. Frightened and shaking in Tyler's, while over the savannah ranged long-legged Terrans with flames in their fists. And these people were his charge, were his to keep safe; he had never thought to delve or probe, had never thought to demand and seek. Perhaps he could have stopped the deaths—how many deaths were there, over the years, over the savannah, over, perhaps, the entire island continent of this semirestricted planet? The governor's hand clenched that of the laboring Hannin, and he felt a deep and abiding shame, felt blame, guilt and, overriding all, a great and terrible compassion. Above the laboring woman, the governor bowed his head and wept.

ALIN'S JOURNAL

They retreat from me, finally. This cave is very dark and very deep, and I lie on my pallet in the darkest, deepest corner, whispering. Small fires lit under natural vents in the rocks. Shadows. The smell of cooking. And many Hanninah leaning against the walls or lying on the stone floors, talking and calling with an unnatural animation in their voices. I fall silent when one of them comes too close to me. I fake sleep, although they know if I sleep or if I wake, and choose to view my pretense with amusement. Amusement? Yes.

Haapati tells me that this cave has sheltered centuries of migrating Hanninah, that each nook and cranny, each ventilation shaft, has been used innumerable times. That the hollows in the stone floor were worn by sleeping Hanninah, one per night, about fifty per migration, one migration per one hundred fifty turns. And at fifty sleepers per one hundred fifty turns per hollows worn thirty centimeters down, how long have the Hanninah been crossing through this pass?

Haapati tells me that Ke'empah has migrated twice. And I believe him.

Haapati tells me all manner of interesting things. Haapati chatters.

Haapati stands guard now at the mouth of the cave. Against what? Against whom? Against Stover, or Quellan? Against Toyon? All day long they have carried me, despite my entreaties, despite my demands. Where is my husband? Ke'empah says, maddeningly, "His trail has parted from ours, for its time was come." What does this mean? Is Toyon dead? My husband dead? Haapati assures me that he is not, that he left the tribes alive and hale. Do I believe this? I woke this morning amid terrifying visions, and when I reached for him he was not there. I cried for him, and the Hanninah moved about me, preparing for the march, ignoring my tears. Except Haapati. Haapati cares for me. Perhaps.

I tell myself that I must not allow my weakened condition to cloud my mind. I tell myself that I must not think of the Hanninah as the proximate cause of my distress, that I must not turn them into monsters.

They have no malice. They have no spite. They have closed themselves to me, now that my usefulness is over, and all except Haapati pay me no attention, simply move around me as though I were an inanimate object, like a pile of pelts, taking up space. But they are not vicious. What they have done to me, they did through . . . curiosity? Ignorance of its results? What explains this?

We are going to the city, Haapati said, after we had reached the cave and I was fed and settled in my place. · A great and dignified migration from nomadic barbarity to civilization, and the rituals of the route herald and create the change. Purge one hundred fifty years of repression. Initiate the ability to feel. Aided and abetted by the yellow pollen and sap of a certain plant, and when Haapati showed me a dried blossom I recognized Rhodes's beloved prayer plants. Yellow pollen, yellow sap. Yellow stew, the one Quellan loved and ate with such delight. Yellow wine. It promotes a bond between those who take it, Haapati said. A religious drug. The Hanninah gather it during their nomadic phase, eat of it during migration, and reseed the great plains when they cross the mountains again.

"Is that why I was with you during the rituals?" I asked.

Haapati nodded.

"It made me able to hear you?"

"And us able to hear you. Your mind was very open during the ceremonies of crossing."

"I thought I was becoming a Hannin," I said.

"Perhaps you are," he replied, as though in comfort. I lay a while in silence, propped by pelts against the wall of the cave.

"Why didn't it affect Quellan and my husband?"

"It did, but to a lesser extent."

"Why? We all ate the same things, didn't we? We all took the same amount of drug."

"Yes, the same amount, but we helped yours."

"What do you mean? How did you 'help' mine?"

202

"Your elder at Eastbase," Haapati said. "The one who burns. He forces it from our stationary tribe and, in the beginning, he would bring many Terrans, one by one, to our camp and make them eat of it. It did not harm them, and their minds opened a very little bit to ours."

I wanted to ask questions, but he gestured to me to wait.

"And then the elder mixed it with some liquid he had brought, and put the mixture into a machine for putting it in to Terrans. He put the machine against the arm of a Terran, and the Terran grew very still. His mind opened completely to us, so that we could explore it as we wished. His mind was a great surprise to us. Then the drug moved away from him, and he woke and craved more."

I thought about this in silence, then said, "You did not show the Eastbase elder that this opening had happened?"

"No."

"And you mixed some of the liquid with my food?"

"With your wine."

"Do you have the liquid?"

"Ke'empah has it. Do you wish to see it?"

I nodded, and he walked across the cave to Ke'empah. They spoke together, and when he came back to me, he carried a glass container of obvious Terran manufacture.

"What is this?" I asked.

"I do not know. It was taken from the elder's flying machine."

I took the cylinder, opened it, sniffed, then plucked the metal knife from my sash and plunged it into the liquid. It hissed and bubbled, and when I pulled it out, the metal blade had corroded to a fine, lacy pattern.

Despite Haapati's objections, I struggled to my feet, crossed to one of the many fires, and grabbed an empty pot from a pile. I poured a millimeter of the liquid into the pot and held it over the flames, and soon greenish clouds lifted from the sizzling liquid and rose through the vent in the rock. Chlorine. Hydrochloric acid. Used, in minute amounts, in the preparation of injections. Used, it appeared, as a potentiator of the Hanninah's yellow drug.

By now the tribe was still and staring at me. I held myself rigidly erect, fighting against the weakness, and walked to Ke'empah.

"You have fed this to me," I said.

"Yes."

"In my wine."

"Yes."

"Why?"

"You are a Terran. Your people have come to our planet, and have disrupted our way of life, have changed us. We needed to know your people better, and we have explored them through your mind. You do not react to the untreated drug the way we do."

"But what will it do to me?"

"We do not know."

I stared at him, then, unable to stand up any longer, I sank to my knees.

"You didn't bother to discover whether it would harm me or not?"

"It does not harm us."

"But we're different from you!"

Ke'empah nodded slightly, but not in concession. His lips pulled flat and wide, and I realized that, for the first time, I was seeing a Hannin smile.

"You don't care what this drug does to me, do you?" I whispered.

"You have been very useful," he said politely. "We have learned much of your culture from you."

"Are you praising me? For what you did to me?"

"How did we harm you? We have shared our religion with you, and our minds have been as open to you as yours was to us."

"But you might have killed me!"

"We didn't."

Again we stared at each other. Haapati stood to

204

one side, as though hesitant to come closer, and the cave was still quiet.

"Haapati said the Terran wanted more. After Stover injected him. He was addicted to this. Perhaps I am addicted to this. Is Toyon addicted too? Is Quellan?"

"No. They did not drink the wine."

"Where are they?"

"We do not need to know. They are no longer of value to us."

"Neither am I, anymore. Are you going to abandon me?"

"No," he said. "Of course not. You have served us well. If you are in need of this drug, we shall give it to you. We are not a violent people." And he turned from me, busied himself with the others, dismissing me from his thoughts and concerns. Haapati carried me to my pallet, took the bottle of acid from me, and went to stand guard at the mouth of the cave.

Tak, the Hannin liquor, is flavored with the drug. And I grew dizzy on the savannah, when Haapati went into trance.

Neither Ke'empah nor Haapati knew that the drug might harm me. They are not monsters. Haapati cares what happens to me, although Ke'empah does not. But they are not monsters.

And addictions can be broken. Addictions can be broken. I will drink no more of their yellow wine. No.

Haapati says:

The weather will change, and it will rain in the desert.

For one hundred fifty turns.

The Hanninah will work metals, will build, will conduct their guild meetings, will marry and procreate and die in their fantastic city. Will farm the newly blooming land.

The weather will change, and the desert will be dry. For one hundred fifty turns.

The earth renews itself, and the Hanninah also renew themselves, purge themselves of emotion, tie themselves to repression so that the memory of their city will remain bright within them. As bright as the machined knives they make in the desert and wear in the plains. As bright as the colors of their sashes. As bright as the explosions of their change.

Haapati says that the great southern icecaps melt now, releasing cold water into the warm ocean. Haapati says that the icecaps are long, thin crusts over the sea, that they break and dissolve easily as Hoep-Hanninah's axial tilt changes. Haapati says that the waters will rise along the continent forty meters in the next ten turns. Great fogs will boil from the oceans, great banks of cloud will move over the desert as the currents shift. Savannah will become swamp. Desert will become farmland.

And what will they do to the Terrans now? I ask. Continue to use them, of course, as they have used Stover as an object for study, as they sent Haapati to Tyler's to study us. As they used me. The Hanninah will pool their knowledge of us and use us for their own ends, and I suppose that we deserve each other.

Haapati says that there is a great debate between the elders now. Their culture has broadened with the coming of the Terrans, they now have the possibilities of trade, of commerce, of an opening to the stars. Some believe that they should change the cycle and remain city dwellers when the cycle turns again, that they should use this foreign knowledge to preserve the city and their lives in it, that the patterns of the Hanninah should shift. There is much argument, conducted silently by Hanninah in trance-states.

I don't care. I am locked and lost within my dark skin, I am abandoned and used and cast aside, I have been rendered worthless. Let them continue their debates, let them change or remain unchanged, it will have no effect upon me. Where is Toyon now?

Haapati comes back from his watch, sits beside me, yearns to hold my hand. He tells me, with shame, that

he is more Terran than Hanninee. He speaks in
Standard, so that the others will not understand. He
tells me that he lost his sack of precious drug in
Tyler's, and that the many years among the Terrans
have changed him to something between what he was
and what I am. I am not sympathetic.

"I feel guilt," he says to me. "For bringing you to
the tribes, for helping them do this to you."

I do not answer.

"I would like to have you for my mate," he says.
"I will take care of you. We are more like each other
than we are each like our separate peoples. I love you."

"What's the word for love in Hanninee?" I ask
harshly, and he tells me that there is none.

"Where is my husband?"

He makes a sudden, familiar gesture with his shoulders, and the mountain seems to shake.

Does it matter where Toyon is? I would not take
me back, were I he. Addicted, sick, half crazy. I would
not go back to him. I think. I would burden him, I
would crush him, he would come to hate me if he
does not hate me already. Standing with dead Taleti
in his arms, and tears on his face, while I scream and
shout and move into orgasmic ritual. How should he
know I was unknowing? How could I have not known
I was being used?

Haapati holds my hand, and I remember now his
care and gentleness, feeding me liquids, seeing to my
comfort, bearing me company as we crossed the thread-
wide path.

Am I to live completely alone on an alien world?

I want Toyon so much my belly hurts, but I leave
my fingers in Haapati's and, in the morning, when the
pain begins, I sip the yellow wine.

CROSSING

Quellan lay on her belly against the slanting rock,

fingers and toes cautiously exploring the tiny holes in which they rested. The sun warmed her back, warmed the rock around her, and as she lay waiting for Toyon's signal she stared at the hardy, minuscule rock-flowers that found lodging in the cracks of the stone. Most of them had feathery leaves, no bigger than one of the hairs of her arm, standing out in rows from the small stalk, and topped each one with rounded, single-petaled blood-red flowers. Others seemed hardier, their multiple leaves almost succulent in their thickness; these raised long, awkward stalks that ended abruptly in blue or purple or green blossoms. Small winged insects fluttered from plant to plant, or crawled over the pitted expanse of rock. She raised her head and watched distant clouds float below her toward far peaks, watched the occasional swooping of birds. The mountain air seemed to magnify things, brought them into immediate and detailed focus, yet always separated from her by a sky-reaching wall of glass. Hundreds of meters below, she saw a dark ravine and the shadow of the trail running through it, but could not tell if Hanninah still stalked along its narrow length.

The day before, she and Toyon had followed Alin and the Hanninah, taking a rough path parallel to the main trail. The Hanninah had stopped for the night in a deep cave and it became obvious why the tribes traveled one by one, for the cave barely accommodated all the members of Ke'empah's group. She and Toyon had found uncomfortable lodging some meters up-trail from the cave, ate their supplement pills, and sipped from a fortuitous spring before wrapping themselves in their molecular sheets and talking of their route. Both had picked up strong feelings of antipathy from the tribe, and agreed that they could not rejoin the Hanninah. Alin seemed too closely surrounded by the Hanninah to venture a rescue during the crossing. And, too, there was no telling where Stover was; they did not want to free Alin only to deliver themselves into Stover's hands. Safer, Quellan said, to wait until they reached the desert, where the tribe was more likely to spread out, where they would have a better chance of spotting Stover when he appeared. And then? And then go rushing in and grab Alin and run like hell, Toyon said. In lieu of a better idea, they left it at that.

The supplement pills provided the substances necessary for life, but did nothing for the dull, empty ache in the belly. Quellan pressed her stomach against the warm stones, feeling the passage of the rope about her waist, and closed her eyes to flowers, sunlight, and sky. The easy trail they had forged during the morning gave out abruptly, leaving them the choice either of scrambling down to the Hanninah trail and taking their chances on not being seen, or of attempting to cross-country over the slabs of the mountain's rim. But the trail whipped and switchbacked around the gorge, exposing it for kilometers in either direction, so they chose the alternate route. Two amateurs, groping and crawling above the lairs of birds. Since Toyon claimed to have some small and distant experience of rock-climbing, he went first, driving pitons into the rock and pulling himself upward, and as Quellan reached each metal stud she would rest, pull the piton from its hold, tuck it into her pouch and, secured by the length of rope about her waist, clamber toward Toyon's latest perch. She would give him the pitons she had salvaged, and after a small rest he would stretch, sigh, study the terrain above them, then carefully pick his way upwards, and soon Quellan would follow.

The rope tugged at her, and obediently she moved up the rock, slowly seeking and finding finger and toe holds. The first piton felt secure under her hand; she rested a moment, then pried it from the rock with the hilt of her knife, shoved knife and piton into her sack, continued. Swing, grip, slide, grip, reach; the universe shrank to the gray rock before her face, the slide and touch of fingers and toes, the grasping of stone against her worn suit and jacket. She stopped at the second piton and, holding it, leaned back and looked around her. The ravine was gone from sight, and the side of the mountain fell in an unbroken, pale slope toward shadowed jungle below. Above, she could see Toyon's head and shoulders against the sky. She pried and packed the piton, continued up.

Within twelve meters of Toyon's perch, she reached for a finger hold and found none. Her fingers scrabbled about the rock, searching, and she looked down at the unbroken slide of rock, the invisible ravine. And knew that if she strained for the hold, if she moved one single muscle, she would loose her grip completely, slide helpless down the mountainside, bringing Toyon with her. She clung desperately to the rock, and sudden moisture on her hands imperiled even the slim hand hold that she had. A cold knot formed in her stomach, her knees chilled. She very slowly looked upward, contemplated the route. No worse than others she had traversed, no worse than holds she had striven for further down the peak. Toyon's rope was secured about the ring-ended piton at the top. He would not fall if she fell. If she fell. But still she couldn't move, and all her mind's wild screaming about the absurdity of her fear only further weakened her legs, her fingers, her rationality.

"Toyon," she whispered to the rock. "Toyon."

The rope tugged briefly at her waist and almost threw her into panic. Only by keeping still, static, unmoving, frozen, quiet. Only. By now she was afraid of breathing, and her lungs began to ache against the slow, cautious pull and push of air.

"Quellan? What's wrong?"

She held her face against stone and could not answer.

"Quellan? Hold still, I'm coming down."

No, she thought. No. The rope trembled against her, small pebbles rattled on either side. Then Toyon was beside her, his hand heavy on her shoulder. She fought against the urge to clutch him in panic.

"I'm afraid," she whispered.

"Afraid? Of what? Come on, snap out of it, you're perfectly safe. It's getting late, come on."

"I can't. I'm afraid of falling."

He forced her face around to him until he stared into her eyes.

"Okay," he said. He pried her hand from the rock, moved it aside, and drove a piton into the stone, then wrapped her hand around the length of metal.

"Pull against that," he said calmly.

"I can't. My hand will slip."

"No, it won't. Come on. Good." He dropped below her, forced her left foot from its hold, pushed it upwards and placed her toes in a cranny. She opened her eyes slowly.

"Now your right hand, about half a meter straight up," Toyon said. Fighting against her terror, she reached, found the hold. "Good. Now the right foot, a little to the left, a bit more, there. Now the left hand, away from the piton. It's all right. Good. The other foot. Now your right hand."

He talked her up the slope to the small ledge, and she hauled herself up the final meters, feeling the terror slide away from her. But there was enough left so that when she reached the ledge she huddled against Toyon's chest and shook.

"Don't worry about it," he said. "It's not that bad. It's happened to me before, in stupider places. You're all right, and you're going to be all right."

She pulled herself away from him, approached the edge, glanced down, saw the piton still affixed to the stones. Saw a way back.

"What are you doing?" Toyon demanded.

"I'm going to get that piton."

"Oh, no, you're not. Forget the damned piton, we don't need any more trouble."

"Toyon, listen," she said, and caught his hands in hers. "If I don't, I'm going to have the same trouble, further up. I know it."

"But it's getting——"

"Late. Yes, I know. But I have to do it."

He grimaced, shrugged, tried to pull his hands

away, then said with weariness, "Yes, I know. Do it, then."

Before she could think, she swung herself over the edge, checked the rope, and moved spiderlike down the slope. Her foot hit the piton first; she moved to the side and down, then wrapped the rope around her shoulder, pried the piton from the rock, and tucked it in her pack. The movement caused her to swing free from the rock, and the terror washed back so thickly that she couldn't scream. She felt the rope burn her arm but hold her, and she took a deep breath, turned, moved back to the ledge where Toyon waited. They stood before each other a moment, unsmiling, then abruptly embraced.

In the three hours before dusk they covered a goodly amount of ground. They separated briefly to search for a sleeping place, and while Quellan clambered over the rocks she heard Toyon calling. She came back quickly.

"Up here," he yelled. She climbed to him, expecting nothing more than a small cup of rock fit for resting, and found him standing at the edge of a drop. Before him, lit in the glow of sunset, lay the harsh, broad expanse of Hoep-Tashik.

They stood together in silence, then Toyon pointed toward the west. "There's the way down."

She followed his gesture to a point where the mountain slid gradually to the plain, and she nodded. "It doesn't seem as far down as it should."

"It's a high desert," he replied. "Maybe three kilometers above sea level. We'll be on it tomorrow."

"And the city?"

He shook his head. "It's too dark to see it from here. I'd guess it's over that way. Look, aren't those the Hanninah?"

"I think . . . yes." The tribe clustered in its bull's-eye circle five kilometers from the plain, fire pit faintly visible. She couldn't tell whether it was Ke'empah's tribe or not.

"We'll follow them," Toyon said. "They're probably all going to the same place."

They moved back from the cliff's edge and found a rocky nest for the night. They ate and drank sparingly from the canteen, then left the glower on for warmth and huddled under their separate sheets. The moons were both crescent that night, casting the palest of glows over the rocks, and stars were thick in the sky.

Unwanted, the terrified moments on the rock face came back to her, and she could not stop her mind from tracing a tumbling descent from the mountain, could not obliterate the fear of falling, the scraping and tearing of rocks against her skin. She twisted uncomfortably under the sheet, sought different positions, tried to force her mind to consider the upcoming descent into the desert, the possibilities of stealing Alin from the Hanninah. But the fear and the death pursued her relentlessly, and she could not evade the terror. She turned again, seeking warmth, and found herself in Toyon's arms.

They lay surprised, rigid. She thought about Toyon's voice guiding her up the rock, about the scene at the river after Taleti's death when she had covered for him. The shadowed hut after Alin's first ceremony with the Hanninah, when her voice and Toyon's had crossed and recrossed over his wife's unconscious form. The bright, dilapidated supply shack at Tyler's, and his huge body filling the door, red beard and red hair; his hands holding a mug of beer.

The wind howled and the ephemera slid away—and they were two small humans, alien and completely alone at the top of the world.

His hand moved and he traced the rope-burn on her shoulder, the scar of the shot she had taken at Eastbase, then pressed his lips against the scar through the cloth of her suit. She moved to let his palm cup her small breast, and as her arms circled him he raised his face, and she searched for his lips beneath the thick, soft beard.

DESCENDING

Toyon wakens early, while the sun is yet an indistinct lightness in the east, and for a moment lies confused amid the twistings of sheet, feeling the warm body beside his. He glances at the browned arm lying across his freckled, red-haired chest, and the color of brown is wrong; the head tucked on his shoulder is sun-whitened blond, rather than springy, reddened black. He untangles himself with care, unwilling to break her sleep, finds his clothes, and hurries into them. The morning air is cold and smells of stones.

He seems to be spending all these mountain dawns alone, perched on a rock and overlooking a scene of interest. Far on the horizon he sees a shattering of light, a whiteness of bleached towers, yet the sight does not move him, and he searches until he sees the already fallen camp of the Hanninah, the beginnings of their march. He squints and peers, but cannot pick out the shape of his wife amid the moving forms. He turns to face south, and finds great gray clouds piled against the mountain's flank, sees the far-off flicker of lightning. Aye, the weather is changing. As Quellan said, as Rhodes said. But this, too, does not hold his interest.

Quellan sleeps. Their coupling had been complicated, intense, a statement rather than a sharing, a substitution, a desperation. He considers casual infidelities over the span of years, considers Alin's own rovings and samplings, and none of these has carried this sense of nonbeing, nor these flavorings of doubt. He has, he realizes, pumped into Quellan his yearning for his wife, as though this surrogate desire could create a bond stretched over a desert and a severing of soul; has made a promise with his hips. An illusion, surely, as all his lustings for Alin's soul have been illusions. She is alone and inviolate, as is he, and her

214

twistings of psyche are not his for the prying or the taking. Love as hunger, love as power, love as yearning for control. He flattens his hands against the stones, tenses his legs, stares out across the desert to the moving tribe.

Bring out the cavalry. Bring on the troops. Suppose Alin does not want to be rescued, suppose that she is happy living this new life, being this new person? The idea startles him, repels him, but holds a fascination that he cannot avoid. He has assumed that she is not herself, that she is in need of rescue and aid, that, once over her current confusions, she will gratefully return to the life she led before, to husband, to empire. Now the assumption seems to him unwarranted, unfounded. She seemed completely within the Hanninah, those last nights at the encampment. Completely one with them, speaking their language, eating their foods, drinking their wines, thinking their thoughts. Suppose that she has chosen this of her own free will. That if I take her from them, she will be not temporarily unhappy, but genuinely unhappy. If I rush in and grab her and bear her away, I will be taking over her life, I will, perhaps, be doing her a genuine harm. Suppose further that my anger and discomfort at these thoughts are purely selfish, stem from the idea that I could be forgotten, discarded, so easily. But also suppose that I am wrong.

Which way? Either way. The decision is not mine to make.

He rises uneasily, paces while trying to work his way out of this net of his own weaving. Quellan sleeps on.

Let her choose. Let Alin choose. Let me be perceptive and watchful and try to see beyond her words and her face, to her mind and her meaning. Let me pry this once, this once let me in to her. For her sake, of course. For her sake. And for mine.

He pushes his hair back from his face and clubs it against his neck. He is reluctant to wake Quellan, reluctant to discover her view of their coupling, reluctant to enter other problems. However, he squats beside her and gently shakes her awake, and in silence they consume pills and water, pack the camp, and stand at the cliff edge. The Hanninah are making good time across the desert.

Quellan tucks the ragged ends of her hair behind her ears, plants her hands on her hips, glances at him obliquely, smiles. "A screw's a screw," she says, and waits for his smile.

"We'd best get to Alin," he says with gratitude, with relief. Together, they make their way down the mountain.

By noon they have reached the desert, by mid-afternoon they are within five kilometers of the moving tribe. The Hanninah make good time, yes, but they are a large group, and their speed is to a great extent determined by the speed of the stragglers. Toyon and Quellan move quickly but cautiously in their wake, keeping to the shallow shelter of a dried water course. When they are one kilometer from the tribe they arrive at a place where great boulders line the banks of the dried stream, and Quellan wriggles herself up the rocks to peer at the Hanninah.

"Toyon," she whispers. "Can you get up here?"

He climbs beside her, follows her pointing arm, sees his wife and Haapati pacing slowly behind the tribe. Alin leans on Haapati's arm, walks cautiously, as though recovering from great weakness; Toyon can see the deep red of her sash and the gleam of a knife hilt thrust under it.

"Let them get a bit more behind the others, and we can rush her," Quellan says. "Get rid of the ape, knock him out or something."

Toyon stares at his wife and does not answer.

"Well?"

"No, a bit further. We don't want to hurt them, not even Haapati. Let's tail them until we find a good place."

Quellan nods an agreement and they slide down the rock.

The sun descends and they move more quickly, completely intent on the two forms ahead, so that when the desert to their immediate right blossoms into flame they stare uncomprehending. The second bolt flashes to their left, and Toyon has barely enough time to see Haapati and Alin scramble under cover, before he and Quellan slide behind a weathered outcropping of soft stone, and grope at their belts for their inadequate weapons.

Quellan's lips move in constant curses, and she pounds the caked ground with her fist. Stover with light-guns, Stover with death, and Toyon sees no comforting forest around them, no rock-slabbed riverbank, no place to hide. He wonders if they can draw Stover's fire long enough for Alin to reach the safety of the tribe, then, considering the Hannin knife that is his only weapon, he wonders if he can draw Stover's fire at all. Quellan, beside him, makes hopeful, useless piles of rocks.

ARRIVING

The infant came, finally, at dusk; its mother's hand clutched the governor's until he felt that his fingers would break, and her shriek blended with the cries of the newborn, creating a holocaust of sound from which emerged, finally, only the gasps of the child. The dead woman's mate had already done what was needed for the infant, and Rhodes gently disengaged the dead fingers from his own and, without speaking, walked through the broken camp and to the air-car.

Aside from the light-gun that Rhodes had taken from Perez, the air-car was devoid of weapons. As the governor finished his inspection, the Hanninah emerged from the camp, threw a few sacks on the waiting porodin, and mounted. The young Hannin, carrying his newborn child, kicked his porod in the governor's direction, stopped beside the air-car, then dropped a sash and a knife at the governor's feet before following the rest of his tribe to the north. The camp, the remaining goods, the dead woman lay abandoned in the rapidly fading light. Rhodes picked up sash and knife, twisted the sash around his waist over his dirty black clingsuit, slipped the knife into place, and climbed into the air-car.

A great calm brooded in the governor's mind as he flew across the savannah, eyes intent on the northward track below him. The time limit on his message to GalCentral had expired while the Hannin gave birth and died, and very soon Agents would arrive at Tyler's port to pursue the trails of his clues until they had discovered all the shapes of the situation. Including Haecker's blackmail, including the cache of documents and cubes that meant the end of Rhodes's career. The governor considered this and cast it aside as of no import. He rode a stolen air-car, he had just entered restricted territory, he had forced an illegal drug into two people, he had held the hand of a dying Hannin, and now he was planning murder, and all of this he accepted with a great calmness of soul. His one desire, now, was to search the sinuous landscape below, his one hope was to find Stover first.

The two crescent moons left little light, but Rhodes flew high and straight toward the rising mountains, settled on the southeastern slopes for the night, and in the morning found and followed the pass, trusting that if Stover saw the air-car, the manager would believe that it was Haecker coming to help, coming to participate. Rhodes flew from the high pass south toward the jungle, then doubled back, cursing the depth and shadows of the ravine through which the trail ran. A flash of red? No, simply the sunlight on a Hannin sash, not the bright red hair of Toyon Sutak. On a far slope, a scurrying, Stover? No, a mountain animal, leaping from rock to ledge with agile bounds. The great stone mouth of an amphitheater gaped below him, and he surveyed it as carefully as he surveyed all else before flying onward. By nightfall, convinced that the Terrans were already across the pass, he set the air-car down and anchored it against the rising winds, battened its ports against the threatened rain, and ate the last of the food he had been given during his death watch. At dawn, he was up again, dipping as far below the fanged peaks as he could. Curving lines of marching Hanninah darkened the trail and straightened as they reached the broad plains, aiming for the gleaming city on the horizon. Lightning flickered against the mountains to the south, and the light dimmed into evening. His fuel ran low and he brought the air-car closer to the desert floor to continue his single-minded search.

Two swift eruptions of fire reddened the darkening sky behind him, to the north, and he spun the car around and sped over the desert. Another gout of flame. He tensed, his long legs tight on the floor of the car, hair in wild disarray; gripped the controls more tightly and squinted into the dusk. He passed to the right of Stover and two companions, banked above the pile of soft rock where Sutak and a woman huddled, then banked over them again and threw them the light-gun before rising again. Further to the north, specks from the line of Hanninah came running swiftly toward the flames. Rhodes dipped back along his path, saw Stover and the other two crouched behind the smooth stones of a gully. One of Stover's companions, a woman, stepped out and began a great waving of arms, gesturing toward a smooth section of land suitable for landing. Rhodes was briefly thankful for the bright, identifying crimson of Haecker's car. With grim satisfaction, he obligingly dipped the air-car toward the earth, dove forward, and saw the woman's eyes open with shock as the nose of the air-car struck her and sent her body tumbling loose and broken through the air.

Stover was already running as Rhodes brought the car around, and the governor chased him across the desert toward the approaching Hanninah. To his right, he saw Stover's remaining companion brace huge legs against the earth and raise the light-gun toward the car, and Rhodes slammed the drivers, desperate to catch Stover before the air-car burst into flames. But the gout of fire hissed along the tail of the car, and Rhodes glanced to his right to see Sutak standing upright, the light-gun in his fist, and Stover's man falling amid a curtain of flame. The governor shrieked triumphantly and opened the throttle, aimed at the fleeing manager, and rammed the car into his running form.

CYCLES

Toyon was halfway to the broken air-car when its door fell open and Rhodes stumbled out. The governor's black clingsuit gleamed with blood, and his right arm hung shattered at his side; as he stepped around to the front of the car, he held his hip with his left hand, and one leg dragged behind him. But the deep gold sash around his waist was crisp and clean, and the knife-hilt gleamed with blood. As Toyon neared, he could see fresh, bright-red bubbles of blood trickling from the governor's mouth.

"Rhodes," he shouted, extending his arms to the man, but the governor shook his head and bent slowly, peered for a long time under the car, then straightened.

"I am glad that you're alive," Rhodes said formally, and the blood ran faster. He raised his head to look beyond Toyon, and Toyon turned to see Haapati running to them across the baked earth. Rhodes smiled, extended his left hand, and fell into the Hannin's arms.

"He burned people," Rhodes said weakly. Then, with satisfaction, he added, "But I killed him, didn't I?"

"Yes, Governor," Haapati said gently, and lowered

Rhodes to the ground. The governor sighed, shivered, and was suddenly very still.

Quellan came up, having checked on Stover's two companions, and knelt beside the governor and closed his eyes. Haapati cradled the governor's body, and the desert was very still. Then the Hannin lay the body on the ground and ran back in the direction he'd come. Quellan and Toyon watched him stop, bend to the ground, and come back with Alin in his arms.

When they were some meters away, she struggled from Haapati's arms and walked toward them, stood beside Rhodes's body and stared at her husband. Her skin had a yellow cast, and lay taut over shoulders and ribs; her eyes were surrounded by deep smudges of weariness. She lifted her knife from the folds of her sash and held it out to her husband, and he looked down at the corroded blade.

"They have this drug," Alin said slowly. "And it doesn't work on us until they mix it with hydrochloric acid. They put it in the stew, and in the wine, but they only put the acid in with my wine."

Toyon remained silent, and Alin sighed, dropped the knife, and leaned against Haapati's shoulder. Toyon stared at her, barely controlling the urge to leap over the governor's body and grab her to him.

"I can't leave," Alin said finally. "If I don't have the wine, the drug, it hurts too much. I tried it. I can't leave."

"We have chemists," Toyon said, trying to drain every inflection from his voice, trying to make the decision entirely hers. "We have doctors. Or—or we can get the drug for you."

"No. It changes me, it makes me hear things. It's— it's . . ." she murmured a few words in Hanninee.

"She says that it is of great beauty," Haapati said, speaking toward the ground. His long arms hung limply, and although he supported her, he did not hold her. As though he, too, Toyon thought, were giving her room for decision. Toyon straightened slightly.

"We can get enough to last until the doctors come

221

up with something, until we can—until you can—until it goes away."

Alin remained silent, her shoulders shaking slightly.

"Hey," Quellan said. Alin raised her head to the fielder. "Hey, love, you want to come home?"

"Yes," Alin whispered. But she did not move until Toyon raised his hand to her. Only then, and with great dignity, did she step away from Haapati, around the governor's body, and fall with a small sigh into her husband's arms. He lowered his face to her dark hair, oblivious to the stares of Quellan and Haapati.

The sky darkened into complete night, and a fine, small rain began to fall.

MORE EXCITING SCIENCE FICTION
FROM WARNER BOOKS